ALSO BY TAYLOR HAHN

The Lifestyle

A Home for the Holidays

A Home for the Holidays

TAYLOR HAHN

ALFRED A. KNOPF
New York
2024

THIS IS A BORZOI BOOK
PUBLISHED BY ALFRED A. KNOPF

ISBN 9780593470701

Jacket illustration by Matt Lamothe
Jacket design by Jenny Carrow

Manufactured in the United States of America

For my mom, who joyfully left her Christmas decorations up until March, and for my daughter, whom I will love just as hard

A Home for the Holidays

Chapter 1

When I was eight years old, Santa crashed in my backyard.

I was asleep, having a scary dream about a bear in my school cafeteria. Bears, fires, and my mom dying. Those were my recurring nightmares.

My mom jostled me awake. "Darling girl, something's happened." I could tell she hadn't gone to bed yet because she was still in her party clothes. Her sparkly bracelets clinked against each other as she shook me. I looked at my Minnie Mouse clock—it was almost two a.m.

Christmas already.

Christmas was my favorite day of the year. Santa always came, though I always missed him by seconds. My mom and I were united in our commitment to catching him. The year before, she'd set up a video camera on a tripod in the living room, facing the tree. It caught him scattering presents before running out the front door. We didn't have a fireplace, so my mom said he used the VIP entrance. I'd heard the door slam, but by the time I jumped out of bed to investigate, falling snow had erased his footsteps from the yard. I watched and rewatched that tape, marveling at the evidence that magic was real.

One year Santa arrived while my mom and I were watching *Miracle on 34th Street* and eating Campbell's tomato soup on TV trays. Reindeer hooves thumped on the roof, and when I looked out our front window to the street, I saw Santa running away from our house like he knew he'd given himself away. It was only ten degrees in Chicago that year and I still chased him for three blocks.

This was going to be the year I caught him. I wasted no time sitting up and throwing my covers back. I'd worn my purple LA Lights sneakers to bed so I'd be prepared for exactly this scenario. "Where is he?" I demanded, like I was a hardened detective about to squeeze a confession from a perp.

"The backyard," she said, and I sprinted downstairs, through the kitchen, and out the back door.

Our yard was a small dark square. Thick winter clouds hid the moon and city stars. But enough light spilled from the kitchen that I could see something red twinkling in the corner. Snow swallowed my shoes and soaked my socks as I ran closer to inspect.

From the back door, my mom asked, "What is it?" She was barefoot, wearing a black velvet dress with shoulder pads.

I picked up a fragment of red glass. "I think it's Rudolph's nose." How would Santa find his way without Rudolph's nose? "This is *devastating*." I'd learned how to spell that word for my last weekly spelling test before winter break. Picturing Rudolph with only the shards of a once-blinking nose on the tip of his little furry face gave me the same seasick feeling I'd experienced when my parents argued over who was going to have me for the summer, or when my mom fell asleep on the couch and I couldn't wake her up, or when she was two hours late to pick me up from school. Like I wasn't on solid ground. Like I didn't know what was going to happen.

"Look over there," she said.

I followed her finger, running to the bushes that lined our chain-link fence, and crouched down. Was that silver wrapping paper? It was all torn and crumpled up. In the yellow light from the kitchen, it looked like wreckage. TWA Flight 800 had exploded over the Atlantic Ocean that year. I couldn't forget the pictures I'd seen on TV.

When my mom gasped, I whipped my head around. Was he here?

"His hat," she said. "On the garage."

I looked up and saw Santa's red hat dangling upside down from a gutter. That could not be good.

"Do you think he's dead?" I asked.

I crept closer. Along the side of the garage, where we kept the trash cans, I found a shiny stack of boxes. "All my presents are here!" I called, falling to my knees in the snow.

"He must have crashed," she called back. "But he made it out okay."

I shaded my eyes from the motion-sensored floodlight. "How do you know?"

"Because otherwise his sleigh would still be here," she said, backlit from the kitchen, a dark and beautiful silhouette.

That answer was fairly logical coming from my mom, a woman who sometimes didn't make sense. She wasn't like other moms. Other moms did mom things, like pack my friends' lunches with Fruit Roll-Ups and heart-shaped sandwiches. My mom wanted to do those things—she bought the snacks and the cookie cutter—but they never happened. Was it really that hard? I wondered. I was only eight, and I was capable of making my lunch every day. Then again, I was one of the most responsible kids in my grade. The teacher usually picked me to feed the class hamster and lead the recess line. So maybe my mom and I were just different in that way. Me, responsible. My mom, forgetful. I suspected other kids' moms remembered to wake them up for school in the morning, so they weren't late. In my house, it was the other way around. I shook my mom awake every morning at ten to eight, when it was time to leave, but it usually took her so long to get out of bed, dressed, and into the car that I missed morning announcements and most of math. But I didn't ask my friends about their morning routine. I wasn't sure I wanted to know the answer.

I was shivering, so I hugged my gifts and carried them inside. One of them was the exact size and shape of a Tickle Me Elmo box, the thing I wanted most. Every toy store in Chicago was sold out. You could get a Tickle Me Elmo only from Santa, and even then, he had to like you.

In the living room, my mom helped me arrange my presents under the tree. We'd gotten it only that morning. Everything in our house ran behind schedule. The tree was lopsided and dry, but my mom had saved it by using twice the number of lights anyone else would have used. It lit up the living room, pinpricks of gold in the dark, like flying over a city at night.

"Do you want to open one?" she asked, prodding my shoulder.

I longed for that Tickle Me Elmo. "I'll wait. It's not Christmas morning yet."

"You've got to let loose a little," she teased.

No, I don't think I can. Only one person in our two-person household could be loose. Otherwise, nothing would get done. I'd never do my homework or get vaccinated or even go to school. I took my role as grown-up very seriously.

I told her we needed to go to bed, and she lay down with me, her velvet dress curled around my flannel pajamas. She was still my safe place. I tried to fall asleep, but she beat me to it, snoring softly, so I was careful not to move a muscle. If I woke her up, she'd stay up all night and sleep until the afternoon, straight through Christmas morning.

At a sleepover two years later, my best friend, Gabby, told everyone there was no Santa, and it turned out all the girls knew that already. I pretended to know that, too, but then I said I had to go to the bathroom so I could cry without their seeing. I felt so stupid. I didn't know what was worse: that I'd still believed in Santa, or how much I wanted to keep believing in Santa. He'd brought an uncomplicated magic to my complicated life. My mom might have forgotten to pay the bills, but Santa was coming. I didn't have to worry or wonder or plan. He would be there, using the VIP entrance, delivering gifts.

When I finally understood, sometime around my fifteenth birthday, that my mom wasn't forgetful, but instead had a problem with alcohol, I reexamined my Christmas memories. Some parents put presents under the tree labeled *From Santa.* Some parents told their kids to leave out cookies and carrots in case Santa and his reindeer got hungry. Some parents even went so far as to eat those cookies and carrots. Those parents were amateurs compared to my mom. She brought Santa to life. I'd cherished him for showing up, predictably, every year on Christmas Eve. I'd cherished him for being the opposite of her. But he was her, all along.

Chapter 2

December 14

Our band, the More the Marry Her, usually played weddings. But around the holidays, we picked up charity galas, office Christmas bashes, and New Year's Eve parties. I liked weddings, but office parties were a blast. No mothers to please, no pressure, just hundreds of overworked employees who'd just gotten their end-of-year bonuses. Antics were guaranteed. Rivals settled the score over cranberry-and-goat-cheese crostini. Everyone jockeyed to bring the boss a cocktail. Secret crushes became dance-floor kisses.

The band had four members—I sang, Dan played bass, Lizzie played guitar, and Ronald played drums. Dan, Lizzie, and I met in college as music majors and initially formed a wedding band to make money after graduation while we figured out our "real" plans. Ten years later, here we were. That Lizzie was my best friend and Dan eventually became my boyfriend proved both that we spent way too much time together and that we had fun doing it. Ronald was a mid-fifties retired firefighter we met on Craigslist who'd replaced our original drummer after she and Lizzie fell in love, then catastrophically out of love, and we all had to choose sides.

Tonight we were playing the holiday party of a huge accounting firm at the Signature Room, the ninety-fifth floor of the famous Chicago skyscraper formerly known as the John Hancock Center, or "Big John." Hundreds of accountants were getting rowdy. Lizzie always predicted who'd end up making out at these things. During our break, she pointed to an older man in a tidy gray suit talking to a younger guy in a blinking holiday sweater. "Those two," she said.

"No way," I disagreed. "The guy in the suit looks like he'd rather be getting his teeth cleaned than having that conversation."

"He's about to. With that guy's tongue."

She was right, of course. By the end of the night, they were making out behind the photo booth. When the lights came on and everyone lined up to get their coats, their hiding place wasn't so private anymore.

We'd finished our last song and begun to pack up. "I don't know why I doubted you," I said, watching them from afar as I zipped my mic into its foam case.

She shrugged as she unplugged her guitar. "Me either."

Outside, freezing in the alley near the service entrance, we loaded our equipment into Ronald's van. He was the only one of us with a house, so we rehearsed in his garage. Lizzie lived in a three-hundred-square-foot studio, and a few months ago I'd reluctantly moved into the apartment Dan's parents bought for him in a new high-rise in the West Loop, with a security desk, windows for walls, and an indoor pool. The bathroom was pristine white, floor to ceiling. I was afraid to get my period in there.

The apartment I'd given up was a one-bedroom in Lincoln Park with creaky wood floors and pale green kitchen tiles. Sometimes I accidentally boarded my old train, and when I realized what I'd done, I went anyway, just to sit in the courtyard and stare at my bedroom window for a while. But financially, it made sense to live with

Dan. Even though, since his parents owned the place, I paid them rent.

"Isn't that kind of weird?" I'd asked when Dan first suggested that arrangement. "Your parents will be my landlords. What if we get married?"

"They're going to give you a discount. You don't have to pay half. Just like thirty percent of the market rate. And if we get married, you can stop."

By no means was I a romantic, but if that was Dan's way of proposing, I'd rather pay rent. I didn't expect to live for free, but it was impossible to relax in my new apartment when Dan's mom stopped by unannounced three times a week and assured me that I should "make myself at home" as if I didn't live there, then circled me like a hawk to make sure I wiped up any droplets of water I splashed on the kitchen counter while washing my hands.

Still, thirty percent was better than a hundred percent, and since I was not exactly flush with cash as a wedding singer, I tried not to think about it too hard.

In the alley, Ronald slammed his hatch. "See you kids on Thursday."

We'd played the usual wedding favorites—"Sweet Caroline" and "Wagon Wheel" and "All of Me"—so many times we barely needed to rehearse anymore, but we still met once a week, mostly because it was fun and the pizza we ordered was tax deductible.

"Can I convince anyone to go to Elsa's for a bite?" I asked. "In the spirit of Christmas?"

"That's a pass for me," Ronald said. He always went home to his kids right after gigs. The band was not Ronald's life. His life was his life, and the band was just a band.

Lizzie was tugging on her knit hat. "I'm in."

"Can we go literally anywhere else?" Dan asked. "That place is everything I hate about the holidays, and the food is disgusting."

I crossed my arms, giving him my best *oh please.* "The food's not that bad. And we only go once a year. It's fun." Elsa's was a German restaurant famous for its over-the-top chintzy holiday decor. Colored lights dripped from the ceiling, fake snow glittered on the floor, and electric reindeer sang carols from the bar. A projector played Christmas movies against a wall, and the mulled wine cost twenty dollars. It was a total racket, but sometimes rackets were rackets for a reason.

Dan rolled his eyes, meaning he'd go, but not without complaining.

We hugged Ronald goodbye, zipped our coats up to our chins, and began the twenty-minute walk.

"Christmas is such a rip-off," Dan continued as we crossed Michigan Avenue. "You can sell carrots for fifteen dollars if you say they're for reindeers."

"We just made four thousand dollars singing 'I Saw Mommy Kissing Santa Claus,'" Lizzie said. "What makes you think we're any different from Elsa's?"

"What we do takes talent," he said. "And I'm allowed to play the game even if I don't agree with the rules."

There were few things Dan loved more than a rant, the exceptions being the Dave Matthews Band, the clear-frame-glasses trend, and his bicycle. I'd learned long ago that the best way to handle Dan's rants was to tune them out.

When we got to Elsa's and the line was a block long, Lizzie raised her brows at him. "I guess the rest of Chicago is fine with the rules."

We joined the end, stamping our feet on the sidewalk to stay warm. Other than the dozens of people waiting, the street was quiet—dark apartment buildings and closed-up shops.

Dan craned his neck to get a better view of the door. "How long are we going to wait? It's fucking apocalyptic out here."

Lizzie checked her phone and admitted, "I might be with Dan on this one. I could wait in this line and get frostbite, or I could answer this booty call from Marcella."

I looked at the text, which said, *Are you feeling naughty or nice?* with the Santa emoji followed by the tongue emoji. "Marcella from the arborists' party?"

We'd recently played the holiday gala of the Illinois Arborist Association, and although we'd agreed when our band first formed and we took ourselves way too seriously that we'd never hook up with guests to protect our "reputation," that rule had long gone unenforced.

"She's more fun than she sounds," Lizzie implored. "Don't hate me. It's been a long, cold winter."

I caved. "Fine. Go. Both of you. I'll eat schnitzel by myself."

Lizzie kissed me on both cheeks. "That's my Uber over there."

Dan kissed my lips. "I'm going to get the train. See you at home."

"Lots of kisses from my deserters!" I called after them.

I waited in line for a while, scrolling through my phone, eavesdropping, shivering. Every so often, I stood on my tiptoes and counted how many people were in front of me. Eventually I had to admit the schnitzel had started to lose its appeal. I was about to call it quits and head home when, up the perpendicular block, I spotted Christmas trees for sale underneath a red-and-white tent lit up with string lights.

Dan and I didn't have one yet because the tree was always a fight between us. He was morally opposed to chopping down trees for entertainment, and I was morally opposed to plastic prelit trees from Target. Not a knock against Target, but the joy of a Christmas tree was picking it out, lugging it home, singing along to holiday music as you strung lights and tried to cover the holes with well-placed ornaments. Taking a perfect tree out of a box and plugging it in just didn't feel right.

The lot was closing. Guys in Santa hats and red sweatshirts were pulling tarps over the trees and turning off the generators. An inflatable Santa melted into a puddle of polyester, one black-gloved hand poking up from the sidewalk like he was reaching for help. I took one last look at the door of Elsa's—still half a block away—and decided to forfeit the schnitzel in exchange for the smell of a real tree. Dan had left me here alone—he had no one to blame but himself.

I jogged up the block toward the red-and-white tent.

"Hey," I said to the nearest staffer in a Santa hat, "got time for one more sale?"

I was dragging my tree toward the train, alone on the street, when my phone vibrated in my pocket. A Chicago area code calling on Saturday night at midnight was unusual enough that I answered. "Hello?"

"Is this Melanie Hart?" a man asked.

"This is Mel. Who's this?"

"My name is Dr. Samuels. I'm a physician at the University of Chicago Medical Center. I'm calling about a patient named Connie Hart."

I stopped walking, my body tensing. "That's my mom. Is she okay?"

"Are you in Chicago? Can you come to the hospital? I'd prefer to speak in person."

"What's wrong?"

"I'd really prefer to talk here," he said. "My shift ends in an hour, but I can wait if need be."

As the words "But I have a Christmas tree with me" came out of my mouth, I wished I could swallow them back down. I'd always remember the first thing I said when I realized my mom died, and I wished it wasn't that.

The doctor sighed. "All right. I'm sorry to tell you this over the phone, but your mother died at the hospital earlier this evening.

We've been trying to track down your number. She's still here if you'd like to say goodbye. I can answer your questions, and our bereavement staff can help you make arrangements. I'll meet you in the waiting room on the fourth floor. Just let the nurses' station know you've arrived. Okay? Ms. Hart?"

A voice—not mine—said, "Okay. Sure. Yeah. Fourth floor."

I hung up and stood still for a while. I couldn't feel my hands and my ears were ringing. What had he said to do?

I looked down at my feet. Surprisingly, they were still there. I started walking, my body floating along the sidewalk. When I looked at my hand, I realized I was still dragging my tree. Nothing felt real.

I walked two miles home. It was after one a.m. when I unlocked the door. Dan was asleep, the apartment lifeless. From the back of a closet, I dug out my tree stand and strings of lights and wrapped them carefully around the branches, pushing the bulbs deep into its heart, using twice the number anyone else would have used. That was how my mom and I always did it.

Chapter 3

December 17

My sophomore year of college, I brought home my first serious boyfriend for winter break, Kamil. Having a man in the house was a new dynamic for me and my mom. She did not date and discouraged me from dating, too. When I'd started hanging out with boys in high school, she told me I was too young to make good decisions. But between the two of us, hadn't I been the one making good decisions for years?

So I had boyfriends—I just didn't tell my mom about them.

But Kamil was the first boy I'd ever loved, and I wanted my mom to see that our relationship was grown-up and real. Kamil was Muslim, so while his family didn't celebrate Christmas in a religious way—we didn't either—they had a big dinner on Christmas Eve with extended relatives, then left on Christmas Day for vacation, always an active one, like hiking, biking, or skiing. He was missing that tradition to be with me. Was I trying to prove my adulthood to my mom or to myself? At the time I thought it was neither. Now I think it was both.

Kamil didn't drink—no one in his family did—and I didn't drink when I was with him either. I hadn't said anything to him about my mom's drinking because I knew he wouldn't understand. He hadn't grown up loving someone with addiction. He'd say, "Why doesn't she go to rehab?" like the answer was that easy. My plan was to hide her habit through a combination of going to bed early and waking up before Kamil to carry the empty bottles to the blue bin out back. I'd also be especially celebratory, so the amount of wine she drank seemed connected to the holidays, an excuse to indulge, and not what happened every night, year-round.

Things went okay in the beginning. Kamil and I went to school locally at Columbia College, where I studied music and Kamil studied creative writing, so I kept us busy seeing friends and showing Kamil my part of the city. But on Christmas Eve, we joined my mom at our neighbor's party.

Clyde, who I'd discovered by then was the one in the Santa suit when I was a kid, had a Christmas Eve party every year. My mom and I were always invited, partly because Clyde was not the type of person to exclude and partly, I suspected, out of pity, since he knew we had no other family.

The party started at five, and by five-thirty, my mom had downed two martinis. I brought her a plate of food from the buffet, but she took only two bites before setting it down. I offered her water, but she asked for wine instead. There were only a handful of people at the party—our neighbors and other teachers from my elementary school, where Clyde taught science—and they circled around my mom, laughing while she told them about the time Clyde saved her from a raccoon that had snuck into our laundry room.

I remembered the story differently.

My mom hadn't come to get me at school that day, so after an hour of waiting by the pickup line, I went to Clyde's classroom and asked if he could drive me home. When we got there, the house was locked, but I knew how to sneak in through the dog door left over from the prior owners by sliding up the plastic partition. Inside, I found my mom on the phone, pacing. It sounded like she'd lost another client, which had been happening more and more.

Clyde had offered to help with my homework, so I let him in the front door, and we sat at the kitchen table. A minute later, we heard my mom scream and ran to find her on top of the washing machine. A raccoon had come in through the dog door because I hadn't replaced the partition. She was trying to poke it with a broom. Clyde ushered the raccoon outside, and we looked at each other in shock, then burst out laughing.

But my mom was sharing only the funny parts.

Clyde wasn't paying attention. He was giving Kamil a tour of his rare book collection. I kept glancing at them, trying to figure out what they'd see if they looked hard enough.

Around seven, I suggested we leave.

"You're no fun," my mom whined. "It's Christmas! Remember when you were a little girl and you'd stay up until Santa came?"

"I have to prep dinner for tomorrow and I want to go to bed early," I said.

I wasn't actually that boring. Normally, I wasn't the last to leave a party, but I also wasn't the first. In my mom's presence I overcompensated, a hyper-serious version of myself.

When she stood up from the couch, she stumbled.

I caught her thin arms, so featherlight a strong grip could break them. "Can you walk?"

"I'm fine," she insisted, but outside it was dark and the sidewalks were icy, so we had to walk in the freshly plowed street. I couldn't support her weight on my own. I looked at Kamil through the white cloud of my breath and admitted, "I need help."

He carried her home, her arm around his shoulders, his arm around her waist.

On Christmas morning, while we were curled beneath the purple comforter of my childhood, Kamil brushed my hair off my forehead and said, "I think your mom has a drinking problem," and I was surprised to feel relieved. I'd kept that secret for so long, and maybe I didn't have to.

Later I found my mom in the kitchen, drinking coffee in her bathrobe. "Was I bad?" she whispered, so quietly I nearly had to read her lips.

I opened the fridge to hunt for breakfast, anger prickling the back of my neck. "You were fine. Everyone was drinking a lot." And then, hoping to avoid another incident, I began a day of trying to feed her. "Let me make you an omelet."

I was thinking about that Christmas as I sat in my car with my phone in my hand, parked on the street outside my mom's house, tallying the people I needed to call with the news.

Clyde had died of a heart attack a few years ago. His kids were grown and gone, and his wife had moved away somewhere. My grandparents had died. So had my only aunt. My mom had a couple of relatives in New Jersey, but they'd never been in our lives. I wouldn't know how to get in touch with them even if I'd wanted to.

That left two people: my dad and Shelly, the accountant for my mom's shuttered business. Shelly liked my mom, so even when the business closed, she kept in touch and always showed up on holidays with platters of food.

I imagined a funeral with the three of us dressed in black, rows of empty seats behind us, and cringed. My mom would have said that was sadder than the death itself.

Did I need to have a funeral? Was it required? My mom would have hated the uncomfortable formality anyway. Too stuffy and melodramatic. She'd want a raucous party or nothing at all.

The only funeral I'd ever planned was for my guinea pig, Cheesehead. He was killed—by me—when I was in the fifth grade. I'd come home from school to find him frozen to death in his cage because it had been so offensively smelly that I'd left the window open in January. My mom drove me to a craft store so I could buy a wooden box and paint to make him a coffin. We buried him in the backyard, only an inch deep because the ground was frozen. My mom asked me if I wanted to say something, but my guilt was so suffocating I couldn't speak, so she stepped to the podium instead.

"Cheesehead, you were not a perfect pet," she said. "You peed on the couch and your cage smelled horrible. But I love my daughter and you made her happy, so thank you."

I shook off the memory and cranked up the heat in my car, cupping my hands around the vents. The preowned 2007 Toyota Corolla I'd nicknamed Lesley Stahl because it stalled out so much had lasted me ten winters. "Please don't quit on me now," I begged, but the weak air was barely temperate.

I reclined my seat and closed my eyes, wedging my hands in my armpits and stamping my feet to stay warm. I accidentally hit the gas and my engine revved.

I jumped ten feet.

My mom always said that—*I jumped ten feet.* She scared easily and so did I. When a car honked, when the doorbell rang, when a door opened unexpectedly. She'd gasp like a knife-wielding, mask-wearing monster from the seventh ring of hell had emerged from the sewer when really it was the delivery guy with the pizza she'd ordered just twenty minutes earlier.

It was one of the traits I'd tried not to inherit, but some things couldn't be helped.

My phone waited on my lap, heavy, pressuring me to make a decision and call someone, so I dialed Shelly first because she was the easier of the two.

"Mel," she answered. "It's been ages."

The news was still so surreal to me that saying the words out loud felt more like I was practicing them in the mirror. *My mom died. My mom died? My mom died!* Over the past few days, I'd had to repeat that fact to myself constantly, hoping that eventually the words that felt like snowflakes, weightless and melting as soon as they touched ground, would solidify into icy truth.

"I have bad news," I said, sounding numb to my own ears. "My mom passed away."

Shelly *mmm*ed. "I thought something was going on."

I fiddled with the heat knob, testing out the old classic of turning it off and turning it back on again. "What do you mean?"

"The last time I spoke to her, she wasn't in her right mind. It was like calling my gran when she went to memory care. Sort of distant, like she only half registered someone was listening on the line. I kept asking her what was new and she kept swearing under her breath, talking to herself. I asked her to call me in the morning and she never did. Oh, I feel awful now."

I was having no success with the heat. My teeth were chattering. Going inside was the obvious solution, but when I looked through the windshield at my mom's front door, a little frostbite seemed worth it. "When was that?" I asked.

"Two weeks ago, maybe? In the evening. I remember I'd just turned on Lester Holt." Shelly's voice got thick with tears. "I should have done something. I should have come over right then and there."

I didn't say so, but I'd stopped answering my mom's evening calls a long time ago.

I pulled my knees up, my shins pressing into the steering wheel. "Shelly, this is not your fault."

She blew her nose. "I know. But it's hard. When someone passes, there's nothing you can do but ask what-if."

A lump rose up in my throat, making it swell and ache, like I'd swallowed a rock. The last time I talked to my mom—the last time I'd ever talk to my mom—was from the home section of Target last week. I was trying to redecorate Dan's bedroom now that I had to sleep in it. The man considered black furniture, a black rug, and black bedding a "bold statement." My mom had an eye for decor and design I did not share. If left to my own devices, I'd end up with purple velvet pillows and a patio table in the dining room and try to get away with calling it eclectic. So I texted her photos of throw pillows and fake plants while we were on the line.

When I sent her the same blanket in four different colors, she said, "It's not the color that's the problem," and I laughed. "No," I agreed, "I'm the problem."

Then out of nowhere she said, "I need to hang up."

"Are you okay?"

"Fine. But I should go. I love you."

"I love you, too," I said, and she disconnected without her usual wish to see me soon and reminder to call anytime.

If anyone should have gone over right then and there, it was me.

I was thankful our last exchange was *I love you,* but loving my mother was a given. It was impossible to stop loving her, but it was so easy to be angry at her.

"If you don't mind my asking," Shelly said, drawing me out of my head, "what happened?"

I peered through the windshield at my bedroom window, where I'd spent years trying to answer that very question.

"She died in the hospital," I said. "But that's all I know. I wasn't there."

"Are you going to have an autopsy?"

"That's for people who drop dead with no explanation, don't you think? My mom wasn't healthy, you know that."

"She looked different the last time I saw her," Shelly agreed. "But of course I didn't say anything. I didn't want to make her feel bad. 'Don't take this the wrong way, but you look like shit'?"

I knew what she meant. At Thanksgiving, I was so startled when I walked in that I thought my expression would have given me away. Her skin looked yellow and waxy, and her body thin but swollen, like a noodle expanding in water. But I didn't want to hurt her feelings. My mom always worried about how she looked, fretting for hours with makeup and hair spray before even the simplest encounter with another person. A visit to the bank, a parent-teacher conference. "She was fragile," I agreed. "I didn't say anything either. I didn't want to make things worse."

Shelly and I were quiet on the line, and I wondered if we were thinking the same thing: that in trying to protect her, we'd let her die.

I took a deep breath and blew it out. "I'm at the house now," I told her. "I've got to go clean."

"Are you eating?" she asked. "I couldn't eat after my mother died."

Nothing tasted good anymore. "I've been surviving on a cheesecake my boyfriend's mom brought over."

Shelly tsked. "You need something spicy to bring you back to life. When's the funeral?"

"I don't think I'm going to have one. She had no friends or family other than the two of us."

"Oh dear. I'm afraid I wasn't much of one in that case. What about your father?"

I pinched the bridge of my nose, squeezing my eyes shut. A pounding headache was waiting around the corner, stalking me, ready to pounce. I could sense it. "He wouldn't come. I'm sure his wife wouldn't let him."

Always full of sound effects, Shelly guffawed. "That's ridiculous. What kind of grown man can't tell his wife not to stand between him and his own daughter? He needs to be there for you."

I laughed.

It came out more bitter than intended.

My parents divorced when I was three. I didn't even remember them as a couple. Until I was ten, I spent every summer with my dad in Florida. But then he married Susan, who had two daughters around my age. Susan didn't want me to come for the summer anymore because she and the girls always spent summers with her parents at a lake in Minnesota. Susan thought it would be more convenient for me to go to camp in Minnesota so they could visit with me "when time allowed" because there was no room for me at the lake house. Susan also thought it was rude for me to call my dad in the evenings because they were having "family time." Was I not family? I waited for my dad to stand up to Susan, but he never did. So I refused to go to camp in Minnesota and went to music camp instead, where I sang away my feelings and didn't respond to my dad's letters. After that, it was easier not to ask for anything from him, for fear that he'd say no.

"Call him," Shelly said. "He might surprise you."

I doubted that, but said goodbye and geared myself up for this phone call by listening to the entirety of Adele's "Hello" at full volume, closing my eyes and losing my thoughts in the lyrics as I sang along, so loud I probably scared the neighbors. Singing was the only way to turn my mind off. Besides, Adele said what I was feeling better than I ever could.

When the song ended, I pressed send before I could change my mind. I held my breath, hoping, though I wasn't sure whether I was hoping he'd answer or hoping he wouldn't.

When the last ring went to voice mail, I let out a pathetic little laugh. Of course he wouldn't answer. He was probably having dinner with Susan.

Leave a message and I'll call you right back, his recording promised. But I hung up. What was there to say in twenty seconds? *Hello, remember me? I need you.*

He used to be there for me when I needed him. It wasn't always like this between us. One summer, flying to Florida by myself, I pinched my finger between two plastic containers on the conveyor belt of the X-ray machine and pain shot all the way up my arm. *Do not cry,* I told myself, *do not cry.* I had to act grown-up so the flight attendants wouldn't think I was a baby and call my mom. I cupped my finger to my chest the whole flight there, gnawing my lip to distract myself so I wouldn't shed a tear. But when the plane landed, my dad was waiting for me at the gate. As soon as I saw him, I burst into tears and launched myself into his arms. I didn't have to be strong anymore. He was there to be strong for me. I could let go and cry.

He got some ice from a Wendy's and held it to my finger until it stopped throbbing while I sat on his lap. I didn't know which one I needed more—the cold or the comfort—but it didn't matter, because he gave me both.

Those days were over.

I turned off my car and emerged into the frozen afternoon. My mom's house, which she bought for us when she and my dad split, was plain and brick with two bedrooms on the first floor and a third in the attic—my room. Every house on the street had that same basic structure: two windows and a front door on the first level, with an attic window like a third eye. Small front lawns and two steps up to the porch. The houses were dressed differently, though—some with American flags, others with gardens, some that needed paint jobs. This was Jefferson Park, where no one had a lot of money, but everyone seemed to have enough to pay the bills and lead a quiet life. I went to theater camp every summer and took dance at the Y. My dad sent a check for three hundred dollars a month until I turned eighteen, and my mom ran her own business called Hart Help, offering transcription and office management services. We came up with that name together when I was little, and we were so proud of ourselves until we realized the double meaning. It took a few years for people to stop calling her about their cardiac issues. Ultimately, she had to put a disclaimer on her website to call 911 in a medical emergency.

When I was a kid, she was always focused on her career. She stayed up late typing with a glass of wine beside her and put on a blazer with shoulder pads after I got her out of bed in the morning. I thought she was the most important person in the world. It wasn't until later that she started losing clients, and I realized that maybe she was only the most important person in the world to me.

I walked up the path to the front door. I put my key in the lock. But I couldn't turn it. *Go in,* I told myself. *It's not that big of a deal.* But my hand refused to obey instructions from my brain. *What evidence of a life interrupted waits on the other side?* it asked. *What had she been in the middle of doing when she'd decided to call 911 instead of you?*

My phone buzzed. *Thank god,* I thought. An excuse to withdraw my key.

You okay? Lizzie had texted. She'd been checking in every hour on the hour.

The wind stung my fingers when I removed my gloves to write her back.

Not sure I can do this, I said.

You don't have to. There's no rush. Do you want my help?

Maybe I'll start with the garage . . . low hanging fruit

Don't push yourself. Just go home and watch TV and eat snacks!!

Later, I wrote. *I think feeling productive will help right now*

I stashed my phone and walked around the side of the house. Like many houses in Chicago, ours had a detached garage in the back accessible only from the alley. We never used it for anything but holiday decorations and stuff we intended to donate but never actually took to Goodwill. I wiped away snow to find the door handle and lifted, revealing piles of cardboard boxes and plastic storage containers. Everything was covered with dead leaves and dust.

I can do this, I told myself. *I have to. There's no one left but me.*

I started by forming piles: *Keep, Give Away, Recycle, Trash.* The air was dry and cold in the garage, but the more I worked stacking cans of old paint and heaving boxes of my high school textbooks, the warmer I got. An hour in, I took off my coat and gloves. Two hours in, I lost my sweatshirt. I opened one box to find the strings of lights we used to decorate our Christmas trees, impossibly tangled, but I kept them anyway. In another box I found the purple karaoke machine my mom bought me when I announced at age seven I was going to be a singer. I plugged it in and pressed the power button, but nothing happened. I carried it toward the giveaway pile, clinging to it, then rerouted at the last second and stacked it on top of *Keep.*

Some of the boxes were easier to empty. Halloween decorations, ratty beach towels. Magazines, receipts, takeout menus. I carried the recycling to the blue bin in the alley and trash to the black one.

How's it going? Lizzie texted during my third hour.

Fine. It's mostly junk. I did find my beanie baby collection though

My mom had driven me all over Chicago for those overpriced bags of sand. Once, Gabby—the one who'd broken the news to me about Santa—flew through O'Hare to visit her grandpa and called me from a pay phone to say a Hudson News had Princess Diana.

This was when you didn't need a ticket to get past airport security. My mom drove us to the airport in the middle of a school day to buy the Beanie Baby, and we had lunch at TGI Fridays. At the time, the excursion didn't seem that unusual to me. What my mom lacked in her ability to keep up with the day-to-day demands of raising a child, she made up for with big special events. On St. Patrick's Day she'd dye all my food green. On my birthday she'd have pizza delivered to school for my whole class. So it didn't matter that sometimes, if I had a fever or a nightmare, I couldn't wake her no matter how hard I shook her. It didn't matter.

omg are the tags still attached? Lizzie asked. *You can buy a new car now!!*

Lol you mean private plane, I joked, but these were worth more to me than that.

Lizzie responded with a gif of Christopher Lloyd saying, "Where we're going, we don't need roads."

I smiled and hearted the message.

The sun set so early in December that I had an hour left at best before it got too dark and cold to work, so I made several trips to my car and the bins in the alley until they were so full the lids wouldn't close.

In the garage, there were still a dozen boxes left, but I could see the oil-stained floor now. Exhaustion hit me like I'd walked straight into a wall. It was time to lie on the couch, watch a sappy holiday romance, and eat snacks.

I grabbed one last plastic container on the way out, the narrow kind for storing files. The long to-do list of death included finding my mom's will, Social Security card, bank statements, and credit cards so I could close her accounts. Years of office management bled into her personal life—her files were always neatly organized and labeled. This box looked promising.

In my car, I deposited the files on the passenger seat and cranked up the heat, refusing to lose faith in Lesley's longevity.

When I checked my phone, I had a text from Dan. *Still on for tonight?*

Shit. I banged my forehead against the steering wheel, having forgotten he wanted to take me out for dinner to "get my mind off things." It had seemed thoughtful at first, but the longer I'd lain in bed over the last few days, the less he was willing to listen to me talk about my feelings, and I'd begun to wonder whether "get my mind off things" meant "move on from this."

When I'd told him the news as soon as he'd woken up the morning after I found out—I hadn't slept; instead, I spent the night decorating the tree in a surreal fog—he'd said, "At least you weren't close."

I'd pulled away from his hug to look up at him. "What does that mean?"

"You weren't best friends. Not like some moms and daughters."

Did we need to be best friends to entitle me to grieve? If that was true, why did my blood feel like wet concrete churning through the barrel of a mixing truck?

On my way home, I wrote back. It still felt strange using the word *home* in reference to Dan's. I felt more like a guest with permission to stay as long as I liked.

Knowing snacks and TV were not in my future, I lost my incentive to leave. Instead, I flipped open the plastic tabs of the file box. Each file was labeled, but not with bank accounts and credit cards. They were full of my childhood projects.

Art, 2nd Grade
Essays, Middle School
Plays, Theater Camp
And *Letters to Santa*

I pulled out the first one, dated 1996.

Dear Santa, I've been good this year. I help my mom with chores she didn't even ask me to do. I finish my homework right away. Ask anyone. The only thing is I miss my dad and I was mad when Gabby won first place on field day. But look no one's perfect okay? If you don't mind I'd really like a Tickle Me Elmo. I know their sold out everywhere but that doesn't matter because you make your own. A karaoke machine would also be useful because I'm going to be a singer like Celine Dion so I have to get practicing. Do you do Hanukkah gifts? If so, Gabby wants a trampoline but her mom won't get her one because she says we'll break our necks. I really don't think a little jumping ever killed anyone, but Gabby's mom says she's the boss. Just think about it, okay? Merry Christmas. Love, Mel.

My mom had saved everything of mine, and here I was, throwing out everything of hers. Like she didn't matter, like nothing mattered.

Tomorrow was garbage day—the bins would be emptied and gone forever. I'd never again hold the sweater she'd worn or the book she'd read or the birthday card she'd written because I'd dumped them in a landfill somewhere. Suddenly, I could barely breathe. How could I throw her away?

I unbuckled my seat belt and pushed open my door, not bothering to turn off the car before running through the side yard and bursting through the gate to the alley. I grabbed the handle of the blue recycling bin and dragged it through the snow to the garage, then went back for the black one, struggling to pull it over patches of ice without slipping and spilling the contents everywhere. My hands were shaking as I lifted the garage door and shoved the bins inside, where they'd be safe, where no one could take them. I yanked the door closed and locked it.

Bent over, hands on my knees, I tried to catch my breath.

The bins would not be emptied. The bins were mine.

I decided not to tell Lizzie about this.

Chapter 4

December 17

Passing the porch on the way back to my car from the garage, I noticed a pink cardboard box. Had that been there when I arrived? It sat on the second step, partially hidden behind a clay pot full of snow.

A note was taped to the top.

I was a friend of your mother's. Please call me.
—Barbara

She left her number in cursive.

Barbara? The only Barbara I'd ever known was the secretary at my elementary school, who wore a red wig and cat eye glasses. She'd hated my mom because I was always late, so every morning Barbara had to write me a hall pass. School secretary Barbara was not sending me a condolence gift.

I lifted the lid to find an apple pie, perfectly golden and charmingly lopsided. It was the first food that had made me hungry in days. But I couldn't handle getting stuck in conversation with a total stranger when I was so exhausted I could barely form thoughts, so I typed the number into my phone and sent a text. *This is Connie's daughter Mel. Thank you for the very thoughtful pie.*

I carried it to my car and set it on the passenger seat beside my letters to Santa. The comforting scent kept me company as I drove to Dan's.

When Dan walked in a couple of hours later, I was horizontal on the couch, watching a Netflix Christmas movie, eating the pie straight from the box. The movie was exactly what I needed. Santa's daughter had gone to study environmental science in San Diego, had fallen in love with an NBA player, and was about to choose between becoming a celebrity wife or a scientist to save the North Pole from climate change.

I heard Dan toss his keys on the counter. "Hello?"

"Over here," I called without getting up.

He rounded the couch and frowned at the pie. "Are we not doing dinner?"

"We are." I dropped my fork in the box and closed the lid. "Sorry. I couldn't stop."

He looked at his watch, still wearing his coat. "It's seven. Didn't we agree to leave at seven? We're going to be late."

I tried to sit up, but I was so drained that it turned out to be one of the top ten most difficult things I'd ever attempted in my life. "Dan, I'm sorry, but is there any way we can stay home? I'm so tired I can't move."

He sat on the couch and cupped my ankle. "I really think dinner will be good for you, babe. It's not healthy to lie on the couch all day. You need some fresh air."

"The air is fifteen degrees, and I didn't lie on the couch all day.

But even if I did, most people would consider that a very normal thing to do three days after my mom died."

He lifted my hand and kissed it. "But you're not most people. You've spent your whole life worrying about your mom and carrying her burden. Now you don't have to do that anymore."

I sat up, easily now. "You're not suggesting this is a good thing, are you?"

"Obviously not. But now you can enjoy your life. Be with me. Focus on your career. Have adventures. That's all I'm saying."

"Was I not doing those things before?"

He exhaled through his nose. "You're not really listening to me, but it's fine. You're tired."

Pushing my blanket aside, I stood up. "I'm not that tired. I'll go change."

In our bedroom, with its black-on-black-on-black aesthetic, I rifled through my half of the closet for a nicer sweater and boots, but there wasn't much I could do to salvage my unwashed hair or puffy eyes. I looked in the mirror and shrugged before returning to the living room and opening my arms to say *Here I am.* "Ready."

He glanced at my lower half. "You're wearing sweatpants."

"These are leggings. I thought we were getting burgers."

His mouth tightened.

"You want me to change?" I asked. "I'll change."

Back in the bedroom, I put on black pants. They were leggings with pockets, actually, but he didn't need to know that.

I must have imagined the burger conversation because it turned out Dan had booked a table at Luna, a prix fixe "performance dining experience" where food was paired with sound and smoke and flavored bubbles and leggings were not appropriate. Rumor had it the meals took three to five hours and cost two hundred dollars per person, not including the wine pairing. I wished Dan had taken me to literally any other restaurant in Chicago. Chuck E. Cheese, the casino for children, would have been a better choice. Dan was myopic when making plans. There were places he wanted to go and things he wanted to do, and it wouldn't have occurred to him that a lengthy, elegant dinner was not the ideal agenda for a person who hadn't had the energy to shower. Usually this quirk didn't bother me. He made plans and I went along for the ride in a way that made life easy. But this time, when Dan disappeared behind his menu without a word, I pushed it back down so he had to look at me and asked, "What's going on? Why are we here?"

We were seated at a corner table by the window—easily a table that required a bribe. The corners of Dan's mouth twitched. "It's a special occasion."

Oh no. My nervous system jolted to high alert. "Dan, if you're proposing, it's really not—"

"I'm not proposing. Jesus. I have some news. But can we order first?"

I appraised him as he perused the wine list. This dinner was a scheme—I just hadn't figured out the endgame yet.

When a man came by and filled our waters, I chugged mine. *He's not proposing,* I reminded myself.

Dan scratched his carefully manicured stubble. "Does a Barolo sound good to you?"

I had no idea what that was. Dan was a self-proclaimed oenophile with a collection of wine in a walk-in closet, all of it biodynamic or grown beneath a waning moon or fertilized with ground-up seashells. Wine had too much baggage for me to enjoy it the way he did. I was too accustomed to proving a point, the point being I was not my mom. But I wasn't immune to being human. There were times—like now, for example—when I, too, wanted to dive headfirst into a large glass of alcohol.

"Sure," I murmured, glancing at the list. Then I saw the prices and nearly cried. "Hold on. We can't afford anything here. Can you just tell me what's going on?"

He snapped his menu closed and pushed it away, nearly upending the breadbasket. "Fine. I got a job."

My eyebrows lifted. "I didn't know you were looking for a job."

"I wasn't. I got recruited."

"To . . . work at a bank? Is that how we're paying for this dinner?"

He glared at me like I'd just accused him of joining the Oath Keepers. "Of course not. To go on tour."

That took a second to compute. The More the Marry Her wasn't going on tour.

Ah.

He meant with someone else. "With who?"

"This band called the Toms." He took out his phone, tapped the screen a few times, and slid it across the table, buzzing with excitement. "I went to school with these guys. They're getting big. They're going on a national tour starting in January and they want me to join their backing band. Rehearsals start right after New Year's in New York. But I was thinking we could go early and celebrate the holidays there. You know, Christmas in New York City? See the big tree and the Rockettes and everything? You always said you wanted to do that. It's the perfect time to get out of town and get you out of this funk."

While he was talking, a woman in all black had silently delivered our amuse-bouches and I'd slid mine into my mouth—a coin of mint jelly with a slice of jalapeño on top. It sat on my tongue as I processed this development, getting spicier and spicier until my throat was on fire and tears sprung to my eyes. I grabbed my water, realized it was empty, then grabbed Dan's and chugged it.

Dan was staring at me like I'd eaten spaghetti with my hands. "Are you okay?"

"I'm coming with you?" I rasped. "Like as your groupie?"

He laughed, patting my hand. "I'm flattered, but no. They need a backup singer. It's like this was meant to be."

I looked at the photo of an indie-rock trio on his screen. They looked like triplets, but that may have been the identical swooping haircuts and matching string instruments. I pictured myself taking up space on their tour bus, trying to fit in. "Are they all named Tom?"

Dan rolled his eyes.

"What about Lizzie and Ronald?" I asked. "And our clients? We have gigs coming up. We've already been paid."

He tore off a piece of bread and slathered it with cilantro-blackberry butter. "There are a zillion wedding bands in Chicago. Lizzie and Ronald can easily replace us, or the clients can hire someone else. It's not a big deal."

"I think it's a big deal." I thought it was a huge deal. Lizzie and Ronald were our friends, not to mention our clients had signed contracts drafted by a very scary lawyer we'd hired, who'd assured us they were ironclad.

The waiter came by and Dan ordered the prix fixe for both of us and the Barolo. We sat in silence until the first course arrived. I looked at what appeared to be a pile of shredded iceberg lettuce, but when I stuck my fork in it, it hit something. I scooped aside the greens to reveal . . . a rock? I poked it. My fork punctured the skin. It was sausage.

The rest of the courses were just like that—sometimes it wasn't clear which part of the dish was edible. One course was served on a platter of spun egg white that turned out to be part of the meal itself, while another was served inside a dark tube that looked like chocolate but turned out to be wood.

While we ate, Dan told me about the tour stops in Asheville, Austin, Los Angeles, Portland, and little towns I'd never heard of, but which he assured me were up-and-coming. He raved about how talented the band was. "They're on another level. Folksy, gritty, electric. It's a totally new sound. I can't even describe it. You have to listen. They're going to be huge, and we'll be in it on the ground level. The best part is they're actually nice guys. And the pay is great. Better than I ever imagined. So yeah, we can afford this dinner."

I nodded, moving a lump of gelatinous carrot cream around my plate. "Wow."

He gaped at me. "That's it?"

"I'm adjusting to the idea," I said. "There's a lot going on right now. This is big news."

I could see the appeal of hitching a ride out of Chicago, preaching the gospel of *out of sight, out of mind*. My mom's house was like a slowly expanding sinkhole trying to swallow me. By hopping on a tour bus, staying in motion, I could outrun it. Whenever the house caught up, I'd skip town again. But the country was only so big. Eventually I'd run out of places to hide.

"I'll think about it," I promised as dessert arrived.

Dan picked up an ice cream cone made of grass. "What's there to think about? You want to be a wedding singer for the rest of your life?"

"I wasn't opposed to it." I licked the ice cream to find it was actually cold whipped cauliflower. "I love our band."

Dan shook his head. "You're crazy if you don't take this job. This is an opportunity to put yourself out there in a real way. You're good enough to release an album. That people would actually buy. Why aren't you even trying?"

Under his scrutiny, my skin began to itch. I wished I were having an allergic reaction to the cauliflower cream. Really, I was allergic to the idea of taking such a risk. I'd spent my whole life avoiding that seasick feeling that said I wasn't on solid ground, that I didn't know what was going to happen, and Dan's invitation threatened to rock my boat, which was barely staying afloat as it was.

"I think whoever thought this would taste like ice cream is crazy," I deflected.

He dropped the cone back on his plate. "Yeah. This place sucks. Not exactly what I had in mind for my big reveal. Sorry."

As bad as his timing was, this job was his dream. I nudged his leg with my knee. "I don't know about you, but I could use a burger."

Chapter 5

December 19

Picking up my mom's ashes wasn't an errand I'd thought much about until it was on my to-do list.

The morning after she died, a woman from the hospital's Care After Death team called to ask what funeral home I'd chosen so they could arrange for a transfer. I hadn't chosen one—I didn't know I was supposed to choose one. The days that followed were a crash course in death logistics. I had to choose a cremation container and an urn. The mortuary sent me a PDF with pictures and prices. I was disturbed to find that the cremation containers were effectively cardboard boxes from Home Depot that cost hundreds of dollars, painted to look like coffins. I ended up paying double for real wood, though the likelihood of fraud seemed relatively high given that I'd never actually seen the container. Still, it was worth it. My mom hated Home Depot.

The urn was harder. There were dozens of options, made of different materials and patterns. Mosaic, mahogany, hand-painted glass. None of them felt right. The material was either too plain or too shiny. The patterns were too busy or too floral. Eventually I chose one I thought my mom would have considered tasteful, knowing I'd never find the perfect urn because even though a person could, in the end, fit into a jar, no single jar could ever capture that person's entire life.

Lizzie insisted on driving me to the funeral home because she didn't want me to run this errand alone. We were due at rehearsal later, so she took me to lunch at Devil Dawgs for Chicago-style hot dogs, after which we planned to "swing by" the mortuary on our way to Ronald's. My one request was that she wait in the car. To the extent a funeral home was bad luck—and no doubt it was for the people who were in there—I didn't want to risk it spreading.

Inside, the waiting room was cold, with classical piano music playing on low volume from an outdated stereo. It smelled like chemicals masked with air fresheners, and all the furniture was covered in plastic. Was there a funeral home in the world that didn't resemble the living room of a 1980s mob wife?

Behind the reception desk, a girl wearing scrubs with her braids in a high ponytail typed on the computer while forking salad into her mouth. Her name tag read: *Intern, Mortuary Science, Malcolm X College.*

I got the heebie-jeebies just knowing what was behind the door marked *Employees Only.* She was brave.

She covered her mouth when I approached. "Sorry. Working lunch. Can I help you?"

"I'm here to pick up my mom. Connie Hart?"

She typed something and read her screen. "She's ready. I'll be right back."

When she opened the *Employees Only* door, I focused on choosing a Jolly Rancher from the bowl on her desk so I wouldn't catch a glimpse of what was back there.

A few minutes later, she returned holding a blue glass urn, the one I'd chosen. A label was taped over the lid with my mom's name, birthday, and date of death. The intern helped me fill out some paperwork, navigating the details with kindness. She reminded me of Dr. Samuels, whom I'd never meet but would always remember.

"This is the death certificate," she said. "Can you verify that everything is correct?"

I took the envelope and opened it. The death certificate said where my mom was born, her parents' names, my name, whom she'd married, where she'd lived. A life, summarized.

There was a section labeled *Immediate Cause of Death,* and there it read: CARDIAC ARREST.

So that was it. Her heart stopped. Maybe I'd never have made it to the hospital even if I'd known.

But my gaze fell to another section beneath it, and my own heart tightened. I had to read it twice.

Other significant conditions contributing to the death: CIRRHOSIS OF THE LIVER. I slid the paper back inside, not prepared to cry in front of this very kind stranger. "It's correct."

She offered me a tissue. "I'm so sorry for your loss. Here . . ." She handed me a white gift bag tied with ribbon. "These are some gifts for your healing process."

In the parking lot, Lizzie waited with the heat on. I folded myself into the passenger seat with my deathly possessions and sat quietly, hugging the gift bag and urn.

"You okay?" she asked.

My body hurt, as if I'd just spent fifteen hours personally digging my mom's grave. Every time I thought the weight of my grief could not possibly get heavier, I was wrong. "I got the death certificate," I said. "It says what killed her."

I handed her the envelope so I didn't have to say it out loud.

Lizzie read it, holding the paper like it was holy. "Are you surprised?"

"No." I wedged the urn between my feet. "I'm pissed, actually. Really fucking pissed. Do you know the last time I asked her about her liver? Less than a month ago. One month."

We'd been standing in the kitchen. She was drinking wine at the table and I was chopping leeks for Thanksgiving dinner. It was shortly after I'd walked in to find her looking so shockingly sallow and bloated. A beloved high school teacher of mine had recently died of liver cancer, and everyone in the neighborhood was mourning him. Noticing the signs of illness all over her body, I seized the opportunity to ask casually, "How's your liver?"

My heart had immediately started racing. Whenever I broached the subject of her drinking, she'd either tell me she'd been cutting back, change the subject, or assure me she was in perfect health. Eventually I started to wonder whether I was the one with the problem. Was I seeing things? Was I too uptight? Was I an ungrateful daughter? I wasn't a doctor. Maybe I was wrong. Maybe all of this was normal.

So I'd stopped asking. I'd added the topic to the List of Things We Do Not Talk About, along with my dad, the closing of her business, and my childhood. Avoiding the topic altogether kept me sane and kept my mom from getting her feelings hurt. On those terms, we maintained a careful, if dishonest, relationship.

Now I had proof we were both lying—to each other and to ourselves.

I wasn't seeing things. I wasn't too uptight. I was right all along. *I was right I was right I was right,* said a voice in my head. Being right had never felt worse.

In answer to my question about her liver, my mom had said, "Fine," quite cheerfully, and started talking about the neighbor's cat. I'd returned to the leeks and we'd moved on. Three weeks later she was gone.

The heat in Lizzie's car was overwhelming. I rolled down her window and welcomed the cold air whipping in.

"My mom made me feel crazy for worrying about her," I said. "Turns out I should have been worried. I should have seen this coming."

We were running late, but Lizzie made no move to leave the parking lot. She turned her whole body toward me, sitting sideways in her seat, and put her hand on my arm. "You're not a doctor. It wasn't your job to diagnose her. Maybe she didn't even know."

"Or she was in denial," I said, my words like an icicle, cold and sharp.

"Or she thought she was protecting you," Lizzie said, her gentleness in contrast.

"This doesn't feel like protection."

My boundaries were my protection. They were survival. They allowed me to love her without my anger being revealed. Now one piece of paper had broken them down.

Lizzie peeked into the gift bag. "What's this?"

I untied the ribbon and pulled out a card. *"Grief is a wound to the soul. It must be tended to with grace and patience. Here are some items to support you on your healing journey."* I pulled out something white and fleecy. "Look, a sad death blanket. And"—I reached into the bag again—"a sad death candle. Am I healed?"

"I don't know, are you?" she asked, eyebrows raised.

"On the whole, I'd say I've probably never felt worse."

"So that candle's not going to cut it, then." Lizzie shifted into drive. "It smells nice, though."

When we got to Ronald's for rehearsal, I brought my mom inside. I couldn't stomach leaving her in the car like a forgotten bag of groceries. Instead, I put her on a shelf in Ronald's garage, next to a toolbox. Ronald restored old cars for fun, so his garage looked more like a mechanic's shop than a rehearsal space. But it was free and his neighbors never complained, so we happily kicked aside greasy rags and random scraps of metal.

Ronald was at his drum set, fully in the zone, eyes closed, headphones on, warming up. But when I tapped him on the shoulder to say hello, he dropped his sticks and swallowed me in a bear hug. "I'm so sorry," he said in my ear. Before any of us knew Ronald, he'd lost his wife in a car accident, when their twins were only babies. He always said she was his guiding light. His grief was so pure I was embarrassed to accept his sympathy. If Ronald's mourning was a gentle violin, mine was a Metallica concert with poor acoustics, noise crashing into other noise. I didn't know where my grief belonged, but I was sure there was some kind of hierarchy—and mine wasn't in the same league as Ronald's.

"You've got to take care of yourself," Ronald said. "Eat, sleep, drink water, exercise. Go to therapy. Book all your sessions a year out and pay in advance so you don't cancel. You're going to want to cancel when you've been going for weeks and you still feel like shit. Do not cancel. It takes time."

"I'll try," I promised. "Right now I just really need to sing."

Singing was my escape. It's why I was a theater kid—because onstage, I didn't have to think. The stage was the most solid ground imaginable, where life followed a script. I didn't write the words, I just sang them.

I was warming up with Sara Bareilles's "Gravity" when Dan walked in looking like he'd killed the class pet. He was wearing a new jacket, I noticed, vaguely military and not warm enough for this weather. And he'd gotten his hair cut to look remarkably similar to the Toms trio. He buried his hands in his pockets. "I need to talk to you guys about something important."

Lizzie's disharmonic tuning withered and died. Ronald set his sticks aside. I steeled, trying to beam Dan a silent message. *Please, not now.*

But he barreled on. "Mel and I are going on tour with a real band."

I jerked my head back. "What?"

"We're leaving for New York in two days." As he launched into the details, he was practically twitching with excitement. "Rehearsals are starting in January, so we're going early to find a place to stay for a couple months and spend the holidays there like Mel's always dreamed of. The first show's at Terminal 5. Can you believe it? Terminal fucking 5! Then we're hitting the road—all the major venues. The Forum, Red Rocks. Insane, right?"

"Dan—" I tried again.

"They called me totally out of the blue and said, 'We need you, buddy.' How could I say no to that?"

Lizzie and Ronald watched Dan pace the garage like tired Americans observing the spectacle of yet another presidential debate. Frowning, exchanging glances of *What is this guy talking about?*

"Dan," I said a little louder.

"So I was like, 'Well, hey, man, I've got to bring my girlfriend,' and it turned out they needed a backup singer. How great is that?"

Lizzie glanced at me with a question mark on her face. In return, I pretended to gouge my eyes out.

"I'm not going with you!" I blurted.

He stopped pacing and gawked at me. "What?"

"I never agreed to go. I agreed to think about it. And I've thought about it, and I'm not going."

He stared at me for several seconds, incredulous. That was how he looked whenever someone didn't agree with him. "Are you serious? Why not? This is a huge opportunity."

"Because I'm already in a band." I gestured at Lizzie and Ronald. "And I need to stay here. I've got a lot of shit going on. I can't just run away."

"It's not running away," Dan argued. "It's running *to.*"

"It wouldn't be that way for me."

Lizzie came to stand beside me and murmured, "Are you sure? This actually does sound like a great opportunity."

"I'm sure," I said. Ronald was right. Grief was automatic, but grieving was a choice, and I needed to put in the work.

Dan stepped closer, speaking only to me. "What's going on here? Are you scared? Because I'm scared. I'm scared shitless. But I gotta go for it. I'll always regret it if I don't."

"Okay," I said, "so go. I'm not stopping you."

He stepped even closer, taking my face in his hands, cupping my jaw. "I'm talking about taking the next step in your career."

"Right," I agreed. "But I'm talking about taking the next step in my life."

We stared at each other—me, trying to stay strong; Dan, apparently waiting for me to change my mind.

Finally he caved, shaking his head in disbelief. "All right. Okay. Fine. I get it. It's not a good time for you. But this is my chance, so I guess we'll do long distance. I'll only be gone, like, eight months and you can stay in the apartment and I'm sure my mom will be glad it's not empty. It'll be fine." He was pacing again.

I caught his shoulder. "Actually, I think it would be better if you go on the tour and I find a new place to live."

His mouth fell open. "You're seriously making me choose? This tour or you?"

I sensed Lizzie watching, gauging whether I needed help. I kept my voice even. "This will be easier. If nothing's changed when you get back, then great."

Dan stared at me, gobsmacked. "I can't believe this. We've been together three years and you're dumping me because I got my dream job?"

"Long distance is hard," I said. "I've done it before. It never works."

Dan started collecting his equipment, shaking his head. He unplugged wires and shoved them in his backpack. "You've never done it with *me.* So how do you know it's going to be hard? And even if it is, so what? Life is hard. Relationships are hard. I thought you knew that, given everything you've been through. I thought you'd be more grown-up about this. I forgot you cut and run. Remind me: What happened to all your other boyfriends? Your dad?"

I clenched my fingers around my mic. "You don't know what you're talking about."

Dan swung his bass strap over his shoulder and lifted an amp in each hand before looking me straight in the eye. I was shocked to see tears. "Is that why you were with me? It was easy? I had an apartment and I was always around?"

I didn't even like your apartment! I wanted to scream, but I wasn't sure whether that made his argument more or less true. "It was more than that and you know it."

Dan let out a bitter laugh as he punched the garage door opener. "I guess that proves my point."

The garage door slowly ground its way up, letting in the icy, chaotic wind.

"Now you're just trying to hurt me," I said, my voice low.

He looked at the ground as he said, "Hurting you would mean you'd let me in, so that's impossible."

Once the door opened, he had to make several trips to the street to load his equipment, extending the agony of this goodbye. Lizzie was trying to catch my eye, but I pretended not to notice. I wanted to believe Dan was having a childish temper tantrum, but I worried these were the most mature things he'd ever said.

When he grabbed his last music stand, he spoke to my feet. "You can come back to the apartment tonight. I'm not kicking you out in the middle of winter." Like he might have considered it in a different season.

"You can stay with me," Lizzie whispered, and I mouthed *thank you.*

Dan turned to Lizzie and Ronald, opening his arms for a hug. "I guess this is it."

"Guess so," Ronald said, and saluted him. Lizzie bent her upper half forward for a stiff pat on the back. The band was being asked to take sides again, and mercifully, they'd taken mine. I hovered, unsure what to do. Dan wouldn't look at me.

He lingered for another few seconds, turning away, then turning back again, as if debating reclaiming the last word. Part of me wanted to embrace him, to say I was sorry, that he was right, that we'd never had a chance because I'd never given us one. But the kindest words I could think of were *Thank you for fulfilling your role as boyfriend and good luck in your future endeavors.* So probably better to say nothing at all.

I knew in my gut this was the right choice, perhaps *because* he was right. I'd never let him in, which wasn't doing either of us any favors. He wanted more from me, and I wanted more from me, too.

Ronald punched the button to lower the garage door. We all watched it grind its way to the ground again, sealing in the silence.

Lizzie turned to me. "What the fuck just happened?"

"We broke up," I said, staring at the garage door like he'd left a Dan-shaped hole in it.

"*You* broke up," Ronald clarified. "The band is still going strong."

He settled himself behind his drum set like he couldn't have cared less that we were one member down. Maybe the band was better off without the shackles of Dan's ego. He'd always thought we were nothing but a gap-filler, a joke band. At the very least, we'd never have to endure another of his histrionic renditions of Jeff Buckley's "Hallelujah" ever again.

"Are you okay, though?" Ronald asked. "That was a trip—and not the fun kind."

I wrapped the cord of my mic around my wrist, tugging it, testing its strength. "Fine," I said, a flat note. "Let's rehearse."

But Ronald didn't pick up his sticks. "What do you say we skip today? Order pizza? Talk?"

I shook my head. "We've got to figure out how to organize our sound with no bass."

He and Lizzie exchanged a look. It was easy to read. *I'm worried. You? Yeah, me too. Are we going along with this?* They shrugged, giving in.

As Ronald positioned himself behind the drums and flexed his fingers, he said, "Dan was right about one thing. No relationship that's worth it is easy."

"You were married to the love of your life," I said. "Of course it was easy."

"She was the love of my life," Ronald agreed. "But we fought every single day, including the day she died."

Lizzie had begun counting me in for "Gravity," but I missed my cue, stunned by Ronald's confession. Maybe I wasn't alone in my noisy grief. Maybe, somehow, Ronald had found a way to turn the noise into music.

Chapter 6

December 19

My mom had been to the hospital once before for what I assumed was a drinking-related health scare, though I didn't know for sure, because she'd never told me. It was the year after Kamil had come home with me for Christmas, and he'd invited me to spend winter break with him in Toronto to meet his family, then join them for snowshoeing in Banff. Snowshoeing was not high on my list of priorities, but Kamil was. I thought we were going to be together forever because I was twenty and in love. And I wanted a normal, simple holiday, without Clyde's party, without transforming into the hyper-serious, hyper-boring version of myself I hated.

But going to Canada meant my mom would have no one. She'd decorate the tree by herself, watch *Miracle on 34th Street* and eat tomato soup by herself, go through the motions of our traditions by herself. I didn't know if I'd even have reception in the mountains to call her on Christmas morning and tell her I missed her.

I tried to convince myself it was no big deal. What was so significant about these two weeks? Why did I think she couldn't survive them without me? She was a grown woman. I'd moved out two years ago. She'd managed just fine.

The night before I was supposed to leave, she called me from the hospital. I stopped packing and rushed over, having flashbacks to my recurring nightmares from when I was a kid—the ones where my mom died. In the lobby, I sprinted past a twinkling tree and a giant menorah to an elevator stickered with snowflake decals. None of the manufactured holiday cheer masked the smell of death and antiseptic.

When I pushed open the door of her room, her chapped lips spread wide into a smile. I hugged her tightly, even though her bones threatened to snap in my arms. When was the last time I'd hugged her like that?

"You're here," she whispered, and kissed me all over my face while I breathed in the chemical detergent of her hospital gown. *You're alive,* I thought. I wished I was seven again, with her body wrapped around mine in my twin bed, my mom, my safe place.

When we let go, I held her hand, something I'd never done as an adult. "What happened?"

She lay back, hair combed and makeup on despite the drab gown and throne of hospital pillows. "I had a little high blood pressure, but they told me I'm fine."

"It must have been pretty high if you're in the hospital." I tried to read the heart monitor that beeped steadily above her head, but had no idea what I was looking at other than evidence her heart was still beating.

I stayed with her that night, telling stories about my new roommate's strange habit of misusing objects. She used a hamper to store food, spoons to apply concealer, and a whisk to paint. On the TV with three channels, we watched *American Icon,* a prime-time national singing contest that debuted in 2002. We'd gotten hooked during season one and watched it together until I went to college. The winner of the first season had gone on to become one of the most famous singers of the last two decades.

"I've always dreamed of you auditioning for this show," she said. "You're better than all these people."

Of course I'd dreamed of this, too, at least once a day since the show first aired. "And have the manager in sunglasses stick a knife in my soul on national TV? I'm not brave enough to do that."

My mom hit me with a pillow. "Are you crazy? You're the bravest person I know. How many times have you sung in front of your entire school?"

She didn't understand that singing in front of the entire school was the opposite of brave. It was hiding.

I plucked exactly two pieces of popcorn and one M&M from our stash on her hospital tray. She had long ago taught me that mixing sweet candy with salty popcorn in a two-to-one ratio was the most satisfying movie snack. "It's just not my thing."

"If you're not going to do it for you," she said, "then do it for me."

Eventually she fell asleep, and I curled up on the reclining chair, trying not to doze off so I wouldn't dream.

In the morning, she woke me up by throwing a bread roll from her breakfast at my head. "Don't you have a plane to catch?"

I sat up, rubbing my neck. "I'm not going, obviously."

She tried to get out of bed, but a nurse checking her vitals pushed her back down.

"You have to go," she insisted. "I'll feel terrible if you stay. Besides, I want to hear all the details about your romantic trip. I'm fine."

"You are not fine," I said like I was *her* mom. "You are in the hospital."

She turned to the nurse. "Am I getting out today? My daughter thinks I'm going to die in here."

The nurse was injecting something into her IV. "Not today, hon. Maybe tomorrow."

My mom opened her hands. "See? I'm fine."

So I gathered my things and put on my coat, but when I looked at her to say goodbye, I couldn't leave. She was going to spend the night alone in the hospital on Christmas. "I don't feel right about this," I said, my eyes stinging with tears.

She held me, kissing my hair. "You have to go and live your life. That's the whole point."

I flew to Toronto with Kamil and cried the whole way there. Snowshoeing sucked. My mom wasn't released the next day or the one after that. She spent Christmas Eve alone in the hospital, then went home on Christmas morning to an empty house.

I broke up with Kamil as soon as we got back to Chicago.

After rehearsal, I insisted Lizzie drive me to my mom's house. She parked on the street and we stared through the windshield at its emptiness.

I unbuckled my seat belt. "I'll be fine. I just need to get over it."

Even though I appreciated Lizzie's offer to stay with her, she lived in a tiny studio with a toilet behind a curtain and ran a dog-sitting business to make money on the side. At any point, she had between two and seven dogs sleeping in her bed. I couldn't take up space she desperately needed.

The fact was, I had a place to stay. I owned a house now. There it was, staring back at me. I'd spent the first eighteen years of my life there. I already knew where the extra toilet paper lived and how to turn on the shower when the knob got stuck. I had plenty of sweatpants and choir T-shirts from high school and probably a tube of toothpaste from back then, too. Now that I wasn't with Dan, I could move in, clean it out, and make it my own. Problem solved.

If only I could manage to get out of Lizzie's car.

"Are you sure? Because we can go to my mom's instead. She's desperate to feed you and she has plenty of space. You don't need to share a pillow with a Rottweiler, I swear to god."

Lizzie was from a huge Filipino family, and food was their love language. At Christmas, her family hosted a hundred people, too many to fit in the house, so they gathered around fires in steel barrels in the backyard. That abundance of togetherness and life couldn't have been in starker contrast to my future.

"Thank you," I said, "but I'm being ridiculous. I have a perfectly good place to stay right there." I gestured toward my mom's house.

Still, I made no move to exit the car.

"You could have gone with him," Lizzie said, her voice as warm as the interior of her beat-up little Honda. "If you wanted to. I hope you didn't stay because you thought I'd be mad. I mean, I would have been, but only for a little while, and only because I was jealous."

I tore my gaze from the drawn curtains to smile at her. "I did do it for you and I'm going to hold it against you for the rest of my life."

She put her bare feet up on the vents. "True friendship. Can't say I would have done the same, to be totally honest. Terminal 5?" Imitating Dan, she added, *"Terminal fucking 5!"*

"But you're braver than I am." I looked back at the curtains. I couldn't remember the last time they'd been opened.

"I think you're doing the brave thing in staying."

"Staying to spend Christmas alone, which is apparently all my fault?"

"Don't listen to him. He's a dick. You're not alone. You have me and Ronald, and honestly, it doesn't get better than Ronald."

My mom's house was the only one on the street without strings of lights. Compared to the merry houses on the rest of the block, with their electronic reindeer and inflatable Santas, it looked so bitter and closed-off.

"True," I agreed, "but Dan's right about me. I kept my mom at a distance. I did the same thing to my dad. I was hurt and angry, so I gave up."

"If you're blaming yourself for putting some distance between you and your mom, you were doing what you needed to do to protect yourself. That's okay. Coming from my family, I've had to pay a lot of therapists a lot of money to drill into my head that boundaries are healthy."

I looked down at my lap, blinking away tears.

Lizzie put boundaries around her life. I put boundaries around my heart.

When I tried to speak, only a whisper escaped around the lump in my throat. "She didn't even try to call me. Probably because she thought I wouldn't care."

Lizzie leaned across the console to hug me. "I'm sure there was an explanation. She could have been unconscious. You don't know."

I pulled away, wiping my face. "Maybe," I played along. "The doctor did say they were tracking down my number."

"See?" She rubbed my back. "Your mom would have wanted to say goodbye."

Goodbye. That hadn't sunk in yet. Sometimes when I got a text or my phone rang, I still expected it to be her.

I bent over to reach for my purse and my mom, forcing myself to stop procrastinating and go inside, but—

She wasn't there.

A vision of her sitting on a shelf next to a toolbox popped into my head.

I leaned against the headrest and closed my eyes. "Shit. No wonder she didn't want to call me. I forgot her."

By the time Lizzie had driven us to Ronald's and back again, it was dinnertime and my stomach was growling. The house loomed, covered with a blanket of snow. *Go in, order food, and go to bed,* I told myself. *Deal with everything else tomorrow.*

Lizzie put her hand on the cold glass of my mom's urn. "What are you going to do with her ashes?"

"I have no idea." I hoped the answer would reveal itself. "She didn't really have interests. The families of hikers and boaters are so lucky."

"I want my ashes sprinkled at Petrillo so I can listen to music for all of eternity."

"That's genius. Can I steal that?"

She pressed her hand to her heart. "I would be honored to spend forever together."

"You mean until it rains," I corrected.

"Then we'll join the lake creatures."

"You mean the sewer creatures."

She laughed. "I can see why you're having a hard time with this. Think symbolically. Not literally."

When I got out of the car, the wind cut through my coat like it was made of Kleenex, pushing me to hurry up the steps and get inside. I dug blindly in my purse for keys and jammed them into the lock.

My mom always insisted I call her when I was five minutes away so she could clean up and wait by the door. I gave her ten or fifteen instead, knowing she needed more time. Otherwise, when I walked up the steps she'd call, "Wait! Don't come in!" and I'd shiver on the porch until she stashed whatever she didn't want me to see and put her lipstick on. Then she'd pull open the door and throw her arms out. "You're here!" she'd shriek every time, then give me dozens of kisses, all over my cheeks, my shoulders, my hair, until I was smeared with her lipstick. I'd come to dread those kisses because she always smelled like wine, a hint of what she was hiding.

But when I opened the door now, the house was dark and silent.

No one called, "You're here!" or threw their arms out to greet me. No one kissed me all over my face, my shoulders, my hair.

I would have given anything to feel those kisses again.

I pressed my fingertips to my cheeks, trying to remember what they felt like. When I couldn't conjure the sensation of her cheek to my cheek or her lips to my skin, I couldn't breathe. I scrambled for air in shallow gasps, falling against the doorframe as the floor tipped. I wanted to scream, but who would hear me? There was nobody home.

I slid to the floor until my breathing returned to normal, then forced myself to move. Sitting still was dangerous. I quickly scanned the house for hazards—a space heater left on, water left running—avoiding everything else. It wasn't too late to call Lizzie and beg her to turn around.

Back at the front door, which opened directly to the living room, I noticed the TV screen was black but illuminated, like it was on, but paused.

I picked up the remote and hit play.

The picture returned. It took only a split second for me to recognize the show—*American Icon.*

My mom had been watching our show when she'd gone to the hospital and never come home. And I hadn't been there for her.

I couldn't stay here. What had I been thinking? I'd sleep better in a dog bed than a room with all of these memories.

I was reaching for the door handle when someone knocked. At first I thought it was Lizzie, reading my mind. "Thank god," I said through the door.

"It's not God," said a woman's voice. "It's the Land Shark."

It took a second to sink in, but I recognized the old SNL reference. My mom had *The Best of Saturday Night Live 1975–1980* on VHS, and we used to watch them together. We had all the skits memorized.

"Who are you?" I asked.

"Candygram," said the woman, just like the skit where the shark tries to convince young single women to open the door. "Telephone repairman. No, wait. Flowers."

Frozen with one hand on the knob, I was suspended in a slice of the universe between the dead and the living. The woman sounded nothing like my mom. She spoke with a New York accent and the flair of my high school drama teacher. But the reenactment of my mom's favorite skit was just like I'd heard her do a hundred times.

"You're that clever shark everyone's talking about," I said, a test.

"Me?" asked the woman. "I'm just a dolphin."

I wondered if I had good and truly lost it, but that didn't stop me from opening the door to the Other Side. For the wild and hopeful second between turning the knob and registering who was standing on the porch, I was sure it would be her.

Instead, I was face-to-face with a stranger.

"Hello, sweetheart. I'm Barbara."

Chapter 7

December 19

Barbara. Barbara of the pie. She was not the secretary from my elementary school who wrote all those late slips, nor did she wear a wig and cat eye glasses. This Barbara had an artistic elegance to her, with an ankle-length velvet coat, tall black riding boots, and turquoise jewelry. Wild gray curls twirled in the wind. I'd never seen her before in my life.

"You sent the pie," I said.

"You never called," she said.

"I texted you."

Barbara wagged her finger. "I don't text. That number is a landline. I know I'm the last person in America with a landline. But I could never get rid of that number in case your mother ever tried to call me."

I held on to the doorframe, guarding the entrance. "Were you expecting her to call?"

Barbara opened her hands, her bangles clinking like the ones my mom used to wear. "Some people happen to get a kick out of reuniting with their former best friend."

Former what? I looked at her more closely, searching for anything familiar. A photo I'd seen. A story I'd heard. I came up with nothing. "I'm sorry. I don't remember my mom mentioning you."

"I'm not surprised, since she hated my guts," Barbara said. "That aside, I was hoping I could convince you to come for dinner."

That was the strangest, least persuasive condolence I'd ever received. "That's nice of you, but you really don't have to—"

"It's not out of generosity, sweetheart. I'd like to know you. And I think you might like to know me."

I took in her lifted chin, her resolute gaze. "Why?"

She clapped, as if I'd already agreed. "It's a long story better told over lasagna. I'm an excellent cook. Did you eat my pie? If you ate my pie, you know that already."

I'd not only eaten the pie but licked the crumbs. "You made that? It was so good I assumed it was store-bought."

Barbara threw her hands up. "Store-bought! I'm offended. Mine are better than store-bought."

"Barbara—"

"Barb, please. You're making me feel old."

What was the nicest way to get this woman the hell off my porch? "Barb, I appreciate—"

"No." The wind kicked up.

I tilted my head. "No, what?"

She crossed her arms and blocked my exit. "I will not accept your polite, however transparent attempt to blow me off."

"I promise I'm not trying to do that." I was. "I've had a really hard day. I was about to leave. I'm sorry, but it's not a good time."

I tried to step around her and close the door behind me, but she darted into my path.

"What happened?" she asked.

It was clear it would be easier to cut to the chase than resist, so I sighed and reached into my purse. "This, for starters," I said, debuting my mom's urn.

When Barb realized what it was, her eyes filled with tears. She pressed two delicate, silver-ringed fingers to her lips and let the impact settle on her, then brushed her cheeks and sniffed. "I always wanted to see Connie again, but not like this."

I hugged my mom to my chest. From a neighbor's house, I heard Christmas carols and laughter. Holiday cheer felt so far away.

"And then," I continued, "after I picked up my mom's ashes, I broke up with my boyfriend, so I'm stuck moving back in here." I gestured vaguely behind me. "So, yeah. It's been a . . . long day."

Barb peered over my shoulder to look inside. "Oh no. There's a dark energy lingering in this house. You can't live here."

I agreed. Homes did have energies. The energy of my Lincoln Park apartment was inviting and cozy. Dan's apartment had no energy at all, which left me feeling empty. My mom's was abandoned but full of ghosts, a haunted house.

"I don't have anywhere else to live," I said.

Barb acted as though she hadn't heard me. "Aren't you hungry, sweetheart? Don't answer that. Of course you're hungry. Your mother just died. I bet you haven't eaten in days. I made lasagna. Not easy to make lasagna from scratch. Took me several hours. Look, I even burned myself." She flashed her bony wrist too quickly for me to notice anything.

"I don't think you've told me how you met my mom," I said, hoping she'd admit they'd met once at the podiatrist's office or something and I'd know she was full of crap so I could safely excuse myself and lock the door.

But unfortunately Barb said, "Connie was my roommate in secretarial school. She was my soulmate. I loved her more than anyone else I've ever known in my life, including my husband, and I'm not just saying that because he's dead."

Well, fuck.

I slumped against the house, defeated. "I'm sorry. I would have called you if I'd known."

Barb stepped closer, into my personal space, but I was trapped against the wall. "Don't be, sweetheart. We hadn't seen each other in thirty-five years. I always thought we'd reunite in our nursing home and spend the days laughing ourselves to death with no teeth and diapers on. When I found out I'd lost that chance, I wished . . . I guess I wished everything were different. Guilt follows grief like a hangover, does it not?"

No one understood that better than me.

"I thought it might be nice for us to toast in her honor," Barb said.

I searched her face for an explanation. "Why hadn't you seen each other in so long?"

Barb flung her scarf over her shoulder and announced in her no-nonsense way, "To be frank, I slept with her boyfriend. I was young. I was foolish. I was trouble."

For the first time in days, I laughed. "So what you're really saying is my mom hadn't spoken *to you* in thirty-five years."

"She had good reason. I'm not denying it." She commanded my gaze with her pale blue eyes, her hair blowing wild. "But I'm offering you a gift. The chance to know your mother as the person she used to be, and I'm the only one left on this planet who can give you that."

I shivered. The longer we stood on this porch, the colder and darker it got.

But Barb was right.

The only other person who knew my mom, really knew her, was my aunt, Joan, who died when I was ten. She'd lived in Iowa, and never married or had children. They used to talk on the phone every night after dinner while I watched Nick at Nite. I'd heard half of the conversation but didn't care enough to really listen. I was too busy watching *Bewitched*. My mom would laugh so loudly from the kitchen that I'd have to turn the volume up. Sometimes she'd smoke cigarettes in the backyard, thinking I didn't know, but the smell seeped in through the windows.

Joan had died suddenly in her sleep. When my mom got the call, we were in a parking garage after a dentist's appointment, and she let out the most guttural, horrible wail, collapsing onto the ground. I was so afraid to see her that way I couldn't move. I'd never heard her cry like that. Minutes passed, maybe an hour. I didn't touch her or hug her or say anything at all. Eventually she collected herself, walked to the car, and we never talked about it again.

I shifted my mom from one arm to the other. "And what makes you think I don't know her already?"

"If you did, her obituary would have been a lot longer than three sentences," Barb said. "You focused on the end of her life. I assure you, the other parts were much more interesting."

I blinked, swallowed. I'd written that obituary in a daze, typed it out in an email, conscious of paying by the word. *Connie Blanchfield Hart died at sixty-five years old at University of Chicago Medical Center. She was pre-deceased by her parents, Mick and Mary Blanchfield, and her sister, Joan Blanchfield. She leaves behind a daughter, Mel Hart.*

"Like what?" I asked. My mom grew up in a town a couple hours away and went to secretarial school in New York. She met my dad and they got married, then divorced, so she moved here and started her business. A straightforward life, possibly boring. What had I missed?

"*Like what?* she says." Barb shook her head at the heavens. "If you have to ask, then you need me more than I thought. Just so you know, I'm not above kidnapping, and this hair would not do well in jail."

My stomach growled again. I looked over my shoulder at the door to the past, then back at Barb and her promise of a different future, one in which I could remember my mom for more than the ways she let me down. Didn't she deserve that? Didn't I?

"All right," I said, locking the door. "But just for dinner."

Chapter 8

December 19

When I was a sophomore in high school, a boy from my French class invited me to a party at his house. I was stunned. I had a heart-stopping crush on him—as did most of the girls and some of the boys. The fact that he'd asked me, the girl who competed in *chorus* competitions, was suspect enough that I was inclined to say no. Gabby urged me to go, probably because she wanted to go and was invited by proxy. So we dressed up in spaghetti strap tank tops and flip-flops from Old Navy, and flat-ironed our hair. My mom drove us to the party and said she'd be back at ten.

The house was on a golf course. Gabby and I walked into a living room with vaulted ceilings and cream leather couches and all the popular kids making out in corners. We knew them and they knew us—we'd all gone to school together since kindergarten—but no one said hi, so we zeroed in on an imaginary person at the bar and beelined over, pretending we, too, were busy. We poured ourselves a red cup of foamy beer from the keg, my first beer ever, then wandered out to the pool, where we knew the girl who'd played Irene Molloy in last winter's production of *Hello, Dolly!*

"Hey, Mel." It was the guy from French class. Edison. *Named after a lightbulb,* he always said, which wasn't exactly right, but no one was going to challenge him on it. "Glad you came."

He sat beside me on the lounge chair, his cargo shorts against my bare thigh. We talked about calculus and football camp and golf—his things, not mine. But I laughed and let him put his arm around me. When he offered me a refill, I followed him to the kitchen, where he poured me a mixed drink with Sprite and tequila. When he kissed me against the cabinets, I was concentrating so hard on whether I was good at it that I didn't ask myself whether I wanted it.

I left Gabby outside by the pool to go upstairs with Edison. His friends flicked their chins up, smirking, as he pulled me into his room. We made out forever, and while I didn't like that his tongue was sandpapery, I liked that it belonged to him. At some point I remembered to look at the clock on his nightstand. It was nine-thirty. My lips felt raw and when I caught a glimpse of myself in the mirror, my face was all red. Would my mom know what I'd been doing? Some part of me wanted her to see me as an adult, because I felt like one.

I let him take my shirt off and put his hand under my bra. We kept kissing and I thought I was getting better, but then out of nowhere he broke away and said, "What's your deal?"

"What do you mean?"

"Are you, like, a prude or something?"

"I don't think so." I thought what we were doing was pretty advanced.

"I just don't think it's cool for you to act like you want more and then change your mind."

How had I acted? I grabbed my shirt and pulled it over my head. Even though he'd just said what he said, I still cared about trying to look graceful as I got dressed instead of like a baby goat who couldn't control her limbs. "I'm sorry," I said, glancing at the clock again. Nine fifty-five. *Thank god.* "My mom is coming, so I should go."

Everyone in the hallway thought we'd done it and clapped as I ran down the stairs and found Gabby swimming in the pool with her clothes on. She saw my tears and lifted herself out to hug me until I was just as wet.

My mom didn't show up at ten. We waited outside, cold, dripping, crying—Gabby out of solidarity—until ten-fifteen, when I went back inside and used the phone to call my house.

She picked up—I heard shuffling and muffled words. But I couldn't understand what she was saying. *Feeding a dog? Basketball? Tylenol?*

"Where *are* you?" I shouted into the phone.

She mumbled something.

"What are you saying?" I had to yell over Nelly singing "Hot in Herre."

Then it clicked. I realized what had been going on my whole life. The wine, the forgetfulness, everything. Maybe I needed to have my first drink to understand. She was drunk. She couldn't have come to get us even if she'd remembered. The voice in my head that had already suspected something wasn't right, that had always wondered what I was missing, finally went quiet. *I can't rely on you,* I thought. *You're not there when I need you.*

A door closed between us, the latch snapping into place. I slid down the kitchen cabinets until I was sitting on the sticky, beer-soaked floor. Gabby found me and dropped to her knees.

"My mom is so annoying," I said, wiping my face with a paper towel. "She's the one who gave me this stupid curfew and now she's not even coming."

"Why not?"

"I don't know. She forgot. She doesn't care about me."

"I'll call my dad," Gabby said. "He's totally watching basketball, pretending he's not waiting up."

I heard Gabby on the phone telling her dad everything—how we had a beer and went swimming and Edison was being a jerk and would he please pick us up because we were cold and hungry and would he bring a snack? *Something good.* It hurt to listen. I buried my face in my knees. I was trapped in my own life. I couldn't wait to turn eighteen, go to college, be free, and never think about this again.

Gabby's dad arrived in fifteen minutes with pool towels and a bag of popcorn. His minivan had a TV in the back and we watched the New Year's Day turkey curry scene in *Bridget Jones's Diary* as he drove, my head on Gabby's shoulder. Gabby was laughing and I was pretending to, hoping to convince them everything was fine and all I needed from them was a ride but nothing more. Because even though I didn't want to go home, I had to. If my mom woke in the night and I wasn't there, she'd panic. And if she panicked, she'd drink.

Outside my house, I could see the TV through our front window. My mom would be asleep on the couch, like she usually was, except this time I understood why, and that made my skin harden. All those times I'd wondered why other kids' moms seemed to be there for them in ways mine wasn't, this was the reason? How could she teach me how to be? I was fifteen. I wanted to be treated like an adult, but I needed my mom. And she'd chosen wine instead of me.

When I let myself in, she was right where I knew I'd find her. I didn't wake her up. Instead, I went straight to bed. We had a little dog back then, a white ball of fluff named Sebastian. He slept on my pillow most nights, so I wasn't alone. That night, I held him in my arms like a baby, crying into his fur. Years later, when he died after a long life of fourteen years, I secretly blamed my mom. Why, exactly,

I couldn't articulate, but it always traced back to that night when he'd been there for me and she hadn't.

I was thinking of Gabby's minivan as Barb drove me in a beat-up version of the same model, only hers smelled like perfume instead of popcorn and chlorine. She was not a good driver. She alternated between speeding and slamming on the brakes to avoid rear-ending the car in front of her, and she had a serious case of road rage. To one sports car that dared change into her lane, she leaned her elbow on the horn and yelled, "Is your pecker too small to respect a van with hips like these?"

Between screaming at strangers, she sang along to the *Chicago* soundtrack at the top of her lungs. She had an incredible voice, very Tina Turner meets Melissa Etheridge. "I grew up in the theater," she shouted over the music. "You're looking at the girl who would have been cast as the original Orphan Annie if they hadn't decided to go with a redhead."

Barb lived in Oak Park, an artsy suburb more like a small town just twenty minutes from my mom's. I'd been there only a few times, but everyone in Chicago knew about Oak Park. It had a reputation for being family friendly, funky, liberal, diverse, and welcoming. Frank Lloyd Wright lived there and designed some of the homes. A high percentage of our wedding couples were moving there to have kids. As Barb navigated the streets, I saw big houses next to little ones, families all bundled up and taking evening strolls, and murals painted on the walls of an elementary school.

While I looked out the window, Barb pelted me with personal questions. Who was the prick I'd broken up with? Who was my favorite musical artist? Had I ever seen *Hello, Dolly!*?

"I was in it," I told her. "I was a big theater kid."

"And how do you pay the bills?" she asked, adding, "I never ask people what they do. People do lots of things, and usually what they do is much more important than how they make money."

"Mine are intertwined actually. I'm a wedding singer."

She gasped, clutching her heart with both hands. When the van veered left, I almost lunged for the wheel. "Connie must have loved that."

I was still eyeing the road, ready to jump in. "Why do you say that?"

"Because of her musical aspirations, obviously." Barb signaled to exit the highway, thank god.

"What musical aspirations?" I asked, but absently, laser-focused on Barb's speedometer.

"She lived and breathed music, sweetheart. You know why you're named Mel, don't you?"

"I don't think there is a reason. It's just a name."

"It is absolutely not just a name." Barb ejected the *Chicago* CD and reached into her console, digging for something. "Aha!" She withdrew another CD, caseless, and plugged it into the slot. When a grungy bassline started playing and a woman's husky voice began half talking, half singing like a female Bob Dylan, she said, "This is Melanie. And *this* is 'Baby Guitar.' "

The bassline continued, peppered with a snappy drum, an electric guitar, and a keyboard. Melanie sang about a woman messing around with her guitar and giving birth to a baby guitar.

"Connie named you after her hero," Barb said, talking with her hands—both of them. "She never talked to you about her music?"

I gripped my armrest. "*Her* music?"

"I'll take that as a no."

Finally she pulled to the curb of a narrow yellow house lit up with Christmas lights. In the front yard, political posters poked through the snow, standing shoulder to shoulder in a silent picket line.

"You like politics?" I asked.

"*Like* politics? Sweetheart, I *despise* politics. But I *believe* in having an opinion. You don't have to agree with my views—although they are the correct ones—but I will not tolerate anyone who disregards the privilege of civic engagement. So tell me the truth. I can always tell when someone is lying. Do you vote?"

Thank goodness I had the right answer to this one. "I do. I love to vote."

She raised one thin brow. "Even in local elections?"

Almost never. "Just the important ones?"

Barb killed the ignition. "Local government is where change begins. The other side of the aisle gets that. Where are you on charter schools?"

"Um." What was the debate about charter schools again? "I'm not really anywhere on charter schools."

Barb kicked open her door. "Don't worry. I'll tell you everything you need to know."

I liked the yellow house as soon as I walked in. It smelled like holiday Yankee candles and baking and a hint of mildew, that distinctive midwestern mix of moisture and must that haunted old houses with basements. I took off my coat and searched for a place to hang it on a rack already stuffed with winter gear.

Barb's insistence that I come for dinner had given me the impression she was accustomed to a house full of people and I was just another mouth to feed, but there was no one else home. Given that a toothbrush sat on the piano and a pile of laundry waited on the stairs, it seemed like she'd been alone for a while. I wondered whether Barb wanted someone to listen to her stories even more than I wanted to hear them.

A golden retriever with gray around his mouth and eyes ambled around the corner with his tail wagging, eager to investigate my pants. "Hi, buddy," I said.

"This is Rudy. My late husband named him Rudolph, likc thc reindeer. He was a Christmas fanatic. It was troubling, really. Imagine a grown man counting down the days with a chocolate advent calendar. It makes this time of year hard, so thank you for your company. Come on, Rudy. Dinner."

My pants forgotten, Rudy trotted after Barb down a short hallway into the kitchen.

Hers was a cook's kitchen, with a huge gas range and jars of different flours on the counter. Stained pots and pans hung from a rack over the island.

"Sit," Barb said. I knew by now that her requests were not optional.

She pointed to a bay window with a built-in bench, where a kitchen table hid beneath mail, mugs, and crossword puzzles.

As she pulled a lasagna from the oven, I inspected the abundance of cow-themed decor—a saltshaker, a cookie jar, a creamer.

"So tell me how you're feeling," she instructed, carving the lasagna with a spatula.

"About what?" I accidentally knocked a cow-print oven mitt off the table. Barb's house was clean but cluttered. No dust. Just stuff.

"Everything," she said, dishing out our plates. "Let's start with the easy one. The boyfriend."

"Ex-boyfriend. And he's going on tour with a 'real' band."

"So you're better off without him."

"How do you know?"

"He's leaving you. Simple." She carried dinner to the table and swept aside the crosswords to make room.

"It doesn't feel simple," I said. "We were together for three years."

"Three good years?" she asked, grating Parmesan.

I picked up my fork. "They were fine."

"So, not good. You know good when you have good." She grated more vigorously, a mountain of cheese growing on my plate. "I loved the wrong man once, but I didn't know he was the wrong man until I found the right one."

"I hope you're right." When she finished, I took a bite. My eyes opened wide. "Oh my god. This is the best lasagna I've ever had. I think it's the best lasagna anyone's ever had."

"I told you."

She sat, then immediately jumped up again to pull half a baguette from the toaster oven. "I learned to cook when I had twelve roommates in New York and we took turns making family meals. We were flat broke—everyone was an artist trying to make it—so we had to get creative. You'd be shocked what I can do with one egg and a head of cabbage."

"When was that?"

She sliced the bread on a cutting board. "I was born in New York and left in 1979. Moved to Nashville, had a short career there, then came here when I got a job with the Chicago Children's Theatre in 1984. I met my husband working the lights. We bought this house when my son was born, fell in love with Oak Park, and never left."

I was scarfing down lasagna, but Barb's still sat untouched. Cooking seemed to be her way of taking care of people other than herself. "A short career in what?" I asked, keeping her talking so I could keep eating.

"Music." She was chopping fresh basil now. "I was a singer."

"I'm not surprised. I heard you in the car. You could put us wedding singers out of business. What did you sing?"

" 'Carry My Heart.' "

My fork froze midair.

"I guess you've heard of it," she said, her voice dry, almost bored.

" 'Carry My Heart'? As in . . . 'Carry My Heart'?" Something clicked. "Hold on. Are you Barbara *Stern*?" My fork clattered on my plate as I clapped my hands over my mouth.

Barb chucked the basil into a colander. "I'm surprised you know my name. Most people don't. They hear 'Carry My Heart' and think Dash Whitney."

"I don't. I hear 'Carry My Heart' and think Barbara Stern." I couldn't take my eyes off her now. This was unbelievable. Was there a Grammy in this house? Could I practice my speech in front of a mirror with it? *Barbara Stern.* Barbara Stern!

"Barbara Stern," she echoed, rinsing her basil leaves. "One-hit wonder."

I stood up for no reason other than I could no longer sit down. "I can't believe this. I'm sweating. I'm actually sweating. I feel like I need to ask you to sign this napkin."

She flung a dishrag over her shoulder. "So you could sell it for, what, five dollars?"

"No," I said, my voice round with awe. "So I could have it."

"Carry My Heart" was an American institution, like Cheerios, like cranberry sauce on Thanksgiving, like dropping the ball on New Year's Eve. More than thirty years after it first hit number one on the charts, it was still the soundtrack for every American-made truck commercial, every middle school slow dance, every rom-com kissing scene starring actresses named Jennifer. You could not go to a department store and ride an elevator without hearing it. You could not listen to the radio without hearing it. I'd just heard it during a YouTube ad for frozen pizza. What a country love song had to do with frozen pizza, I had no idea, but that wasn't the point. The point was "Carry My Heart" evoked longing, whether you were longing for love or DiGiorno's. It was the song of my first date, first heartbreak, first karaoke performance. I had sung it hundreds of times, because it was on our standard wedding playlist, and if we dared skip it, brides always demanded it. They longed for the chemistry between Barbara Stern and Dash Whitney. You could feel it when they sang together, their voices raw and imperfect but powerful, like lovers in bed.

Dash Whitney was the man who transformed country music in the late nineties with his album *Honest Man*. Thanks to him, country music wasn't just for boys in pickups anymore. It was for Wall Street, women, even the White House. Bill Clinton invited Dash Whitney to perform at the annual White House Christmas party. I watched it on TV. *Honest Man* won a Grammy in every major category and continued to be one of the highest-grossing albums of all time. But following "Carry My Heart," Barbara Stern dropped off the face of the earth. Only Dash Whitney's star power lasted. But his chemistry with Barbara Stern propelled him to fame in the first place. He would have gotten nowhere without her.

And now she was feeding me lasagna.

I'd managed to sit down but couldn't eat. "You went to secretarial school?" I asked. "Why?"

"Secretarial school was before. Connie and I dropped out after one semester. She went back to finish. I didn't." Barb slid a second helping onto my plate.

"Why would you? You were famous!"

"I was never famous. That song was famous."

"Your voice is the reason that song is special."

"I think the lyrics are what make that song special."

"I think you're being modest."

Barb finally sat, tasted her lasagna, and made a note in the margin of the recipe lying open on the table.

"I assure you," she said, "modesty is not my best quality."

It occurred to me that given that song's notoriety, I'd have expected our plates to be made of solid gold, but Barb's house was charmingly shabby. "Did you make any music after that?"

"No."

"Why—"

She snapped her cookbook closed. "Finish eating and we'll go to the living room. I have something to show you."

Torn between the best lasagna of my life and Barbara Stern, I ate as fast as I could, then helped her carry dishes to the sink and followed her to a cozy room full of knickknacks and crochet blankets, with floral-papered walls and a short, squat Christmas tree with no decorations on it yet. While I inspected the pictures in frames on the mantel, she lit a fire, then her collection of Yankee candles on the coffee table.

"I like your tree," I said, touching the soft, prickly needles.

"I always pick the weird ones. I don't want it to look like the lobby of a Macy's. You can help me decorate it." She gestured at a silver menorah on the piano. "I'm Jewish, and my children are mitzvahed, though they haven't set foot in a temple since. But the tree reminds me of my husband, and my grandson likes it."

On the mantel I'd seen a picture of a little boy in a snowsuit, holding a sled taller than he was. "Where does he live?"

Barb fluffed the throw pillows and gestured for me to sit down. "Everywhere. My daughter travels for a living. My son lives in Chicago. Unfortunately he's married or I'd have set you up already. No children, though. Six years and no baby. I mean, what, do they not fuck?"

I'd just taken a sip of water and nearly did a spit take. I knew only one other person like Barb, and that was my mom. She liked to be a tad outrageous. Like on parents' night at my middle school, she'd call all my male teachers Mr. Handsome, and I'd want to move to another planet.

"Make yourself comfortable," Barb insisted. "I'll be right back."

I perched on the edge of Barbara Stern's sofa. My butt was on a cushion that had also touched Barbara Stern's butt. Had it touched

Dash Whitney's butt? Were they friends? Would *he* let me borrow a Grammy to practice my speech?

Barb reappeared and handed me a photo album. It was old, with cardboard pages and adhesive plastic film. I opened it to find my mom in a yellow halter top and feathered bangs, leaning against the hood of a white Oldsmobile, beaming. She looked so radiant I couldn't breathe for a second. Like a different person, someone untethered and unburdened. On the bottom corner of the page, *1979* was written in pencil.

Barb lowered herself into an armchair by the fire and spread a blanket across her knees, finally sitting still. "That was the year I met Connie."

Chapter 9

December 19

I asked Barb to tell me the whole story, from the beginning, leave nothing out.

"I was born in New York City," she said, and I laughed. "What? That's the beginning."

"No, please, continue." I cozied up with the blanket she'd given me. "I'm ready. I was also born in New York, by the way."

Seated in her armchair, legs gracefully crossed, she smiled. "I figured. Technically, I'm from Long Island, but nobody needs to know that. I was the only child of two parents who seemed surprised I belonged to them. My father was always busy selling cars or playing cards or betting his cars in his card games and losing them, and my mother was usually busy walking. She walked everywhere, all the time, as if she had to remain in motion or whatever she was walking away from would catch up to her. Nobody paid me any attention, which only made me more desperate for it. If I got famous, I figured, everyone would want to know me. So when I was seventeen, I dropped out of high school and moved to the city for Broadway."

With the fire haloing her in warm light, I could picture her onstage, beneath the hot beam of a spotlight, younger and hungrier, but with exactly the same attitude.

"That's when I lived with twelve roommates," she went on, her bangles jingling as she talked with her hands. "Singers, ballet dancers, jazz dancers, actresses, models. We all had something to prove. There are some artists who want to prove their talent to themselves. I was nowhere near that evolved. I wanted to prove my talent to the world so someone would love me."

Watching Barbara Stern tell the story of her life was like tuning in to *Where Are They Now? One-Hit Wonders* on VH1, only I got to ask the questions. I was mesmerized by the honesty of her answers and the melody of the way she said them, set to the rhythm of the fire popping and crackling. Barbara Stern made music just by opening her mouth.

She adjusted her shawl and reached for her tea. One of her silver rings flashed in the light cast from the flames. "To make money I was a cocktail waitress at the Harvard Club. I'd never have gotten the job if they knew I was Jewish, so I told them my name was Barbara Stanley and got hired on the spot. I was stunningly gorgeous, and this head of hair would have landed me a lot more than a waitress job if it hadn't been for my last name. Other girls had to sleep on a pillow of pencils to make their hair look like mine. I auditioned five days a week—for Broadway, for off-Broadway, for off-off-Broadway, for so far off Broadway I was back on Long Island. But in three years, I only managed to get cast as the understudy to Young Sally in *Follies,* ensemble in *Chicago,* and one week as Frances Perkins in *Annie* because both the real Frances and the understudy Frances had chicken pox. The directors told me I was too Jewish for the non-Jewish roles and not Jewish enough for the Jewish roles. 'Exactly how Jewish am I supposed to be?' I asked them. And they'd tell me that if I wanted to change their minds, I could meet them in their office."

I shook my head. "I'm sorry."

"I wish this was a story of how it used to be," she said, "but unfortunately not much has changed."

The length of time for which Barbara Stern could sit still expired. She knelt beside two cardboard boxes marked *Christmas.* "Let's talk and work."

My knees cracked more than hers as I joined her on the floor and we attempted to untangle strings of vintage bulbs.

"One night I was in the bath trying to soak the pain from my feet," she continued. "My feet never had a day off. In the mornings, I had dance classes; in the afternoons, I had auditions; and in the evenings, I worked. I ran my fingers through my hair and it all came away in tangled clumps like seaweed. I couldn't have that—my hair was my best feature. I decided then and there to go to secretarial school."

"Why secretarial school?" I asked. "You could have stayed in art. Been a dance teacher or something."

We freed a string. Barb plugged it in and we stood on opposite sides of the tree, passing it back and forth, wrapping from the bottom up.

"Secretarial school was a big deal back then," she said, disappearing behind the branches. "You had to be pretty and type ninety words a minute. My plan was to graduate, get a job, marry my boss in six months tops, and then I could go back to auditioning without worrying how I'd eat." She peered at me around the tree, her eyebrows raised. "And I was a feminist."

I laughed. "I'd be lying if I said I hadn't considered marrying a man with health insurance just so it would be easier to sing for a living."

"I don't blame you. But when I moved out of the apartment I shared with the other Broadway girls, it felt exactly the same as giving up my dreams. It was like going to my own funeral. The secretarial school was on Ninety-Sixth Street and I cried the whole way uptown. But then everything changed."

She handed me the bundle of colored lights, a faint smile on her mouth. "I met your mother."

I was holding the lights, but I'd forgotten what I was supposed to do with them.

"Your mother had unpacked her record player before she'd unpacked any of her clothes. And that's when I knew. My Broadway era might have been over, but my Fleetwood Mac era had just begun. Look at this." She reached for the photo album on the coffee table and showed me the next picture. My mom was lying on her back in the grass, wearing white heart-shaped sunglasses and smoking. "How could I not worship her? She had ideal traits for a hippie. Straight hair, flat chest, long eyelashes. I had to draw mine on like Twiggy. We never went to class. We were having the time of our lives. We slept all day and danced all night. Your mom had a 1.9 GPA and I was squeaking above passing with a 2.7. We didn't fit in with the girls who spent all day practicing their penmanship. We thought those girls had been brainwashed by the man, and those girls thought we were lesbians. In school, they taught us to respect our bosses, sit up straight, and take notes in shorthand. That last bit was actually useful, but the rest would make Connie roll over in her grave."

Barb stopped and glanced at me. Perhaps we were thinking the same thing: that Connie wasn't in a grave. She was sitting on the kitchen counter next to a bunch of overly ripe bananas. "Figure of speech, sweetheart," she said, her voice gentle.

She handed me the album and I flipped through the pages. My mom wearing denim cutoffs and white cowboy boots, my mom doing a handstand in Central Park, my mom asleep on her textbook. She brimmed with so much joy, even with her eyes closed, that she looked nearly unrecognizable.

Some of this sounded vaguely familiar. My mom told me she never went to class and nearly flunked out. "She told me about secretarial school," I said, "but I guess I wasn't paying attention."

Barb was unwrapping a tiny ballerina ornament from newspaper. "Daughters have a blind spot when it comes to their mothers. They don't see us as people. I have a daughter. I would know. When she got her first period and I taught her how to use a tampon, she was shocked to find out I had mine, too, like I'd ceased to be a woman."

I swallowed a threat of tears, knowing I'd had the same blind spot. My mom's divorce, her love life—I'd analyzed those things only in relation to myself, how they affected my life. I'd never spared a thought for her heartbreak, her womanhood. God forbid, her sex life.

I turned the page, pushing the thought away.

The next photo showed my mom and Barb wearing Irish dancing costumes, laughing through a jig. I had no context for what I was seeing. The woman in the photo may as well have been a model who posed for stock images in picture frames. "I should have asked her more about her life."

Barb handed me the tiny ballerina to hang. "What do you want to know?"

I searched for the perfect branch. "Why'd she drop out?"

"By winter break that first year, we were on academic probation anyway, and Connie didn't want to go home for Christmas. As I'm sure you know, Connie's parents were very religious. But their form of religion was more punishing than uplifting. Her mother went to mass every day to atone for her sin of having had a miscarriage, and her father believed it had happened because she wasn't a virgin when they got married. The only reason Connie ever would have gone home again was to see her sister, Joan. But Joan promised that as soon as she graduated from high school, she would enroll in secretarial school, too, and come live with us."

I'd frozen in the middle of hanging my ballerina. "No," I said, "I didn't know that. That's so awful." How had I missed such a defining part of her experience?

I asked my mom once why we didn't go to church. I was in middle school, and all my friends were talking about youth group at the

Baptist church, where they had water-gun fights and boy-girl dances on Friday nights. *My parents were Catholic,* she said, which wasn't an answer to my question, but she gave vague answers like that when she didn't want to discuss something, so I dropped it. Later, the youth group leader got arrested for buying liquor for eighth graders, and I was grateful for the freedom to make decisions based on what I believed, not on what a youth group leader had told me was right or wrong.

Barb unwrapped more ornaments—a football, a bear skiing, a picture frame made of Play-Doh. They told a story, but it wasn't one I'd read before. The story of a family that wasn't mine.

I accepted the picture frame from Barb and found a branch to hang it. "My grandparents died when I was really little," I said. "I barely remember their funerals, but I do remember that my mom didn't cry."

Barb lowered herself into her armchair. The way she sat in front of the fire was so elegant, with her long dancer's legs and her shoulders-back posture, as if she were still onstage. "When her mother lost the baby, their priest told Connie that to cry meant you were questioning God's plan. She never cried again."

"She cried when Joan died," I said.

Barb's fingers touched her lips. "Joan died? When?"

"More than twenty years ago."

I was surprised when Barb's eyes filled with tears.

"Did you know her?" I asked.

Barb shook her head, gazing at the fire. "I never met her, but I heard so much about her, I felt like I did. I was always jealous of Joan. I viewed her as my competition for Connie's full and undivided love. I can only imagine how losing Joan must have felt for Connie."

Barb understood right away what I hadn't: that without Joan, my mom had no one. "I didn't get it."

"You were just a kid. What were you supposed to do?"

I shrugged, digging through the box of ornaments so she wouldn't see me blinking away tears. Had I been a terrible daughter? I held up the football and tried to smile. "Were you a football family?"

"Heavens, no. Do I look like I'd wake up at the crack of dawn to paint my face and go tailgating? That's not a football. That's a rugby ball. My husband was English, which was for the best. When we met, he'd never heard 'Carry My Heart.' It kept my ego in check."

Barb took the ball and hung it right in the center, over the heart of the tree.

We unwrapped ornaments for a while, listening to Rudy snore.

"If you never met Joan," I said, "does that mean she didn't come to live with you in New York?"

"We didn't stay in New York. Instead of going home over winter break, we got in the white Oldsmobile Connie inherited from a dead uncle and started driving west. We packed everything we owned in the back seat like we knew we were never coming back. Ah, here. This is the one I was looking for."

She handed me a small white cowboy boot with red roses painted on the side, and my breath caught. I recognized it. We had one, too. It was in one of the boxes I'd planned to give away before I changed my mind.

"We got them that Christmas in Nashville," she said. "The same day we decided to stay."

Instead of hanging it on the tree, I set it on the photo album, standing up, the shoe of an invisible person. "Why Nashville?"

Barb opened the second box to reveal dozens more mismatched ornaments. "We'd been driving for days, listening to Joni Mitchell, Crosby, Stills, Nash, and Young, Patti Smith, David Bowie, Simon and Garfunkel, the Rolling Stones. Windows down even though it was freezing, music so loud we couldn't hear ourselves think. We were twenty-two, high on freedom and our own beauty. Secretarial school was a million miles away. By the time we got to Nashville, we'd forgotten about it completely. Music felt as alive as any other human being there. It lived, breathing and taking up space. We went to the strip to hear the next big thing, and it turned out *we* were the next big thing. Connie couldn't sing worth a damn, but I was good enough for both of us. We got onstage and sang 'Dreams' by Fleetwood Mac and remembered that we'd had them once."

I wasn't even pretending to hang ornaments anymore. A miniature croissant dangled from my stunned fingers. "I know what yours were," I said in a hush. "But what were my mom's?"

"Do you like Carole King?" Barb swept to the stereo, and a few seconds later, Carole King played the opening chords of "I Feel the Earth Move." Barb danced around the living room as she continued. "*Tapestry* meant a lot to all of us, but it changed Connie in ways even I couldn't understand. It was raw, gritty, and powerful. Carole's voice didn't tell stories—her voice was the story."

"That album will never get old," I agreed. "In two thousand years, highly evolved humans with brains the size of basketballs and solar panels on the backs of their ears will still listen to 'Will You Love Me Tomorrow?' and start crying."

Barb laughed, still dancing a swaying, finger-snapping routine. "You got it. And Connie was always a great writer. Her letters to Joan were like little novels with scenes and characters and dirty poems she'd made up. Carole King planted the idea in Connie's head that she could write songs and I could sing them, and we'd be like Simon and Garfunkel but with better hair and sex appeal."

"I can't believe she never told me this. I've wanted to be a singer my whole life."

Barb twirled. "It didn't work out. She was embarrassed."

"Embarrassed? Of what? It's amazing."

Embarrassing were the complicated fantasies I used to have about going to a Céline Dion concert and singing so beautifully from my seat in the nosebleeds that she'd invite me onstage and ask me to finish the concert for her. This was not embarrassing. My mom had the guts to take a risk like I never could.

"But we failed," Barb said.

"What happened?"

She reached for the photo album and flipped to a picture of the two of them wound together on a faded, ripped couch in a crappy apartment, innocence replaced with exhaustion. "We got jobs as typists so we could pay rent. For a year, we worked too much to write a single song, but neither of us was willing to admit defeat. We were as stubborn about losing as we were afraid to succeed. Were we happy? No, we were miserable. But we were living in the world as adult women, and that was something. We went on dates almost every night. Connie liked that southern men called her *miss* and I liked that they called me *yankee.* Being kissed in a pickup truck spoke to some feminine urge to be rescued on horseback we didn't know we had, and that we'd deny if asked. We independently decided to lose our virginity on the same night when we were twenty-three, having come to the conclusion that sex was the key to unlocking our music. Shockingly, it was not."

Barb kept passing me ornaments, but I paid no attention to where I shoved them. One shaped like a baguette—I was sensing a theme—ended up on the same branch as a frog prince, giving the impression the frog had a large, flesh-colored erection. I quickly moved the frog to the back to avoid scandal.

"Then I got a new job typing a novelist's dictated manuscript," Barb continued. "It was a misogynistic tome full of women with large breasts and no brains. But he paid me triple what my last boss paid, and he knew people. He got us a gig at a club at the very end of the strip, where nobody went unless they'd already been kicked out of everywhere else. Of course, we had nothing to sing, so Connie wrote us a song. Not that I could have done any better, but the song needed work. 'Beep Beep,' it was called, inspired by our road trip. *Big sky, empty road, wonderin' why he never showed.* But it was our chance, so we gave it everything we had. I thought I was going to die from singing my beating, bloody heart right out of my chest. When we finished, no one even clapped." Barb chuckled, shaking her head. "I wasn't a rock star, I was a typist, and not a very fast one."

Outside, it had begun to snow and the fire had shrunk to embers. Even Rudy was cold. He burrowed himself under a blanket while Barb threw on another log and stoked the flames. "When a man approached us," she said, "we should have known. But one look at his face and I was a goner. Denim jacket, cigarette. I'd learned by then that sex was better with older men. The lines around their eyes directly equated to the notches on their bedposts. This man had one line for every woman he'd made weak in the knees. He shook my hand and spoke to something broken in me. That I wanted to be somebody because it meant I wasn't nobody. He said, 'My name is Ernest, and I want to make you famous.' Connie stuck her hand out and said, '*Us.* You want to make *us* famous. *We* are the Secretaries.' So Ernest became our manager, and the man who got between us."

She lifted the last ornament from the box—a miniature platinum record—and handed it to me. I found the only empty spot left on the tree. We stepped back to admire our work. Colored lights, snow out the window, Carole King, and a roaring fire. My mom would have loved it. I hadn't cried yet, not really, not in the uncontrollable way I needed to. When it happened, I couldn't stop, and Barb held me like a mother would.

Chapter 10

December 20

I let Barb put me to bed in the basement. I couldn't have made it to my mom's if I'd wanted to. My body was empty and weak, as if I'd cried out all my strength. The days of sleeplessness and to-do lists and cleaning and pretending I was fine had caught up to me. I wasn't fine. I never had been.

Even getting down the stairs was a challenge. I held on to the railing while Barb held on to my waist. The fold-out couch was already made up, like she'd planned for this all along. Under other circumstances, I'd have thought that bordered on creepy, but right now, I was grateful. I sat on the edge and she wrapped my shoulders in a blanket, then kissed my temple. "You keep this," she said, handing me the photo album. "I've looked at it a thousand times and it always tells the same damn story. Are you okay?"

I didn't know what okay was anymore. "I think I need to get some sleep."

"There's a toothbrush and a towel in the bathroom," she said, "and enough blankets to warm all the nuns in Westminster in the closet. I left a pair of my daughter's pajamas, too."

I couldn't look at her as I nodded, knowing that if I saw the tenderness in her eyes I'd cry again. She lingered, resting her hand on my shoulder, before climbing the stairs. "I'm a night owl," she called. "If you need anything, I'll be in the bath. My feet have been killing me since 1978."

When I curled under the blankets in a stranger's pajamas, in a stranger's bed, I set my mom and the photo album on the mattress beside me, wishing she could explain how I'd ended up here. But only the album could speak for her now, so I started turning pages. The woman in those photos wasn't the woman I knew. They were both dead, leaving me with twice the grief.

I woke up under warm blankets, blinking myself back to reality. Where was I?

The photo album. It was splayed open on the mattress, right where I'd left it. Last night rushed back in snapshots, scenes cut from a movie. Decorating the tree. Barb, holding me.

I rolled onto my other side, clinging to sleep. Even though a spring dug into my hip, my body didn't feel like wet concrete anymore; my head didn't throb. Finally, I'd slept more than a few hours.

Closing my eyes, I breathed deeply through my nose. Barb's basement smelled exactly like ours. Earth, mildew, boiler heat. It was comforting. Growing up, we'd occasionally have tornado warnings, a blaring siren that came from who knew where, like the trees had mouths or the streetlights were sentient. Did those citywide alarms exist anymore? Our phones warned us now. But there was something perversely exciting about it. My mom and I would hear the alarm and hurry into the basement with potato chips and watch *The Best of Saturday Night Live* tapes until the warnings stopped. I was always a little disappointed when they were over.

I must have dozed off again thinking about the Land Shark because when I woke up, I was hot and my phone said it was past eleven. I sat up and stretched. Last night, I'd been too wrecked to pay attention to what was down here. It was partially finished, one side carpeted and the other concrete. The finished side had a kitchenette, my bed, and a classic brown La-Z-Boy. On a card table sat a small TV with a built-in VHS just like the one I'd had in my college dorm, only mine was purple and covered with pictures of Abercrombie models. The arrangement was modest but homey, and nicer than most apartments I'd rented in my twenties, despite a few mysterious puddles on the concrete floor.

I went to the bathroom to brush my teeth, wash my face, and change back into yesterday's clothes before going upstairs.

In the kitchen, any indication that Barb had spent hours cooking that lasagna was gone. She'd mentioned she was a night owl. I pictured her on her hands and knees, scrubbing the floor at one in the morning while singing along to "It's the Hard-Knock Life" from *Annie.*

"Hello?" I called.

No one answered.

I poured myself coffee and spotted a note. *My son is coming home today. You'll get along famously! Went to market for supplies. Do me a favor—go to Bun in the Oven and buy some rugelach. His favorite. Fresh air is good for the soul!*

Her son? Now I was encroaching on a family holiday. I typed Bun in the Oven into my phone. It was half a mile away on a street of shops and restaurants. I could walk around, get some breakfast, run her errand. Fresh air probably was a good idea. *I'll do this,* I told myself, *then go.*

Last night's snow was bright and sparkling beneath a blue sky. My breath clouded as I walked, heels crunching on the salted sidewalk. I filled my lungs with icy, clean air. *I'm alive. I am breathing. I am still here*. Eventually I would have to find a way to move through a world that would continue to spin whether I was ready or not.

Bundled children made snowmen in front yards as their parents shoveled or hung lights. I waved. The street looked vaguely familiar. In middle school, I had a friend from music camp named Megan who lived in Oak Park. Her parents were still married, and they kissed on the lips in front of the kids. Megan's mom made us snacks shaped like animals and her dad took us to get ice cream and see movies on hot summer days. My mom had just lost her biggest client for missing deadlines. The company claimed she'd cost them a lot of money. She hadn't told me about it, but I heard her on the phone. This was after Joan died. Without their nightly phone calls to fill the hours after dinner, she filled them with wine instead.

I'd been going to Megan's every weekend, thinking her family was perfect, until one day Megan spilled cranberry juice all over the kitchen floor. I didn't think it was a big deal. The floor was linoleum. I grabbed some paper towels and dropped to my knees. But Megan's mom threw a bottle of Lysol at Megan's head and called her a stupid idiot. When she cried, her mom told her to shut up. I went home and hugged my mom for a full minute. She'd never once yelled at me, never got angry when I spilled. I'd focused so hard on what was wrong about our life that I hadn't noticed what was right about it.

In the cold sunshine, I kept walking until I reached a quaint street of shops and cafés. Garlands decorated bright front windows and the gas lamps were tied with red bows. I poked around the shops for a while, hoping to find a thank-you gift for Barb. But I didn't know her well enough to choose anything with meaning and I suspected she'd be offended by anything as impersonal as a candle or a picture frame, so I left the shops empty-handed.

The smell of coffee and baking led me to Bun in the Oven, a cozy café so crowded with warm bodies that the window was fogged. I joined the line, reading coffee puns on kitchen towels for sale by the register. *Java nice day! Mugs and kisses.* I ordered a peppermint latte, a breakfast sandwich, and a box of rugelach, and carried my number to the only seat left at the counter facing the window.

The stools were close together. I squeezed in carefully to avoid disturbing the man beside me, who was intensely focused on his screen, typing to save his life. Best not to bother someone in the zone like that.

Before I could look away, he caught me.

I smiled quickly. "Good morning. Or, wait, afternoon."

He grinned back. "It's always morning when they serve all-day breakfast."

I laughed. "True."

Waiting for my food, I scrolled through apartment listings on my phone.

But then he spoke to me again.

"Do you mind if I use that outlet?" He pointed to the floorboards near my feet.

"Of course." I moved my knees out of the way so he could duck beneath the bar. His sweater stretched, exposing a glimpse of neck meeting shoulder. His dark, wavy hair was just on the edge of needing to be cut. I glimpsed his gold wedding ring as he plugged in his laptop charger. Thankfully my sandwich arrived, so I stuffed a bite in my mouth and pretended to text.

"Thanks," he said. "I hate paperwork. Are there any jobs that don't involve paperwork?"

"Hm. I doubt Banksy's doing paperwork."

He laughed. "Unfortunately I have no talent. What do you do? Does it involve paperwork?"

"I'm a wedding singer, and yes. Invoicing."

He threw his hands up in mock defeat. "See? Even the cool jobs are the worst."

"What do you do?"

"I'm a doctor." He rubbed his face with both hands, and I realized that despite his good spirits about it, he seemed tired and a little miserable. "They don't teach you about insurance in med school, and they don't warn you that for every hour you spend seeing patients, you spend two hours doing paperwork."

"That's too bad. I thought being a doctor was exactly like *Grey's Anatomy*. They never do paperwork. They're too busy falling in love and losing limbs in freak plane accidents."

"Doctors don't usually lose limbs at the hospital, but they do fall in love. I married one." He swiveled his stool around to look at the menu above the register. "Do we think this place has beer?"

"I think this is more of a tea-and-scone type establishment."

"Damn. A scone after hours of checking off boxes just doesn't land the same way." He swiveled back and closed his laptop. "I'm sorry I'm complaining so much. It's been a week."

"Same."

"Do you want to complain about it? I'm all ears."

"Sure. My mom died."

He buried his face in his hands. "If I were flexible enough to put my foot in my mouth, now would be the moment."

I laughed. "Yeah, you should probably start stretching. What happened to you this week? Flat tire?"

He nodded. "You could say that. The air went out of my marriage."

I looked up from my plate and found him watching me this time. His eyes were comfortable, soft, and inviting. Bedroom eyes. I bet he could tell a patient's family their loved one wasn't going to make it, and they'd feel safe to cry on his shoulder.

I tore my gaze away and picked up my sandwich. "Well, aren't we co-presidents of the Doomsday Club."

"No," he said, his voice dropping. "I've lost a parent. It's worse. If anything, I'm the treasurer."

I laughed. "Deal. Math is not my forte. What kind of doctor are you?"

"Oncologist. I lost my dad to lung cancer."

"Are you subconsciously trying to save other people because you couldn't save him?"

When I heard the words that had come out of my mouth, I felt my eyebrows go up and up and up. They, too, were surprised. I forgot to blink, then blinked repeatedly.

"I'm sorry," I said. "I have no idea where that came from. I think medical professionals call that projecting. Or this tea is spiked with truth serum."

He laughed. "Don't worry about it. You're almost spot on. I'd say it's fifty percent me trying to rewrite history and fifty percent that when he was going through treatment, I thought it was all really interesting. I research immunotherapies now."

"I have no idea what that is, but you've successfully convinced me I'm talking to a very impressive person."

When he smiled, my stomach floated up like its tether had been cut. I reached for my latte with both hands and ducked my face into it.

"Right back at you," he said.

"I'm not saving lives with my rendition of 'All the Single Ladies.'"

"I bet you've saved some pretty bad weddings." He glanced at his ring, then closed his fist. "Do we think this is a BYOB scone place?"

I shrugged. "Better to ask for forgiveness than permission."

"I'm procrastinating going home, if you couldn't tell."

"Me too. I'm staying with someone I barely know."

He raised a brow, teasing, like I'd had a one-night stand or something. Even the vaguest allusion to sex in this stranger's presence made my neck get hot.

"It's nothing like that," I hurried to explain. "She was a friend of my mom's and she's a little intense. It's a long story."

He grinned and opened his hands. "The longer, the better."

"Procrastination. Right. I can help with that." I swiveled my stool back and forth, debating how much to reveal. I didn't know him, but that was kind of freeing. "A few days after my mom died, my boyfriend told me he got a job as a bassist on a national tour, so we broke up."

"Your boyfriend sounds . . . very cool. I'm intimidated."

"Ex-boyfriend," I clarified.

"Still intimidated. But go on."

"So then I had no place to live, except I did—do—because I could move into my mom's house."

"He's the one leaving town, but you have to move out? That doesn't seem right."

My turn to raise a brow. "Who's in your house?"

"My wife, but I never liked our house. It's a 'smart house.' I opened the door with my thumbprint and the fridge spoke to me if I left the door open. I just want a regular key I can lose and to discover I've left the fridge door open when all the food goes bad. You know what I mean?"

I nodded. "My ex's apartment was in this super-high-tech new construction building downtown, and it had these very intense electronic toilets that looked like spaceships. It was like peeing in a Tesla."

"Does your mom's house have a remote-control TV or something?" He covered his face. "Bad example."

I laughed. "Believe it or not, she did live in this century."

"But you didn't want to stay there?"

I picked at the bread of my sandwich, tearing off little pieces. "It was complicated with my mom. There's a lot of history in that house.

To be honest, we weren't very close. I thought that would make it easier in some ways, but now I think it's harder. At the same time that I'm realizing she's really gone, I'm dealing with where it all went wrong."

"It's like getting your appendix out, only to get an infection at your incision."

I looked up at his bedroom eyes and nodded.

"When my dad died," he said, "I went backpacking in Southeast Asia for six months. I couldn't be in Chicago if he wasn't here. I got on a plane and told myself that was healing."

"Did it work? Because this woman showed up at my mom's claiming to be her best friend from thirty years ago and I ran away with her. She's basically the equivalent of my Southeast Asia."

"I felt great while I was gone. Then I came back."

I laughed. "So, no."

"I had a lot of complicated feelings, too. My dad was a lifelong smoker and it killed him, so I was pretty angry about that, but also devastated. He was my flawed hero."

"I'm angry, too," I admitted. "And now I feel guilty about my anger and angry about my guilt and it's a vicious cycle and I should just stop."

He was quiet for a second, then grinned, as if with sudden inspiration. "I'm going to repeat something my therapist said. All feelings are valid. The hard work is processing them as they come instead of trying to push them away."

"Did it ever get easier?"

He twirled an empty mug between his palms. "Yes and no. I still think about him all the time. I still want to call him after every Cubs game to hear him complain. I went to therapy for a long time, and I think I could start the whole process over from day one and still have plenty to talk about. But life does adjust to a new normal, and eventually it doesn't feel so hard to function." When he held my gaze, it felt like he was holding me. "You will feel joy again, I promise you that. You won't always feel this heavy."

Tears sprung to my eyes. I tried to hide them, but he rested his hand on my wrist and gently squeezed. "Can I get you a tea or anything?"

I grabbed a napkin. "I'm all right. I have this very cold peppermint latte."

"We can do better than that." He pointed through the foggy window at a pub. "See that place over there? They have the best fried pickles you'll ever have in your life. They have medicinal properties. I've conducted extensive research. Would it be weird if we went together?"

"I think we are well past weird, given that I'm crying in front of you and I don't even know your name. But . . ." I pointed at his ring, drawing my eyebrows together. "You're still married and I'm not interested in any funny business."

"I assure you I am no good at funny business. I'm not even sure I'm good at boring business."

The thought *you're good* popped into my mind, but I punted it away. "Okay then," I agreed, sliding off my stool. "I'll test your theory about these pickles. But you should know I'm an expert on all things fried."

I put on my coat while he unplugged his laptop. I was wrapping my scarf around my neck when I noticed his box of rugelach. "Funny. I have one, too. Must be good."

"They're my favorite," he said, buttoning his coat. "Whenever I come to see my mom, I have to stop."

Click click click click click. My brain exploded in pops of light like a paparazzi attack. "Hold on. I'm sorry if this is an insane question, but are you by any chance Barb's son?"

He looked at me like he was considering making a run for it. "Uh—"

"I'm sorry," I stammered. "If you have never heard of a woman named Barb, forget I said anything. She was a friend of my mom's and she told me her son was coming for dinner, so she sent me here to get this." I held up my box.

His eyes widened. "Right. That was . . . thoughtful." He held up his box. "Now we've got two."

It took a second to click; then I nearly collapsed with relief. "So you *are* Barb's son. Wow, thank god. I thought I was the one who needed to do foot-in-mouth stretching."

I thought he would laugh, or at least smile. I'd have even settled for a pity chuckle. But instead he considered me with a line between his eyebrows. "So you're staying at my mom's?"

"No," I hurried to say. "Only last night. It was more of an accident. We just . . . got to talking." *Crying.* "Anyway, I'm leaving later today."

He nodded, sliding the strap of his briefcase over his shoulder. We stood there, blocking the flow of traffic out of the café, looking at each other.

I stuck out my hand. "I'm Mel, by the way. My mom was Connie. Maybe Barb told you about her."

His palm was warm and his grasp comforting. I had that feeling again, that he was a bedroom I could curl up in.

"Henry," he said.

I forced my hand into my pocket. "I've never called a doctor by his first name before. It feels illegal."

Finally he laughed. We smiled at each other, dressed to leave, but not leaving. I started sweating beneath my scarf.

"Should we go home?" I asked, then panicked. "Not home for me. Home for you. I mean, should we go back to Barb's?"

He checked his watch. "She has been known to call every hospital in Chicago if I'm late. Maybe the fried pickles will have to wait."

I nodded, still looking at him looking back at me. *Turn away. Open the door. Go.* But instead, an uncontrollable force possessed me. I lunged forward and gave him a hug. For a moment, it was just me clinging on like a child to her parent's leg. Then his hands wrapped around my back. He held me while I closed my eyes and breathed in his sweater. I heard the clink of ceramic mugs and the clatter of forks on plates. I heard Michael Bublé singing "Silver Bells." I heard his heart beating. The café continued the bustle of breakfast, but I was here, holding on.

Then I snapped out of it and removed myself from the café without looking back.

Chapter 11

December 20

Usually, when a pushy mother wanted me to meet her son, that son was not a handsome doctor.

Outside, my hot, burning humiliation turned out to be the most effective coat. By the time I'd walked back to Barb's, I was wearing only a T-shirt.

Before going in, I stood on the porch, wondering whether to call an Uber and eliminate all risk of further embarrassment. What would I succumb to next? Booping him on the nose? Fist-bumping? Worse?

But Barb threw open the door, making me jump.

"I'm furious with my son for letting you freeze your tush off out there in the snow!" She steered me inside and straight to the kitchen table, where Henry was waiting.

I couldn't look at him. I wasn't sure I'd ever be able to look at him again.

Barb deposited a bowl of soup in front of me. "Fate is a funny bitch, isn't she? Although I still don't understand why you were going to go out for beer when there's beer here. And your mother."

"Sometimes a man needs to go where there's beer and no mothers," Henry said.

I stood, scraping my chair against the wood floor. "Excuse me a second. I need to change."

As soon as I escaped into the hall, I heard Henry say, "Mom, please."

"What?" Barb asked, all airy.

"You know what."

My skin melted off my face.

In the basement, I took a thirty-second shower, braided my hair, and scrounged a little makeup from my purse. Then I made the bed and packed my few belongings, including my mom, before going upstairs. Just outside the kitchen, I took a deep breath. I would have lunch, thank Barb for everything and promise to call, then leave.

"I thought you flew the coop!" Barb cried when I walked in. "I kept your soup warm. Sit. Henry was just catching me up on life as chief of Integrative Oncology Research and vice chair of the University of Chicago's Comprehensive Cancer Center, not to mention my son." She tousled his hair, and he ducked out of her reach like a kid would. Funny how even successful doctors reverted to acting like children in the presence of their mothers.

As I focused hard on my soup, Henry gave updates about life at the hospital, including a new trial he'd gotten approved. He said he'd taken Dylan, his nephew and Barb's grandson, to a Blackhawks game, and that Dylan and Summer were heading to Montreal next. "Summer's a tour manager," he explained to me. "She and Dylan live on the road." Then he said he'd been to a Bruce Springsteen concert. He didn't mention his divorce, but that was none of my business. Barb filled him in on the neighborhood gossip, then complained about the House of Representatives for forty-five minutes.

"Anyone want seconds?" she asked, clearing plates. "Dessert? Tea? Eggnog?"

I jumped up. "Please. Let me." I took the plates from her hands and carried them to the sink.

"You don't need to be so polite, sweetheart. I'm not the queen." Suddenly Barb gasped. "Speaking of the queen, where's Liesel?" She looked through the bay window to the street like Henry might have forgotten her in the car.

"Right. About that." He briefly glanced at me. "We're divorcing."

Barb's shock registered before her hands clasped over her heart. "Oh, sweetheart. I'm sorry. So this wasn't a surprise visit simply because you love your mother."

"No," he said. "I thought I'd spend the holidays with you while I find a new place."

I tried to keep my face still. So he wasn't here only for dinner—he was staying. *But I'm leaving,* I reminded myself.

Barb threw her arms wide. "I'm elated. Not about your divorce, of course. Are you all right? Are you seeing a shrink? You've got to take care of yourself, darling. Do you want to talk about it? I'm here if you need me. Counseling, on demand, for the low price of telling everyone at my funeral how wonderful I was."

Henry stood up, collecting our napkins and water glasses. "There isn't much to talk about. Liesel decided she didn't want children anymore."

A soapy plate slipped through my fingers and clattered in the sink. "Sorry," I muttered. "Clumsy." I pretended to see something fascinating out the window so they wouldn't notice my face burning. What did I care whether Henry wanted children? I didn't! I was merely surprised there was a woman in the world who didn't want to have this man's baby.

"Oh, Henry," Barb said. "You know I want fifteen grandchildren, but I'll understand if you want to stay married to Liesel."

Henry laughed, patting her on the shoulder. "Mom, I don't know how to say this, but I promise I'm not getting divorced for you."

"In that case, you've got plenty of time," Barb said. "One of the great injustices in life is that men have all the time in the world to have children. All they have to do is marry younger. But if you bring home a cheerleader who just graduated from college, I swear to god. Mel, how old are you? Oh, don't give me that look, Henry, I'm just curious."

I studied the soapy water swirling down the drain. "I'm thirty-three."

"Practically a newborn baby," Barb said. "What time is it? The sun is setting soon. Let's get ready." She swept out of the kitchen with her entourage of dangling shawls and clinking wrist bangles.

Alone, Henry met me at the sink.

"I'm sor—"

"I'm sor—"

We exchanged a smile.

"You first," I said.

"I just wanted to say I'm sorry for crashing your party."

"I'm sorry it's so weird I'm here. I'm going to leave tonight, I promise."

Henry lifted a dripping plate from my hand and toweled it off. "Rudy's groomer sleeping in my bed was weird. This is not weird."

I raised a brow. "Do I want to know?"

"My mom hates being alone, so the first time my sister and I were with our respective partners at Christmas, she invited a bunch of strays. Her bank teller. The groomer. The guy from the cheese-and-wine department at her market. I hope you're not leaving on my account."

"No. Well, sort of, if I'm being honest. It's just silly that I'm here when I have a perfectly fine house."

"You don't have a perfectly fine house. It sounds like you have a place you could stay, but you're not ready."

Through the window, violet-gray clouds blew across the sky. Here I was cocooned in home cooking, blankets, and a different version of my mom, the one I wish I'd seen. I pictured letting myself into the cold emptiness of my mom's house and shivered. But how could I stay here? Henry and Barb weren't my family and this wasn't my home.

Our fingers touched when I handed him another plate. "What happened to 'Southeast Asia doesn't fix anything'?" I asked.

"Southeast Asia doesn't fix anything in the long run, but neither does spending the holidays alone. I couldn't live with myself if you left just because I'm getting divorced. Besides, you know my mom would never allow it."

From the living room, she called, "Am I lighting these candles alone or what?"

"Almost done!" Henry answered. Then, to me, "Stay. Honestly, you'd be doing me a favor. My mom will only want to talk about my divorce if you leave. It'll be nice to have a buffer."

I handed him the last dish and turned off the water. "Do you want to talk about it? It's only fair that I return the favor."

"Not really, no." He toweled off a mug and returned it to the cupboard.

The kitchen was clean(ish) and Barb was waiting and the sun was setting and we really should have gone to the living room, but I didn't move and neither did he. Once again, our goodbye stretched on for an eternity.

"I'm sorry about the hug, by the way," I said. "I don't know what came over me. That was hug by fire."

He leaned against the counter and crossed his arms, smiling. "I liked the hug. There's strong medical evidence that hugs reduce blood pressure and strengthen immune systems."

I laughed. "In that case, you're welcome."

He gestured for me to lead the way. "After you."

We met Barb at the piano, where the silver menorah reflected the light of the fire. It was the fourth night of Hanukkah. Barb turned the lights out and lit the candles while Henry said the prayer. I'd never seen the ceremony before; it was peaceful and beautiful. Henry's voice was soft and melodic, and when he finished, we stood in silence for a while, in the dark, watching the flames twirl and the wax drip.

When Barb exclaimed, "Gifts!" Henry and I jumped.

"We always get each other a silly little something for each night of Hanukkah," she said, flipping the lights on. She and Henry exchanged packages wrapped in shiny blue paper. Then Barb handed me one, too, and I wished I'd bought that picture frame after all.

"I'm sorry," I said. "I don't have anything."

"Your presence is the ultimate present, sweetheart." She tore the paper on Henry's gift to reveal a box of lightbulbs and laughed. "Henry loves a practical gift. How many doctors will it take to screw these in?"

Henry went next, unwrapping *The New Yorker Book of Doctor Cartoons*. "The answer is probably in here somewhere."

They both looked at me. My heart pounded as I peeled mine open. It was a small picture frame, just one inch by one inch. My mom's face beamed at me in front of a plain background.

"That was from her student ID," Barb said. "Look how beautiful she was. I was so jealous I could barely stand it."

My mom had long, straight dark hair and a huge, openmouthed smile. She looked youthful, ready to take on the world.

Henry leaned closer. "You look just like her."

It was too hard to look at. I put it in the pocket of my sweatshirt.

"Thank you," I said, both for the compliment and the gift. "I think I should take off."

Barb reacted like I'd said I didn't plan to vote in the next election. "*Leave?* I made pot roast!"

"You two should be alone. I don't want to interfere."

"Go get the album," Barb instructed. "I need to show you something."

"I looked at it a hundred times last night. I've seen everything."

"Not this. I'll meet you in the kitchen."

I collected the album from where I'd left it on my pillow, but I couldn't open it. I couldn't bear any more evidence of the person my mom had been. Of her vulnerability or what she'd desired and dreamed about and lost. That person had loved her best friend, her sister, music, and maybe life, too, at least the parts of it that promised something. Her innocence was a slap to the face, painful and awakening.

Upstairs, Barb was standing at the island, where she had scattered the ingredients for mashed potatoes. I handed her the album and she flipped through it until she found what she was looking for. "Here."

When I took it back, the album felt heavier in my hands, loaded with secrets. The photo she'd flagged was taken from the stage looking down at a crowd. It wasn't well lit—the faces were shadowed and obscured by other faces. "What am I looking at?"

Barb withdrew a huge chef's knife from a wooden block. "Ernest. Our manager. You'll know him when you see him."

Henry and I bent closer to the photo. I was focused, but not so focused that I missed how he smelled like winter, like a favorite sweater, like crawling into bed. His nearness made my skin tingle.

"Bottom right," Barb said, pointing with her knife. "Cowboy hat."

"Almost all of these guys are wearing cowboy hats," Henry said.

"No one wore it quite as well as he did," Barb said.

I inspected each face carefully, playing *Where's Waldo?* Only I didn't know what Waldo looked like.

Then my eyes caught on someone familiar. His square smile, his long sideburns, his jaw with two sharp angles like the bottom half of a bucket.

I peeled back the plastic cover and unstuck the photo from the cardboard page to hold it closer to my face. It was old, sun-washed and faded, but I was pretty sure I knew that face. I was pretty sure everyone in America and probably thirty other countries knew that face. "Oh my god," I blurted. "Is that Dash Whitney?"

Barb chopped a potato in half with a vicious *thwack*. "The man, the myth, the legend."

"But you said his name was Ernest."

"It was. Would you become famous with the name Ernest?"

I processed that information for several seconds. "Dash Whitney," I clarified, "as in Dash Whitney, managed my mom's band."

Thwack. "I'd like to think it was our band," Barb corrected, "but yes."

"How is this possible?" I glanced at Henry, but he didn't look as shocked as I felt. *Of course he doesn't,* I reminded myself. He'd known his whole life his mom had a relationship with Dash Whitney. This was news only to me.

"It's possible the way anything is possible. Connie's dreams were not a joke. She was *this* close." Barb wielded her chef's knife as she pinched her fingers. "If not for Dash Whitney, né Ernest, she'd have had a completely different life and so would you. For one thing, you'd be sitting in a mansion made of diamonds, wearing a feather boa made of clouds."

I had to sit down. My legs felt like mashed potatoes. I lowered myself onto the bench below the bay window and hung my head in my hands. "This is bananas."

I heard the *thwack, thwack, thwack* of Barb's knife as she continued. "Ernest said he had connections at record labels in Nashville and Los Angeles, but that we'd get only one shot and we weren't ready. We had to be irresistible to get noticed, he said. I remember thinking, *But you noticed us.* Weren't we irresistible already? But that was his game. The more he told us we weren't good enough, the more we needed his approval. He critiqued our clothes, our hair, our dancing, always dangling that illusory phone call to his friends. He held our self-esteem and self-worth in the palm of his hand with the same nonchalance as he held his whiskey. Like he forgot he'd ordered it in the first place. I didn't even sing because I loved it anymore. I sang so Ernest would look at me."

I stared at her, struck by the casual way she tossed potatoes in a bowl while revealing such explosive emotional truths. "So he was an abusive asshole," I said.

"He owned us," Barb agreed. "Our bodies, our dreams, our futures. In my defense, I did wonder why, if he was as connected as he claimed to be, he spent so much time with two secretarial school dropouts. But I took it as further evidence that he thought we were special. We'd talk about what we were going to do when we got rich. I was going to start my own theater, Ernest was going to buy a ranch and racehorses, and Connie was going to travel the world. Obviously, those dreams only came true for one of us."

I'd read about Dash Whitney's seventy-acre luxury ranch and horse rescue in *People* magazine. It was where he made whiskey and earned millions of dollars in royalties while he drank coffee on his porch. "Okay, but you did record the most famous country song in America. Why aren't *you* filthy rich?"

She waved her knife around the kitchen, gesturing at its charming glory. "Are you suggesting my house needs work? I'm only joking, sweetheart, don't look so terrified. I barely made a penny off that song because I was uneducated, unrepresented, and didn't know what I was signing. All I cared about was that Ernest wanted to sing with me. I'd have done it for free."

"Have you done anything about that?" I asked. "I'm sure you could hire a lawyer."

"I've been telling her this for years," Henry said, not looking up from his cutting board, where he was slicing chives into miniature rings with the precision of a surgeon. "She deserves her share of the pie."

Barb *thwacked* her chef's knife through another potato. "Recording that song was a mistake. I want nothing to do with it. And I have plenty of pie. Apple pie. Homemade and better than anything money could buy."

I noticed the muscles in Henry's jaw flex as the steel of his blade severed another batch of chives. Did it bother him to hear this much about his mother's relationship with a man who wasn't his dad?

"Christmas of 1982," Barb said, "Connie was going to visit Joan, but Ernest wanted to take us to the piano bar at the Fairlane Hotel so we could sing for the recording industry bigwigs who drank there. He wanted us in miniskirts flanking his arms, so Connie canceled her trip. Ernest fed us dirty martinis and watched us sway on the dance floor with our arms around each other. We didn't even sing. I felt more like a sandwich than an artist. But I didn't care if I got famous based on sex instead of talent, as long as I got famous. That was the way the world worked. I was only twenty-five, but I was old enough to understand that."

Barb had given up chopping. She told the story gazing out the bay window, as if the past were a play she could step into and rewrite.

"That night Ernest passed out drunk on our couch with his cowboy hat covering his face—a habit of his. In the middle of the night, I put on my robe and went to make sure he was alive. At least that's what I told myself I was doing. Then I heard them. Connie and I both had the same idea, but she'd gotten there first."

My limbs felt like anchors weighing me down. "You're telling me my mom was sleeping with Dash Whitney. Whose poster I had in my bedroom. Is he the one you had an affair with?" I glanced at Henry. "Sorry."

He shrugged and kept chopping. He had a small mountain now. "I'm used to it."

Barb set aside her knife and knelt at my feet, taking both my hands and looking me straight in the eyes. "Ernest had Connie, but one half of us only made him feel like half of a man. I should have told him to hitchhike to hell, but I was desperate for validation. I wish I could tell you I'd made the choice because I was selfish. That would at least mean I had a backbone. But Ernest wanting me meant I *was wanted.* Can you understand that?"

It was hard for me to imagine that kind of betrayal. Lizzie would never do that to me, even if she liked men. Gabby and I had crushes on the same boys in middle school, back when sharing a crush was like sharing a diary. That was different. That was fun. This was cruel.

I searched her eyes for a reason to say no, *No, I can't understand,* but I saw only remorse. "How did my mom find out?"

"She caught us. Red-handed. Packed her bags and never spoke to me again."

It wasn't like Barb had hid this from me. Within minutes of showing up on my mom's porch, she'd told me the truth. Still, picturing the version of my mom in those photos losing her best friend, her boyfriend, and her dreams all at once made my chest ache. Barb must have read it on my face because she squeezed my hands.

"What did Ernest do?" I asked.

"He sat on the couch like he had nothing to do with it. I think

Connie expected it out of him. She was angry, obviously, but he'd betrayed a romance. I'd betrayed a friendship, which is much worse."

I shook my head, blinking away tears. "You were young. He preyed on you."

"He did," she agreed. "But I wish I'd had the strength to fight back. Can you forgive me, sweetheart?"

I pulled my hands from hers to wipe my face. I wanted to say yes, but I couldn't. Forgiveness wasn't mine to offer.

"I know you wish things ended differently," I said instead, using a napkin to blow my nose. "I wish things ended differently, too."

I wished for so many impossible things. I wished my mom were alive. I wished I understood why she died. I wished I'd had the chance to ask her these questions myself. I wished I could tell her I didn't know what I was doing when I played *Honest Man* on repeat. I wished I could say I was sorry for how lonely that must have made her feel, like she didn't matter.

Slowly, I lifted my heavy body. "I need to be alone for a while." I sensed Henry's eyes on me as I turned away. If I left now, would I ever see him again? He was tangled up in this mess.

Barb caught my arm. "Are you leaving?"

My mom never spoke to her again because of this. Why should I?

"I only agreed to come for dinner," I said, my voice as aching as my goodbye.

Her stance was one foot forward, a hand outstretched, like she was already considering coming after me.

I went to the basement and lay down with my arms curled around my mom, longing for her in the deepest parts of my body, bottomless voids I didn't know I could feel. My tears slid sideways, wetting the pillow, until the fabric was cold and sodden against my cheek. I wasn't crying because Barb had an affair. I was crying because I didn't know. I didn't know anything about my mom's life, and whose fault was that?

I could leave. I had every right to get my things and go. But where? And why?

My mom deserved to be known for what she was instead of what she was not. If I left now, I'd never find out. This was the gift Barb had offered me—the truth, whatever it was.

I fell asleep, and when I woke, the cold glass of my mom's urn was warm from my body. I put her on the nightstand beside her picture, the school photo Barb gave me. "All those times I listened to Dash Whitney," I said. "Why didn't you tell me?"

But she just beamed back. I'd have to find the answer some other way.

I went upstairs, just in time for pot roast.

Chapter 12

December 21

At the kitchen table the next morning, in my borrowed pajamas, I flipped through the photo album again, hungry for details of my mom. The way she wore her hair. The denim vest she paired with all her outfits. Her white cowboy boots.

Henry sat beside me, reading the paper, and Barb across from him, reading a cookbook.

We all looked up at the creak and swish of the front door opening.

"Who on earth is that?" Barb asked. "Are we getting robbed at eight a.m.?"

A woman's voice said, "Dylan, hang up your coat," followed by the clomping of boots and the muffled thud of something heavy landing on the floor.

Barb leapt out of her chair and rushed to greet her daughter and grandson. Henry smiled at me and followed.

I lingered at the door to the hall, peering in.

Summer had Barb's wild spirals of hair, only hers were bleached blond, and her arms were painted in colorful tattoos. Dylan was a miniature Henry, with dark hair past his ears, straight brows, and a pointed chin. He wore a puffy camouflage jacket twice his size.

When Summer noticed me, she said, "Hey, stranger. Who are you?"

"This is Mel," Henry said. "She's staying with us."

I curled my arms around my middle, covering the band T-shirt Barb had lent me—without Summer's permission, probably. "Hi. I'm crashing your holiday."

"You're not the first and you won't be the last. This is Dylan." Summer nudged him. He didn't look up from his video game. "Hang up your coat," she said again.

Dylan managed to wriggle himself out of it without ever taking his eyes off the game.

"Dylan's about to reach the last level of Super Mario Party, so he'll say hi later," Summer explained.

Henry pointed at their two huge suitcases. "I thought you were going to Montreal."

"Change of plans," she said. "Dylan and I have some super exciting news." She raised her brows at Henry in a message that said, *You better act like this news is exciting or you'll be hearing from my lawyer.* "Don't we, Dylan?"

Catching the hint, Barb threw her arms wide. "I can't wait to hear all about it. Let's go sit. I have cinnamon rolls."

Figuring Summer wouldn't want to share her not-so-exciting news with a complete stranger, I quietly retreated, tiptoeing toward the basement door.

Barb's voice stopped me. "What, are you sick of us?"

"I thought Summer might want some privacy."

"Families don't give each other privacy except in the bedroom and the bathroom."

I had to laugh as she shooed me into the kitchen. "*Your* family doesn't," I teased. "Some families do."

"I'm not even sure I stand by my own rule. What if I die on the toilet? No one would know."

At the table, Summer plucked the video game from Dylan's hand and replaced it with a glass of milk while Barb produced a platter of cinnamon rolls she must have stayed up all night making. Dylan used his fork to scrape his roll clean of frosting, then licked it like an ice cream cone. He had the same eyes as Henry, the color of a forest floor.

"So what's this big news?" Henry asked.

"We're moving in!" Summer said, full of false cheer. "Surprise!"

"Hurrah!" Barb cheered, nothing false about it. "It's a Christmas miracle."

"I hope that's all right, Mom," Summer added quietly.

"Don't be ridiculous. I'm thrilled. I'm beyond thrilled. But why? What happened to Montreal?"

Summer kissed Dylan's hair. "Montreal isn't home. We need a home."

"What about work?" Henry asked.

"I quit," she said, pouring herself coffee. "I'm going to try something local. Managing, agenting maybe. The music scene here doesn't get enough credit."

"Music is in our blood," Barb said to me. "Summer's been sneaking into concerts since she was twelve. I pretended I didn't know because secretly I loved that about her."

Summer's thick brows danced over the rim of her mug. "That's how we know Henry was switched at birth."

"I did get kicked out of group piano when I was seven because I was so bad the other parents thought I'd make their kids worse," Henry admitted.

"I can identify the babies that came out of my own body, thank you very much," Barb said. "Henry was born this serious. He didn't even cry. He just shook my hand."

Dylan set down his milk. "What did I do?" he asked his mom.

"Ate, slept, and pooped, just like now." She poked his belly, and he doubled over in laughter.

"In case you're wondering which one of us is the more interesting sibling," Henry said to me, "Summer calls Lenny Kravitz 'Len.'"

"Is that the only thing you know about my job?" Summer chucked a piece of cinnamon roll at him. Within half a second, Rudy trotted in to eat it.

"Is that not the coolest part of your job?" Henry asked.

"Mom has Madonna's cell phone number," Dylan interjected, back on his video game.

"Fair point," Henry agreed. "But does she know her last name?"

Summer rolled her eyes. "You're not even a dad. You have no excuse."

Henry ruffled Dylan's hair. "Uncles are allowed to make lame jokes."

"Beg to differ," Dylan said, his delivery dry and perfect.

"Henry has plenty of time to work on his dad humor," Barb said.

Summer paused mid-sip of coffee. "What does that mean? Are you having a baby?"

"Far from it. We're splitting."

A line appeared between Summer's brows; then an identical line appeared between Henry's.

"What?" he asked.

"Honestly? I'm sorry, but I think this is good news."

"I'm not sure whether that says more about you or me," Henry said, eating his cinnamon roll with a knife and fork.

"Having a conversation with Liesel was like taking a class from Miss Manners," Summer said. "Did she pluck her eyebrows using a ruler? I just think you need someone a little more fun to balance you out."

"Liesel is the chief of her department," Henry said. "She didn't have time for fun."

Summer nudged Dylan. "Everything can be fun when you're with the right person. Right, my guy?"

But Dylan was absorbed in his game, his little thumbs dancing and punching.

Henry frowned. "I have plenty of fun."

Summer gestured at his slumped-over posture. "You're sitting there like a grump."

"I'm getting divorced. How am I supposed to sit?"

"That's an even better reason to let loose," she insisted. "Dylan, now that we're staying in Chicago, you can help Uncle Henry live a little."

"I want to live a little," Barb said. "Can I come?"

"Given that we'll be living here," Summer said, "you've got a standing invitation."

Barb beamed around the table, her house suddenly full. "Have I won the lottery or what?"

"Just for now," Summer clarified. "We're going to find a really nice apartment where Dylan can have his own room and go to a special new school. Isn't that so exciting?" She nodded around the table with a smile plastered on her face. *Now is the time to agree this is very exciting!*

"Mom promised I can build a fort wherever I want in our new apartment. Even in the bathroom. A toilet fort." Dylan held up his cinnamon roll like it was a live slug. "Do I have to eat this?"

"No, babe. You can be excused."

He scraped his chair back and bolted to the living room. Seconds later, the TV turned on and he started singing along to a theme song.

Summer's head collapsed on the table. "Mitchell is a fucking dickhead who hasn't paid child support in two fucking years. Dylan needs to go to that special school I can't afford, but apparently Mitchell doesn't give a shit that Dylan can't read. Mitchell probably can't even fucking read." Summer lifted her face and added, "Dylan's been going to online school. I thought that was a workable solution given my schedule, but now he's way behind and it's my fucking fault, so Mitchell's blaming me and won't help with tuition. He's such an asshole."

"Have you talked to a lawyer?" Henry asked.

"Justice is prohibitively expensive. Every lawyer I talk to wants thirty percent of whatever they collect. I need that thirty percent. That's the whole fucking point." She licked frosting off her cinnamon roll just like Dylan. "I'll figure it out. If we stay here for a little while at least I can save some money. That school is not cheap."

"I'll help you," Henry said. "Whatever you need."

"And I'll talk to Mitchell," Barb said. "He'll be paying by the end of next week."

Summer hung her head in her hands and laughed. "I don't doubt that. Just don't get yourself arrested."

They reminded me of Lizzie's family—teasing, loving, fast-talking. Until the cranberry juice incident, I'd spent so much time comparing my family to Megan's, thinking the perfect family had a mom who sliced cold watermelon and a dad who played catch in the front yard. Then I thought the perfect family had to be one that never yelled like Megan's mom had, never hurt each other's feelings, never even had problems. Maybe I still had it wrong. Maybe the perfect family wasn't one that avoided the darkness altogether, but helped each other through it.

Barb reached across the table and squeezed Summer's arm. "It takes a village, sweetheart. Thankfully, we are a village."

I decided to tag along when Henry took Dylan sledding that afternoon.

"I've never been sledding before," I told them as we dressed in our winter gear by the front door.

Henry helped me into my coat. "Really? What did you do as a kid?"

"Mostly choreographed dances to the Spice Girls in my bedroom. Is that not what you did?"

He bent to help Dylan with his boots. "I just looked at their pictures in my bedroom."

"Gross," Dylan said.

"Is sledding hard?" I asked. "Should I be scared?"

"It's like the easiest thing ever." Dylan shoved me out the door before I even had my boots zipped up. "So easy a baby could do it."

"I'll let you in on a little secret," Henry said as he locked the door behind us. "Sledding is just sitting while holding on."

"I don't know," I disagreed. "It might be one of those things you have to learn when you're young or you'll never be good at it, like French."

Henry unlocked his Jeep with a beep. "If you have a butt, you can sled."

I laughed. "Low barrier to entry. My kind of sport."

Based on the hard time Barb and Summer were giving Henry about being too serious and never letting loose, I'd begun to think maybe he was more buttoned-up than the person I'd glimpsed in the café. Dr. Henry, MD. But when I saw the inside of his car, I smiled. The open, honest person I'd seen in the café was the real Henry, not the other way around. His car was a disaster. Not one, but two banana peels were stuffed into the cup holders. Empty seltzer cans rolled around on the floor. Something white—cream cheese?—was smeared on the dash, like he'd changed a song while eating a bagel. I pushed aside a bottle of contact lens solution to sit in the passenger seat. If Dr. Henry, MD, wasn't hiding anything, maybe I could open up, too.

From the back seat, Dylan asked, "Can you make my butt hot?"

Henry turned the seat warmer on. "Do you want your butt hot, too?" he asked me.

It sounded like dirty talk coming out of his polite mouth. "Yes, please."

We drove a short distance through the neighborhood to a park with a snow-covered hill crawling with children in brightly colored jackets, sledding down and climbing back up. Their happy screams brightened the gray landscape of the winter day.

Henry killed the ignition and unbuckled his seat belt. "Ready?"

Through the windshield, I watched an older kid torpedo into a younger kid's sled, sending him flying. "Are you sure this is safe?"

Dylan answered, "Ish," and kicked open his door. "Race you to the top!" He jumped out and took off running.

"Could we get hurt?" I asked.

"Definitely. But I'm a doctor." Henry grinned at me sideways.

"Will immunotherapies help my broken back?"

"No, but I still remember how to make a tourniquet."

"You're really selling this."

"Do you want to abort the mission?"

"No way." I kicked open my own door. "I'm not a quitter."

Outside, my butt missed the seat warmer. Henry led the way up the hill, dragging a blue sled. By the time we reached the top, my jeans clung to my legs, soggy and freezing. Everyone else was wearing snow pants—I was woefully unprepared.

Looking around, I saw we were the only two people over the age of ten. "You bring a lot of women here?"

"You're the first," Henry said. "Would it make a good date?"

"I guess that depends on how good you are at this. No one wants to date a bad sledder, because it means you don't have a butt."

Henry grinned, then arranged the sled on a plateau facing forward. "Hop in, Dylan. Pressure's on."

Dylan was insatiable—he raced up the hill after each run, dragging the sled, demanding Uncle Henry get in and go faster this time. They sledded again and again until they were both red in the cheeks and winded. Dylan climbed the hill a final time and collapsed in the snow with his arms and legs splayed. "I'm too old for this much fun," he said.

When Henry made it to the top a few paces later, he nudged the sled toward me. "Your chariot awaits, milady."

"I'm not getting in there alone. I'll crash into a tree."

Henry frowned at the sled. "It'll be a tight squeeze if I get in there with you. Are you okay with that?"

"I will take your cooties over certain death." I climbed into the sled. When Henry didn't join me, I glanced back and found him hesitating. "Get in, Speed Racer."

"If you insist." Slowly he lowered himself into the back of the sled, and I understood what he meant by *tight squeeze.* His chest hugged my back, his legs straddled my hips, his hands grazed mine when they reached for the steering rope. My skin heated, no seat warmer needed. Against me, Henry didn't move a muscle. If not for the beat of his heart against my back, I'd have thought he'd turned to stone.

This was a bad idea.

When he finally said something, I felt the words in his breath on my neck. "Do you mind if I get you in position?"

I glanced over my shoulder and met his gaze, the only thing blazing on this cold hill. "Yes. I mean no. No, I don't mind."

"Hold on here." He guided my hands to the side. "Put your feet on the footrests." He lifted my right calf to reposition my foot. "If you want to slow down, lean into me. If you want to go faster, lean forward and bend down. Think aerodynamics."

"I'm going to go out on a limb and say it's unlikely I'll want to go faster."

Henry chuckled, low and vibrating in my ear. "Are you nervous?"

"A little. Are you?"

"Yeah. But not because of the sled."

Dylan let out an exasperated "Will you just go already?" and we both laughed.

"Sorry," Henry called. "I'm a chicken."

"It's okay to be scared, Uncle Henry. It happens to the best of us."

Henry moved us forward until we hit the slope and tipped downward. As it began to slide, he lifted his knees and pulled them in tight against my legs, holding me safely in place. With one Elvis-like thrust of his hips, he lurched us forward, off, racing down the hill. I gripped the sides for dear life, but as the sled picked up speed, the wind whipped in my hair and bit my cheeks and I remembered: *I'm alive. I am breathing. I am still here.*

I leaned forward, into the wind.

The hill wasn't as tall as it looked from the top. After only seconds of flying, the sled slowed as the ground flattened. We inched to a stop on a wide expanse of snow, breathless. I looked at Henry over my shoulder and found him watching me, waiting.

I beamed. "You were right."

"That it was easy or that it was fun?"

"Both. Let's do it again, but faster this time."

Chapter 13

DECEMBER 21

After a dinner of chicken pot pie, Dylan went to bed, Barb went upstairs to take a bath, and Summer challenged Henry to a game of Scrabble. I joined them in the living room on Summer's instruction that I referee so neither of them lit the Christmas tree on fire in a competitive fit of rage.

"I hope you've cleared your calendar for the next six hours," she said, unfolding the board.

"The only thing on my agenda is going to the kitchen for more of this." I raised my bowl of the best cherry cobbler I'd ever had in my life, warm and paired with vanilla ice cream.

"Where's Mom?" Summer asked. "She usually hovers around telling us what word to play."

"She's in the bath," Henry said, lighting a log in the fireplace.

"Ah. That explains the weed smell. Ready?" She held out the velvet bag for him to draw a tile. "Dammit. You first."

Henry chose his seven tiles and arranged them so far from Summer that even if she could have caught a glimpse, she'd have needed glasses to read anything. "Mel, get your dictionary ready. Summer thinks you can put *anti* in front of any word in the English language for more points. As in antiholiday. Antifood. Antiwin."

"Henry is willing to die on this hill because he doesn't want to admit he lost the last game we ever played with our dad. Hanukkah is not a Scrabble word. Neither is Christmas. Scrabble is an atheist."

Henry was about to take a sip of water but paused to say, "Don't you mean antigod?"

As he contemplated his first move, Summer turned to me. "So what's the connection between you and our mom?"

"Our moms were the Secretaries," I said. "Did Barb tell you about them before?"

Summer unfolded herself from her armchair to peruse Barb's liquor cabinet, picking up and putting down all the bottles of sherry. "Oh, yeah. Mom said they were like Ann and Nancy Wilson from Heart. Have you ever seen the music video for 'All I Wanna Do Is Make Love to You'? Iconic. It's about a girl who picks up a hot hitchhiker for sex. They perform in eighties business suits while playing the electric guitar and crying. I love to imagine Mom like that, wearing shoulder pads and jamming out. It kills me." Summer selected the only bottle of regular wine and poured everyone a glass.

"She's told us a lot of stories," Henry said to me. "She swears she was going to replace Barbra Streisand in the movie *Funny Girl* until the director found out she was only nine."

Summer handed me my glass and resumed her seat in the chair near the fire. "She claims she sat next to Lee Strasberg on the subway and he told her to call him, but then she dropped his card through a manhole, went down into the sewer to get it, but a rat had eaten his phone number off."

"There were only so many times ten-year-old me could listen to her talk about taking dance lessons from Bob Fosse before I needed to go play with my baseball cards," Henry said. "She traffics in stories of almosts and what-ifs."

I burrowed deeper into the couch, pulling my blanket to my chin. "You don't think those stories are true?"

"I don't think she's lying to us per se," Summer said, rearranging her tiles. "She might be lying to herself, though."

"Her opinion *is* her truth," Henry said. "If you don't agree with her, it's not that you have a different view. It's that you're wrong."

They exchanged a look I couldn't read.

"Henry's mad at her for never doing anything about the money from 'Carry My Heart,'" Summer explained. "Our dad had a business cleaning pools that went under when he got sick. He didn't have good insurance, his bills were astronomical, etc., etc. Classic American bullshit." She swallowed a big sip of her wine. "It was hard. She was going to lose the house, but Henry paid it off."

Henry focused on his rack. "And now you and Dylan need money and she still won't do anything about it."

Summer shrugged, playing her first word. "It's her money."

"No, it's not. That's the problem. If it were, you know she'd give it to you."

She flung a tile at him. "I thought you were giving me the money," she teased.

"You know if I had ten million dollars, Dylan would be going to the most expensive school in the world, but unfortunately only one of us is sitting on that gold mine." To me, Henry added, "When we were growing up, it seemed like our mom was trying not to earn money to prove a point. But we never understood what that point was. And still don't."

"She hates Dash Whitney," Summer said. "And she's stubborn."

They refilled their racks and contemplated their next steps as the fire cracked and popped behind them. I didn't say anything, but

I sided with Henry on this one. Enough women in music had had their voices co-opted. Barb had a chance to take hers back. Why hadn't she? If she hated Dash Whitney that much, why not squeeze him for everything he was worth?

"So, Mel . . ." Summer said, the change in her tone evident. "How long are you staying?"

I set my empty bowl aside and reached for my wine instead. "I should have left by now, but your mom keeps feeding me."

"That's how she sucks you in."

"When my ex leaves town, I'll go to his place for a while."

Henry arranged his tiles on the board with little clicks. "Mel's boyfriend is going on tour. What's the band called?"

"Ex-boyfriend. And they're called the Toms."

"I know the Toms," Summer said, penciling down Henry's points. "They suck."

"Really? Dan said they were the next big thing. A 'totally new sound.'"

"Sure, they're a totally new sound," she agreed. "Making music sound like garbage."

I settled into the cushions and sipped my wine. It tasted like your basic grocery store wine. Dan would have hated it, which made it even better. "He wanted me to join the tour and sing backup."

Summer finished her turn and sat sideways on her armchair, legs dangling over the side. "I didn't know you were a singer."

"She's incredible," Henry said, without looking up from his rack.

"How do you know?" I asked.

Summer cackled. "Busted. He definitely googled you."

Henry played a word. O-O-P-S.

"Do you tour?" Summer asked.

I shook my head. "Purely local. Mostly weddings and events. The occasional festival, like the craft beer one in the summer. Sometimes the Renaissance festival, which is always a wild time."

Summer leaned forward to inspect the board. "Do you want to go bigger?"

"No. I mean, I *have* memorized my Grammy acceptance speech, but haven't we all done that?"

"I've got mine down to forty seconds so they don't string-instrument me offstage," she said. "Henry doesn't have a Grammy speech. He's got a Nobel Prize for Science Guys speech."

I laughed as Henry tapped the side of his skull. "It's a lecture, and it's an hour. Wanna be my date?"

Summer flashed two tiles: N, O. "I'm busy that night."

"Have you guys ever met Dash Whitney?" I asked.

"I've worked for him," Summer said. "My first job on the road was with a country music festival. My mom told me not to take it because he was the headliner. Of course that only made me want to take it more."

"What's he like?"

She lifted her mass of curls and secured them with a clip. "Your typical diva. You know he screwed over Mom. Dash Whitney fucks a lot of people, and I mean that in both the literal and the figurative sense."

On the board, Henry added a word that Summer challenged.

"*Sackbut* is not a word, you doink."

"A sackbut is a brass instrument from the Renaissance era. Ask Mel." Henry grinned at me.

I typed it into my phone. "Hm. If I say it's a word, will you still help me meet Dash Whitney?"

She narrowed her eyes. "What are you plotting?"

"I need to talk to him. Can you pull some strings?"

"He's playing the Jingle Ball downtown now that he's the country Michael Bublé. If you want, we can go."

I sat up straight. The Jingle Ball was a holiday festival with multiple stages, carnival games, and booths selling roasted hazelnuts and eggnog. It happened every year at Millennium Park downtown.

"When is it?"

"Tomorrow."

Tomorrow. This was my idea, but tomorrow was too soon. I thought I'd gear up for it, have time to practice my speech in the mirror.

"Earth to Creeper," Summer said, chucking another tile at Henry's head. "Stop staring."

I glanced over just in time to see Henry look away.

"Would you both come with me?" I asked.

Summer shrugged. "Why not? But we can't tell Mom. It's not worth the drama."

"I'm in," Henry said.

The three of us looked at one another across the fire like we'd made some kind of summer camp pact to invade the boys' cabins and short-sheet their bunks. My knee bounced until I couldn't take it—I stood up and started pacing. I was a live wire, buzzing.

"You okay?" Henry asked.

"Dash Whitney was my idol," I said. "I'd have given my Princess Diana Beanie Baby to meet him. But now I also hate him?"

Henry caught my gaze. "He's your flawed hero."

I nodded. "So how do we act around him? Are we nice? Do we egg him? What's the plan?"

"We'll be fair," he said. "Maybe he's remorseful and wants to make it right. Maybe he even wants to pay Mom."

Summer raised her eyebrows and nodded. "Sure, Mister Rogers, good luck with that."

He checked his watch. "Time for me to hit the twin bed. Selma Blair and Sarah Michelle Gellar are expecting me."

"Henry still sleeps beneath the beguiling stares of a *Cruel Intentions* poster he hung up in the eighth grade," Summer explained.

He grinned. "I hung it with only the purest of intentions. So—" He inclined his head toward me. "We ride at dawn?"

I laughed. "See you then."

Summer drained the last of her wine. "I don't think we need to leave until, like, two-thirty."

When they'd gone upstairs, I hurried to the basement to text Lizzie. *I have news. It's explosive.*

She answered right away. *Dan got fired on his first day . . .*

Lol

No

Well maybe but that's not it

I had already filled her in on the appearance of Barb in my mom's driveway. *The manager of their band was DASH WHITNEY. Yes THAT ONE. And they were sleeping together!!!! Should I be concerned that when I was thirteen I was in love with the man my mom dated?*

Dash Whitney released his third album right when I hit puberty. He was too handsome to be anything but famous, the way it was impossible to imagine one of the Hemsworth brothers not as a movie star, but as a dad at your kid's school who sometimes chaperoned field trips. My fantasies stopped involving Céline Dion inviting me onstage and started involving Dash Whitney inviting me to the Valentine's dance and serenading me in front of the entire grade. I taped his poster on the underside of my bunk bed so I could look at it while I was falling asleep, and when my mom discovered it, she was furious. The tape had peeled off the paint, so we couldn't sell it when I grew out of it. *She doesn't get me,* I'd thought, stewing in bed that night. Apparently, I was wrong. She knew what it was to be obsessed with Dash Whitney. When she tore that poster down, she was only trying to protect me.

Lizzie sent back a gif of a dog cocking its head to the side and the words *say what?*

This was before he was Dash Whitney. His name was Ernest. We're going to meet him tomorrow at the jingle ball. Do you want to come?

It had been years since Dash Whitney had released new music. He'd moved on to less artistic moneymaking endeavors—game shows, a whiskey label. And last season he joined *American Icon* as the reasonable judge, alongside a former girl-band pop star from the early aughts who told everyone they were a winner in her heart and the grumpy manager who never took his sunglasses off, who'd been on the show since season one. In addition to his contract, the Pepsi cup he drank from must have earned him a zillion dollars a week.

But perhaps the biggest shift in Dash Whitney's career was the move toward Christmas music. He'd released at least five Christmas albums in the last five years and played a sold-out show in New York every year, during which fake snow fell on the audience and little kids got to join him onstage. If he was headlining the Jingle Ball, he had indeed usurped Michael Bublé as the angel—or devil, depending on how you looked at it—of December.

Lizzie responded to my text with a screenshot of the cover of the eighties movie *Ernest Saves Christmas.*

Did Ernest successfully save Christmas? she asked.

Tune in to find out, I wrote back.

Chapter 14

December 22

Weather-wise, it couldn't have been a worse day for the Jingle Ball. When we woke up, wind rattled the windows and whistled in through cracks in the sill. As the morning progressed, sleet blurred the panes and spattered on the shingles. By two-thirty, the ground was ice and the clouds were nearly black. We reluctantly packed our bodies into layers of warm clothes and tried not to think about it.

"Why on earth do you want to go to the Jingle Ball when you could stay here and bathe in soup?" Barb asked when I borrowed her snow boots.

"I've got friends working this gig I haven't seen in ages," Summer covered for me. "And Henry's working on having more fun."

"At an event for children?" Barb asked.

"We're meeting him at his level," Summer said.

Outside, it was bone-chillingly cold. We ducked beneath our hoods and ran to Henry's Jeep, where he cranked up the seat warmers and drove to pick up Lizzie at twenty-five miles per hour with his hands locked in the ten-and-two position. When we finally parked outside of her building, she dashed out, her Santa hat the only bright spot in otherwise gray misery.

I kicked open the back door and she jumped in.

"Remind me why we're doing this?" she asked, shutting out the wind.

"We're gathering intelligence. Henry, Summer, this is Lizzie. Lizzie is my best friend. These are my new friends."

Henry waved to Lizzie in the rearview. "Great to meet you."

Summer twisted around, bleached curls exploding from beneath her knit hat. "Hey there."

There was no mistaking what happened next. A current passed between them, so unsubtle that Henry and I exchanged a smile before he rejoined traffic.

Not three seconds passed before I had a text from Lizzie, just the staring eyes emoji.

He's married, I wrote back.

And her?

Single I think

Lizzie hearted the message and stashed her phone. "I was sure you guys would bail. This weather is disaster-movie-esque."

"You know my teenage self would have gone streaking through the Arctic Circle to meet Dash Whitney," I said.

"He would love that," Summer said, her bare feet on the heat vents.

"Never meet your heroes," Lizzie warned.

"Don't be surprised if he hits on you even after he finds out he also dated your mom," Summer added.

"In this getup?" I gestured at the lumpy knit sweater I'd layered over Summer's band T-shirt before zipping on Henry's hoodie. To complete the ensemble, Barb lent me the hot pink hat she'd knitted for the Women's March and a pair of her husband's shearling winter gloves.

Without looking, Henry said, "You look great."

A nanosecond later, my phone buzzed. Lightning Fingers had sent another text.

Married Henry has a crush

He does not, I typed back.

He's chauffeuring you to Santa's birthday party on the coldest day of the year.

I snorted. When Henry looked at me in the mirror, I forced a cough. "Something in my throat," I lied.

Summer wasn't fooled. "They're texting about us," she commented, tuning the radio away from the holiday station.

I could feel my scalp sweating, but Lizzie only shrugged. "Just the basics. A/S/L."

Summer twisted around, one corner of her red lips turned up. "Thirty-four. Woman, hear me roar. And currently, my mother's house."

Henry and I locked eyes again, grinning.

We found parking close to the event, since we were the only people in Chicago crazy enough to come. Our umbrellas threatening to flip inside out, we picked our way through icy patches, Lizzie holding my arm, me holding Henry's, Summer holding Lizzie's, until we reached the VIP entrance. Summer briefly chatted with the guy manning the gate. He handed us each a backstage pass and let us into a covered area built of scaffolding and black curtains, with portable heaters every few feet. It was at least tolerable. "There's a bar set up for the talent over there," he said. "Don't get too wasted. This is a family thing. They'll kick you out."

"Clearly he's never experienced children at the holidays," Summer said as we walked to the bar. "The parents will be the drunkest ones here."

Henry rubbed his hands together. "Can I make anyone a cocktail?"

"A doctor and a mixologist?" I teased. "You should put that on your Tinder profile."

"Should I add a picture of me in this?" He unzipped his coat to reveal a bright red sweater featuring Macaulay Culkin slapping his cheeks and the words *Merry Christmas Ya Filthy Animal.*

I laughed. "I'd swipe right."

When he turned away, Lizzie leaned into my ear. "Tinder? Swiping right? You said he was married. Is he a swinger or something?"

"They're getting a divorce," I admitted. "But married is married."

"Okay, so? The destination is single. Hop in the car."

"Dan and I broke up three days ago. My wound hasn't healed."

Lizzie pinned me with a look. "Your wound was a paper cut. At least have sex with him. He looks like he'd be good at it."

From a few feet behind him, I watched Henry's hands move across the bar, measuring, stirring, pouring. Deft, like a doctor's.

I bit my lip, grinding away a stir of desire. "I can't," I said. "We're friends."

"Why does that matter? I have sex with a lot of my friends."

"Because the window for casual sex without it getting complicated is small. If you don't nail it, you're screwed."

Lizzie hid her laugh as Henry turned around with our drinks.

"Where to first?" he asked.

"Food!" I blurted before Lizzie could suggest the Bone Zone and I'd have no choice but to die. From the glint in her eye, I knew I'd saved my own life.

Summer hung backstage with her friends while the three of us wandered around, playing a few games, stopping to watch a high school choir perform Christmas carols, eating roasted hazelnuts and soft molasses ginger cookies. At a petting zoo, we fed carrots to a real reindeer. The sleety wind was relentless, forcing us to run from tent to tent. An hour in, we were soaked and frozen. I bought a dozen hand warmers from a table of Girl Scouts and Lizzie and I stuffed them in our bras, while Henry put his in his back pockets. "A portable seat warmer," he said with a smile. Remembering the way he'd asked if I wanted my butt hot, I suddenly no longer needed mine.

More families arrived, almost everyone decked out in light-up Christmas gear. At the smaller stages, up-and-coming artists sang morose acoustic versions of the classics, making Frosty the Snowman sound like he'd just been dumped at the altar. One TikTok-famous singer stunned us with his rendition of "Blue Christmas," and when a mariachi band played "Feliz Navidad," Henry grabbed my hand and pulled me into a circle of dancers. As the flow of foot traffic skirted around us, I let my head fall briefly on his shoulder and closed my eyes. In those blissful seconds, we were an island, this was a regular date, my mom was alive, and Dash Whitney didn't even exist.

Then a toddler riding a giant candy cane took my knees out and I fell into Henry's chest.

"Whoa," he said, catching my shoulders. "You okay?"

I straightened, not wanting to be that girl in a rom-com who stumbles into a man and forgets to get up. "Bad dancer."

He smiled. "Beg to differ."

When Henry captured my hand and held my waist to keep dancing, I considered finding that toddler to pay him five dollars.

Later we found a bar in a tent, where Henry and Lizzie discovered they shared a passion for eggnog, the two of them making increasingly ridiculous toasts with every sip. Lizzie toasted "to all varieties of soft cheese except blue, which can go to hell" and Henry toasted "MySpace Tom for making sideburns cool," at which point he said, "I should switch to hot chocolate so I can drive us home."

"I'll drive," I told them. "Knock yourselves out."

Watching them make each other laugh, my best friend and my new friend, warmed me in a way no layers of sweaters or portable seat warmers could. The snow looked pretty as it fell around the tent. Coming here was worth it, if only for a break from . . . everything else.

Twenty minutes before Dash Whitney was scheduled to headline, we headed to the main stage. Following the directions Summer had given us, we found someone named Craig at the backstage entrance. He wore all black and had at least six lanyards around his neck, with two phones in one hand and a walkie-talkie in the other. Just standing next to him made me feel like I was late for something.

"If you walk fast, you might catch a glimpse of him leaving the greenroom," Craig said, checking his Apple watch. "Just don't be assholes about it. No selfies. No autographs." He held the door to let us pass and we scurried in like teenagers sneaking into an R-rated movie.

My first experience in a greenroom was at a local news station when our band played "Santa Claus Is Coming to Town" for a holiday segment while fake snow blew around the studio. I'd been disappointed to find it wasn't actually green, with lots of snacks and beautiful people lounging around. Instead, it was a windowless room by the copy machine with a few bottles of water and an outlet. At least Dash Whitney's was slightly more glamorous: a trailer with his name on the door.

I raised my fist.

But it got stuck, an inch away from knocking.

Dash Whitney was not just the first age-inappropriate man I'd ever had a crush on, whose songs I'd sung in the shower for fifteen years, whom I watched every week on *American Icon,* wondering what he'd say if I ever got up the guts to audition. He was the man who'd taken an album's worth of photographs of my mom onstage, radiant under a spotlight, happier than I'd ever seen her. The pictures were captured through the eye of someone in love.

My heart started pounding. Before I realized what I was doing,

I found Henry's hand and squeezed. A second passed, and he squeezed back.

Staring at the door, I admitted, "I'm not sure if I'm more afraid he will remember her or that he won't."

But I didn't have time to debate it because a woman in a white pantsuit and big gold jewelry answered the door. That this woman drove a Tesla and lasered off her freckles was written all over her finely blended microhighlights. "Can I help you?"

"We're here to meet Dash Whitney?" I sounded like I was in the sixth grade, calling him on his parents' landline.

"We have a personal connection," Henry added, because he hadn't had his brain replaced with sparkly gel pens. "He used to know our mothers."

The woman blocked the door with one tan hand. "That's very sweet, but Dash Whitney is a busy man who has known a lot of people." Her tone was cloying, like *we* were toddlers with candy canes.

"Right," Henry agreed, "but my mother is Barbara Stern."

If the woman didn't know who that was, she was bad at her job. If she did, she had a very good poker face. "You can wait at the exit of stage left if you'd like his autograph after the show. Please—" She wiggled her fingers at a snack table. "Help yourselves to some cookies."

I was gearing up to make my case when there was movement in the door and Dash Whitney filled up the frame, so broad-shouldered he had to turn sideways to fit through it. Even if I didn't recognize his long sideburns and square jaw, I'd have known I was in the presence of a celebrity. You could smell it on him—money, talent, fandom. It was in the way his leather jacket fit his shoulders, impeccable to the stitch but somehow relaxed. It was in his smile, so easily given. When you were Dash Whitney, you had plenty to smile about.

He was as handsome as I'd imagined, but something about those glittering green eyes made the back of my neck prickle.

"Hiya, kids," he said. "What can I do for you?" His warm, casual greeting was just how he presented on TV—like the only good guy in an industry full of jerks.

I noticed Henry did not offer his hand. "We wanted to introduce ourselves. I'm Henry. My mom is Barbara Stern."

"Well, I'll be. How is Barbie?" Dash's pleasant face was unaffected. "Haven't seen her since the day she stormed out of my studio. She always did have a flair for the dramatic."

"I'd say you deserved however she left, don't you think?"

Dash tipped his head back and let out one amused, unbothered laugh. "Is that what she told you?" He pointed one finger with a gold football ring on it between me and Lizzie. "Do either of you ladies want an autograph?"

I elbowed Lizzie. We needed to stall.

"Uh—" She produced a cocktail napkin. "Here."

Dash held out his hand like he expected someone to stick a pen in it, and perhaps unsurprisingly, someone did.

As Dash signed, Henry continued. "Before 'Carry My Heart,' my mom and her mom"—he nodded at me—"were in a band that you managed, the Secretaries."

On the napkin, Dash's pen paused. "I usually don't forget pretty faces, but that doesn't ring a bell. The Secretaries? No, son. Sorry. Anyone else?" He glanced around, pen waiting. "You don't have to sell my signature on the internet or anything. You can just keep it. That's how these things used to work."

I handed him my backstage pass. "Thank you. I'm a huge fan."

He smirked at that.

While he scrawled, I searched his face for some sort of sign. But what was I looking for? How could he give me an answer if I didn't even know the question? I was the one who wanted to talk to him in the first place. But now that I was standing in front of him, I couldn't express what I needed. *Help me understand,* I wanted to say. *Help me understand so I can forgive us both.* I swallowed, fighting tears. I couldn't let him see how desperate I was. Henry must have noticed because I felt the pressure of his hand again, holding me steady.

I breathed.

When Dash Whitney handed back my pass, his expression said *you're welcome.* "Don't spend it all in one place."

I looked down to see what he'd written. *Sweetheart—thanks for being a fan. D.W.*

I wanted to rip it in half. I would have if it weren't made of plastic. He was going to placate me with the same blasé bullshit tagline he'd signed a million times? He meant something to my mom, and she meant something to me.

"My mother is Connie Blanchfield," I said.

His jovial expression flinched so quickly I'd have missed it if I weren't so focused on reading him. "What about her, little miss?"

"You used to date her. Or at least sleep with her."

Though his celebrity grin remained plastered on, it wasn't as effortless. His eyes roved my face, forehead to chin. Then he looked me in the eye for the first time. His teeth clenched, his jaw flexed. The final curtain dropped on his crowd-pleasing demeanor. "Excuse me, kids." He stepped out of the trailer, pushing us aside. "I've got a show to play. Nice to meet y'all."

The white-suited woman appeared at my elbow and pulled me out of the way. A makeup artist dabbed Dash's face with a sponge and a photographer snapped behind-the-scenes photos as he sauntered toward the stage, trailed by a team of assistants, one of whom seemed there just to hold his bottles of water. It all happened so quickly, and then he was gone.

Lizzie gaped in the direction of Dash's retreating army. "What the fuck was that?"

"He recognized you," Henry said. "He definitely recognized you."

They were right. Something about my face bothered him. Scared him, even. I glanced at Lizzie, who said aloud what I was too afraid to think.

"Wait. Is Dash Whitney your father?"

The ground shifted. If not for Henry holding my hand, I might have collapsed.

"Let's get out of here," he said, and I focused on the warm strength of his fingers all the way back to the car.

Chapter 15

December 23

The last summer I spent with my dad in Florida, Susan and her two daughters had already moved in. She had redecorated. The fuzzy black and white pillows I loved because they glowed radioactive green under my black-light lava lamp were gone. I slept in a room with a white wicker daybed and white lace bedding. The previous summer, my dad had bought me two blue parakeets, but they were gone, too, replaced with a cat that sat on the windowsill hissing at neighbors walking by. Everything my dad and I had loved, Susan had gotten rid of.

She wouldn't let the two of us be alone either. If my dad suggested we go to our favorite hot dog place, she'd be sitting in the car when it was time to go, then say she wasn't hungry when we ordered. Our annual tradition was to go deep-sea fishing. Susan insisted on coming and got seasick in the first fifteen minutes, sending us back to the marina. Our deep-sea fishing trips had been perfectly preserved ecosystems, and she'd disrupted them.

Even at ten, I understood Susan wanted my dad all to herself. She wanted to pretend her daughters were his daughters, that they were the perfect family, and my mom and I were a threat to the charade. Susan would take her daughters out for dinner, then invite my dad to "stop by" after work, so the four of them would end up eating without me. If my mom called, Susan would tell her to call back later because I was busy with "my sisters." When it was Susan's birthday in July, she told me to draw her a card with our "family" on it, smiling and holding hands, then emailed a photo of the card to my mom. I waited and waited and waited for my dad to give me a sign that I was still his number one girl, but at the end of the summer, with my suitcase by the trunk of his car, he knelt down, grasped my shoulders, and told me to go tell Susan I loved her. I knew then who he'd chosen to be his number one girl.

Maybe if I'd been older or at least tougher, I'd have said no. But I thought it was his job to say no for me, to be on my side, to have my back. As my dad, wasn't that one of his main gigs?

I missed my mom as I hugged Susan stiffly and told her I loved her, trying not to cry. Maybe the man I'd worshipped and missed and loved and wished would come home wasn't my dad, I thought. Maybe he was my father, but not my dad.

My coffee was cold when I took a sip. I'd been sitting at Barb's kitchen table for who knew how long, remembering. My body was somehow both drained and heavy. I'd barely slept, eventually giving up and getting out of bed before the sun came up.

But I was yanked back to the present when Henry walked into the kitchen wearing scrubs. I glanced down at myself.

My flannel pants were tucked into my socks.

"Morning," he said, his hair damp from the shower. "You're up early."

"Couldn't sleep."

He paused with one hand reaching for a mug and looked at me. "I can only imagine. Are you okay?"

I blinked, nodded. "I'm fine."

That line appeared between his brows, the one that said he saw right through me. "I'm beginning to think you say that even when it's not true."

I was pinned beneath his gaze for a second. "I've been better," I admitted.

He lifted the coffeepot. "Can I solve any of your problems with caffeine?"

"Just one of them." I held out my mug for a refill. "Wow. You have arms."

He laughed. "Indeed. Two of them."

"They're very doctor-y."

He contemplated his forearm. "Is that a good thing?"

"Whenever you see doctors on TV, their arms are always super capable looking. Like, strong, clean, tan, not too hairy. I swear they audition TV doctors just by the attractiveness of their arms. I have remembered this *Grey's Anatomy* scene for fifteen years where McDreamy crossed his arms and smiled. That was it. That was the whole scene. And the patient was healed."

Henry opened the fridge and leaned in, but not before I noticed him blushing. "I promise you I'm not that good of a doctor."

His hand on the door caught my attention. "Hey. You've lost a piece of jewelry."

"Yeah. It was time."

Maybe my hand in his had left an impression. It had for me. I could almost still feel it.

He pulled out the cream cheese, a tomato, and a jar of capers. "Can I interest you in a bagel?"

"I will never say no to a bagel," I said. "So what happened there? If you don't mind my asking."

He sliced an everything bagel like he did everything else: with his full attention. Only the line between his brows said he'd heard me. When he finished, he crossed his arms and smiled.

For a split second, I was healed.

"I don't mind. We always planned to have kids, but when it came time to try, it wasn't working. Liesel was facing possibly years of treatments and interventions, and she didn't want to do it. I want kids, but I wasn't going to pressure her into medical procedures she didn't want to have."

My skin broke out in a hot tingle. "I'm so sorry. I shouldn't have asked."

"Don't be." He turned back to the counter, depositing our bagels in the toaster. "That's the technical reason, but I think the baby was more of an out. She's decided to move to Texas to open a women's clinic, and that's what she always wanted to do. But none of this would have ended our marriage if we'd had the kind of love that wasn't a question."

From behind, I watched his shoulders move as he sliced our tomatoes. "Does that exist?" I asked.

He shrugged. "I think so. I hope so. My parents had that. Did my mom tell you they never spent a single night apart their entire marriage?"

"How is that possible?"

He still faced away, slicing with precision. "Even when he was in the hospital, she slept in bed with him. I hated it because I thought she was going to tear his IVs out. But she said that at the end of her life, she wanted to look back and know for sure that she'd never wasted precious time."

Suddenly his hands gripped the edge of the counter. Was he picturing Barb and the man I'd seen in photos in a hospital bed together as he lay dying? Grief surprised me in the strangest moments, too. Last night, I'd been washing my face when I got makeup on a towel, and it transported me into my mom's bathroom, where she'd taught me how to rub off lipstick with lotion and a tissue. *She's gone,* I'd thought. *I'll never talk to her again. How is that possible?*

I wanted to go to Henry, wrap my arms around him from behind, rest my cheek on his back, and say, *I know. It sucks. I'm sorry.*

He picked up his knife again. "You don't think love like that exists?"

"I don't know," I admitted. "I want to believe it. But I've never seen it."

Instead of saying anything, Henry turned to look straight at me.

My stomach zoomed up, like a buoy underwater.

When the bagels sprang out of the toaster, he smeared them with cream cheese. "When my wife and I were residents, medicine was all we talked about. Then having a baby became all we talked about. When that ended, we had nothing left to talk about. Our house was extremely quiet. We even watched TV muted with subtitles on because we didn't want to disturb each other."

I couldn't help but laugh. "You're not serious."

"It was like a mausoleum housing our dead romance." He carefully arranged the tomatoes and capers and finished them off with fresh pepper. "What about you? Was there more to the story than a national tour?"

He carried our plates to the table and sat across from me. Both of us folded our bagels back together to eat like a sandwich.

"I didn't think so at the time," I said, "but in retrospect, yeah. Dan and I had very different opinions about things. He thought our band was stupid. He thought a lot of the things I liked were stupid. But our relationship was so easy. We spent every weekend together doing weddings, and we knew all the same people, so it was too convenient to walk away from until he was leaving town and I would have had to put in real effort to keep it going. Isn't that terrible?" I took a bite—warm cream cheese, salty bagel, sweet, crunchy tomato. "Wow. I see there are two chefs in the family."

"My skills begin and end with bagels," he clarified. "I know what you mean about proximity. It would never have been possible for Liesel and me to date if we weren't at the same hospital. We were working hundred-hour weeks, but at least we could have lunch in the cafeteria."

"Easy and worth it aren't the same thing," I said, thinking of Ronald.

Henry's eyes locked on mine. "Which one are you looking for?"

My self-conscious desire to look away was overwhelming, but I forced myself to stay as I answered, "I want worth it."

He nodded. "Me too."

"I've pushed away a lot of people because they let me down. When things got hard, I gave up, and I don't think that was the right answer."

There was that line between his eyebrows again. "I think there has to be a balance between protecting yourself and accepting people for who they are."

His words settled on me like a blanket. I tried to take comfort in them, but the voice of my guilt was louder than the voice of reason. "I hope you're right," I said. That would mean I was not a bad daughter—a bad person—for setting boundaries.

We finished eating, but neither of us made a move to get up from the table. The sky had lightened a few shades, but the house was still sleeping.

On the bench, I hugged my knees. "Did you have fun yesterday?"

His face broke into a smile. "Don't tell Summer, but I haven't had that much fun since I ate a weed brownie at a Green Day concert in 2009. Is that sad?"

I laughed. "Very."

"Did you have fun?"

"I don't know. I can still feel the burn of Dash Whitney's evil eye. Is finding out my entire life might have been a lie fun?"

He hesitated, frowning at his coffee. "I'm not sure how to ask this."

"Just ask it," I said, waving a hand. "We're way past formalities."

"Is there another dad in your life? Or no dad?"

Henry had a way of drawing the truth from me. I heard myself answering before I had time to reconsider.

"He hasn't been much of a dad, but yes. I know him. His name is Philip, and he lives in Florida with his wife. He and my mom were married but they divorced when I was very little."

"You don't have a relationship with him?"

"When I was a kid, it was great. I spent every summer with him—" I cut myself off. "I'm sorry. You don't want my life story."

"I do, actually." He waited for me to go on, cupping his mug in one hand but not drinking it. He gave me his full attention.

The way he looked at me was too kind, too curious, too *sexy*. I needed a distraction before all that nervous energy racing through my veins made me do something crazy, like kiss him before I'd brushed my teeth. I jumped out of my chair and busied myself in the fridge.

"You were warned," I said, as cheerfully as I could. "I spent every summer with him. After he got remarried, I felt like if he had to choose between me and his new life, he'd choose the latter, so I never asked him to make that choice." I settled on orange juice and poured myself a glass. "I just backed off."

"I'm sorry," Henry said. "You shouldn't have been in that position."

I shrugged, as if I didn't care. "Maybe my dad knew something I didn't."

When I sat down, Henry reached forward and touched my fingers. I wasn't expecting it. My guard was down. I looked up and met his eyes and tears filled mine, just as they had when my dad picked me up at the airport all those years ago. I was safe. I didn't have to pretend anymore.

"That must have hurt," he said.

I nodded, brushing my cheek. "It did."

After a while, we got up to wash and dry the dishes together, like that had become our ritual.

"Dash Whitney aside," he said, "how are you feeling about your mom being in a band?"

I took a deep breath, considering. Given everything that happened over the last few days, I'd barely had time to process. "We had a lot more in common than I thought. I wish I'd known. Maybe we could have recorded a song together, like Naomi and Wynonna Judd." I laughed, picturing us with big red hair and my purple karaoke machine.

"Have you ever considered writing your own songs?"

"Why, because I'd have a lot of material?" I teased.

He lifted a dripping plate from my hands. "No. But I think you'd be great at it. You're very insightful and self-assured."

I laughed loudly, one big *ha!* that might have woken up the house. "What on earth has given you that impression?"

"Your videos, for starters. I watched them all. You're a force up there onstage."

I'd been cold earlier, but now the kitchen was too warm as my body bloomed with heat. As I turned back to the sink, my shoulder brushed his arm, and instead of pulling it away, I leaned closer. "Thank you, but no. Hell no. Singing my own songs would be like publicly singing my deepest, darkest secrets while naked under a spotlight."

"Is the audience also naked? Because I've heard that's supposed to help."

"I think what you're describing is open mic night at a nudist colony."

"I can't decide if that's an experience not to be missed or one to be avoided at all costs."

I handed him the last mug. "That depends on your level of comfort with sax and treble."

He smiled, drying his hands, then checked his watch. "I should go or I'll be late."

"Right. You're off to save lives. I also have a very busy day ahead of playing video games with Dylan, so I should get going, too."

He lifted his coat from the back of his chair and shrugged it on. "Same time tomorrow?"

I nodded. Considering I'd already revealed to him some of my deepest, darkest secrets while, if not naked, then braless, I may as well have written him a song. If he wasn't running, then neither was I. "Same time tomorrow."

Chapter 16

December 23

After Henry left for work, I drank my coffee, listening to the tick of the clock above the bay window until I heard footsteps and murmurs upstairs, the sounds of a family waking up.

Since Summer and Dylan had arrived, the yellow house itself seemed happier. Before, it was a house waiting for its family, the way a loyal dog waits by the door. But now, when Dylan ran down the stairs shouting, "Can we have pancakes?" and Summer trudged in grumbling about coffee and Barb preheated the oven, the house settled back with a sigh, satisfied.

We spent the morning around the island while Barb cooked and the rest of us pitched in as unqualified sous chefs. We sang along to Mariah Carey's *Merry Christmas* and James Brown's *Funky Christmas*. First, she made banana-walnut pancakes—her husband's favorite—then flipped through *The Joy of Cooking* and landed on raspberry thumbprint cookies. "Your mother loved these," she said to me, whipping around the kitchen collecting ingredients and throwing them on the counter. The flour bag tipped and spilled. The jar of jam slid off the edge and Summer caught it right before it hit the ground. Barb didn't care if her house got messy. She'd just clean it up again. The house was a place for people to gather and live, not a place to look pretty. Hers overflowed with food and pictures and knickknacks and memories. Cookies filled up Tupperwares and casseroles crowded the freezer. When I opened the fridge for butter, a glazed ham fell out. Abundance made this house a home.

"What's all this food for?" I asked, holding up a container of dumplings. "Are you hosting a party we haven't been invited to?"

Barb was kneading dough. She gestured around the kitchen with one floury hand. "I cook for the people I love, sweetheart. Some of them just aren't here anymore."

I shouldered up to her at the island and read the recipe, the page smeared and stained. "I didn't know these were her favorite. My mom hated baking."

She folded sugar into the mixture. "I didn't say she baked them. I said she ate them."

"Do you mind if I do it?"

She slid me the bowl. "Of course not."

But when I stuck my hands in, I wasn't sure what to do next. Squeeze it? Barb looked like she was squeezing it.

"How was the concert?" she asked.

I glanced at Summer, who drew her finger across her throat.

"We met Dash Whitney!" I blurted. *Sorry,* I mouthed.

Barb's hands fell limp as she looked between us. "On purpose?"

I nodded. "I'm sorry we didn't tell you. It was my idea. I wanted to talk to him."

"And did you tell him to take a long walk off a short pier?"

I glanced at Summer for help, but she only shrugged. *Told you so.*

"He seemed to recognize me," I admitted, "and when I mentioned my mom's name, he couldn't get away from us fast enough. Does that mean anything to you?"

Barb turned her back to me. Without saying a word, she opened the fridge, withdrew a package of chicken breasts, laid it on the counter, and started whacking it with a wooden mallet.

Summer flinched. "Jesus, Mom. Are you having a rage blackout?"

Whack, whack, whack. "I'm not surprised he ran away like a coward," Barb spat. *Whack, whack, whack.*

Summer whispered in Dylan's ear and he took off running. A second later the TV turned on.

"This sounds crazy," I said to Barb. "But is it possible he's my father?"

She dropped her mallet, out of breath, and lifted her eyes to mine. "It's not crazy. I'm sorry, sweetheart. I've been wondering ever since you told me you were a singer."

Gooey dough squished through my fingers. "Oh god," I said. "So you think my mom and Dash Whitney kept . . . even after?"

Barb lifted her bony shoulders. "How could I know? But I do know Ernest had power over us. It's not hard to believe Connie might have taken him back. If it were me, I probably would have."

I almost dropped my bowl. Barb reached out and caught it just in time. "Sit down," she said, guiding me to the table. My legs were numb and shaky. When she brought me a towel, I let her wipe my hands like I was a little girl.

I shook my head at the floor, blinking away tears as I said, "I can't believe she hid this from me."

"You don't know that she was hiding this."

"Did I even know her?" My voice cracked, throat aching.

"Here's the thing, sweetheart." Barb knelt and took my hands. "Motherhood changes who you are. The Connie you knew wasn't the Connie I knew. Unless you've got a time machine, you'll never know my Connie, just like my children will never know me at twenty-two or understand the decisions I made."

"I'd have liked to know you, Mom," Summer said from the island. "I bet you were cool."

"Define cool. I've always had great hair and a great ass, but I didn't love myself. I think truly cool people love themselves enough that they don't put up with bullshit. Like you."

Summer crossed the kitchen and dropped to her knees to embrace her mother, who still knelt at my feet. They hugged tightly, not letting go. I lifted my knees to hug myself, having no one else. No matter how much I wished I could fit in, I was still an outsider in this house, among this family. They were blood. Watching them hold each other was like looking at a painting. How beautiful, how evocative. A mother seeing her child. Her child feeling so seen.

When they let go, I bumped my socked toe against Barb's shoulder. "You don't put up with bullshit, Barb. Even I know that."

"Not anymore I don't."

She sent her affection my way next, grabbing my face with her warm floury fingers and kissing both my cheeks.

Just like my mom used to do, but not quite the same.

After lunch, I snuck into the living room and plugged in the Christmas tree before curling up on the couch. It was gray enough outside that the tree glowed, even in the daylight.

Barb and Summer were in the kitchen singing show tunes theatrically and cracking themselves up. When they started on "Matchmaker," I pictured them with kitchen towels tied under their chins like scarves. I wanted to join, but I needed a few minutes alone.

Barb thought Dash Whitney could be my father.

Did I want her to be right?

The allure wasn't that he was famous. The allure was that if I had this shiny new parent, I didn't have to deal with the one I already had.

I opened my phone and searched *Dad* in my texts, scrolling through our history. The last time I'd heard from him was a month ago, on my birthday. He called but I hadn't picked up, so he sent a text. *Happy birthday! Hope to talk to you soon.* I hadn't responded. I hadn't responded to the one before that either. *I read this great book about American history as told through the music of the times. I think you'd like it.* I had no idea what book that was. I'd never asked.

I still hadn't even told him my mom died.

I was so stiff and impenetrable in my conversations with him. It was like reading the back of someone's hand. If I wasn't going to give him the chance to be my dad, could I at least give him the chance to tell me the truth?

I scrolled to his number and pressed send.

This time, he answered on the first ring, his voice high with surprise. "Mel? Is that you?"

"Merry Christmas, Dad."

"Merry Christmas, honey. It's been a long time."

I curled deeper into the couch, resting my head on the arm, hugging a blanket. "Yeah, I know. I do want to catch up, but I'm also calling to tell you my mom died." The way I referred to her as "my mom" instead of "Mom" was a phenomenon I'd noticed in all my friends with divorced parents. There was a possessiveness implied. She belonged only to me, no longer to him.

Still, he sounded heartbroken when he said, "Oh my god. That's awful news."

I'd told myself I wouldn't cry, but hearing his voice was like seeing him at the gate, launching myself into his arms. Tears slid down my cheeks, salty on my tongue.

"It happened last week," I said, wiping them away with my sweatshirt. "I called you, but you didn't pick up."

"You did? Did you leave a message? Susan and I just got back from a cruise. We didn't have any service out on the ocean. I had no idea. I would have called you back."

"No, I didn't." The living room was cold without Barb's usual fire. I shivered.

It occurred to me that I didn't leave that message because I was afraid he wouldn't call me back, and then how would I feel? But he didn't call me back because I hadn't left that message. It had been a while since I'd taken Psychology 101, but I still knew that destructive little trick was called a self-fulfilling prophecy.

"Leave a message next time," he said. "I'm old-fashioned. Are you with Dan for the holiday?"

I cringed at the reminder of how little he knew about my life lately. "We broke up, actually."

"Jeez, honey." I remembered how my dad tugged the hair on the back of his head when he got bad news, though based on the last photo he'd sent me from deep-sea fishing, he had a lot less of it these days. "Why don't you come here? You can't be alone after all this."

"Find me a find!" Barb and Summer sang in the kitchen. "Catch me a catch!"

"I'm not alone," I said. "I'm with this woman who used to be my mom's friend. Barbara Stern."

He was quiet for a few seconds. The singing in the kitchen grew louder, more dramatic. "Barbara Stern. That name rings a bell."

"Probably because she's famous. She sang that song with Dash Whitney. 'Carry My Heart.' "

"Hm. Can't say I know it."

That made me laugh. "You must have been on that cruise for a really long time."

"Five weeks."

"Five *weeks*? Did you cruise to the moon?"

He chuckled. "The Galápagos. The girls are into bird-watching."

I shifted onto my back to stare at the ceiling. "Susan's daughters went with you on a five-week cruise? Do they not have—" *A life?* "Jobs?"

He dropped his voice. "Don't tell Susan I said this, but they're not as self-sufficient as you."

I closed my eyes, unsure that was a compliment. Maybe they weren't as self-sufficient because they didn't need to be. They didn't get left out of family dinners. They were always invited to the table. "Dad, I need to ask you something. Did my mom tell you about her band?"

"Of course. Your mother had just moved back to New York to finish school when I met her on the crosstown bus."

"What'd she say about it?"

He whistled. All his noises and mannerisms were coming back to me now. "That was thirty-five years ago. But I remember she said she'd learned her lesson. I said, 'Connie, you gave it a go. You're braver than most. I could have never gotten onstage like that.' But she'd decided becoming a secretary was the better choice, and I didn't disagree with her. I was studying accounting. We both wanted an uncomplicated life." He paused and lowered his voice again. "That was where I went wrong, by the way. With your mom, with all of it. When things got complicated, it was easier for me to pretend they weren't."

So we had that in common. Who was I kidding in thinking I was not related to this man? We had the same earlobes.

"Did she ever see either of her bandmates again? Barb or Ernest, their manager?"

"Not that I'm aware of. We lived in New York. We didn't have the money to go anywhere. But—now hold on—I've got something." I heard movement through the line, a door, a rustling, a slam. "She gave me a book once as a gift. It's full of songs she'd written. I'll mail it to you."

I sat up. "Really? I'd love that." I gave him Barb's address.

After that, the conversation dwindled. I chewed my bottom lip, waiting for him to say something, but it seemed as though he was waiting for me to say something. There was so much ground to cover, I didn't know where to begin.

He whistled again. "You know, the name Barbara Stern is stuck in my head. Who did you say she was?"

"They met in secretarial school and started the band together."

"Huh. I'll have to think on that."

"Call me if you remember anything else. I'm trying to figure out—" *My life.* But I didn't say that. Why couldn't I say what I wanted to say to him? It was like the words got stuck behind a wall of panic. "What happened with my mom and her manager."

"I will," he promised. "If it's okay with you, I'll call for other reasons, too."

I lay down again, remembering the way I'd lean against him while he read to me before bed, and closed my eyes. What if, for once, I said exactly what needed to be said? The antiprophecy. Or maybe it was still a self-fulfilling prophecy, but in a good way, where you ask for what you need and get it.

I braced myself. "Dad, I'd really like it if you played a bigger role in my life. I'm willing to make more of an effort if you are."

He made a strange wheezing sound. At first I thought he was choking; then I realized he was crying. He cleared his throat, tried to speak, then cleared his throat again. "I would like that very much."

Tears blurred my view of the ceiling. I blinked them down my temples, into my hair.

"I'm sorry about your mother," he added. "I loved her."

"Someday I'd like to know what happened there. The real story. None of this 'we weren't meant to be' crap."

He chuckled and blew his nose. "Fair enough."

In the background, I heard a woman's voice that sounded like

Susan's high-pitched, *who, me?* aloofness. "I don't mean to keep you from your Christmas plans," I said.

"You are never keeping me from anything."

So I curled onto my side, balancing my phone on my ear. "Then maybe we can stay on the phone for a little while longer."

Chapter 17

DECEMBER 23

I ended up talking to my dad for two hours. We covered that book he'd recommended, which led to a conversation about the newspaper, which led to a conversation about recycling, which led to a conversation about rising sea levels in Florida, which led to the lengthiest conversation of all, about ceviche. When we finally hung up and I checked the time, I realized I was late.

Every year, the day before Christmas Eve, Ronald had a blowout party at his house, and our band always performed. It had become my favorite tradition. This year's theme was *A Christmas Story,* but in my fog over the last two weeks, I'd never planned my costume.

Summer's ever-rotating wardrobe of coolness sprung to mind. I went to the bottom of the stairs and called, "Summer! Could I come bother you for a minute?"

I hadn't been upstairs before. When she invited me up, I stopped on the landing, where four doors faced a short hallway.

One of them was Henry's.

His twin bed, *Cruel Intentions.*

I felt like I was fifteen and his parents weren't home.

I jumped when I heard, "Over here," and looked toward the voice to see Summer hanging out of her doorframe, looking killer in a cropped leopard-print sweater and gold hoops, with her blond curls barely restrained in a red bandana.

"I have nothing to wear to a costume party," I explained.

She stepped aside, holding her door open. "Enter my studio, if you dare."

I walked into the type of room I'd always imagined high school girls had until I became one and still had my Harry Potter shrine featured prominently. The walls were papered with album covers and concert tickets. Wooden beads hung over the closet instead of a door. Miniature paper lanterns zigzagged the ceiling, and incense must have been embedded in the carpet because I didn't see any burning, but I smelled that unmistakable haze.

The bed was a double, and Dylan's fire-truck pillowcase lay next to Summer's lavender silk one. I swallowed a stone, remembering my mom's soft snore on those nights she shared my bed.

"What's the theme?" Summer asked, winding herself cross-legged on her papasan chair. Another enviable vestige of 2005. Gabby had one and we'd lived in it, our hips smashed together as we cast love spells on our crushes from a book we'd pooled our money to buy from the New Age section at Borders.

"*A Christmas Story,*" I said. "So I guess I should be the leg lamp? Do you have any fishnets? Everyone goes all out for Ronald's parties. I can't throw on a Santa hat and call it a day. He has a closet full of backup costumes for people who show up wearing nothing and someone has definitely barfed eggnog on them."

Summer had already unfolded herself from the chair and started opening drawers. "You don't want to be the leg lamp. Everyone is going to be the leg lamp. You want to be Mother."

She gestured for me to sit on her bed while she gathered supplies—

a curling iron, hair spray, a long gold chain, a gray cardigan. What she didn't have, she borrowed from Barb's closet—after frowning for a while at my bottom half, she disappeared and returned a few minutes later with nylons and a wool skirt. Then she popped the lenses from a pair of sunglasses and dangled the frames from the gold chain before sliding clogs off her own feet and instructing me to put them on.

When I turned to the mirror, I laughed out loud. I looked perfect. Exactly like a woman who spent the entire day cooking red cabbage because her husband liked it, only to have him display a scandalous lamp in the front window.

"You're a genius," I told her.

"Your hair needs to be way frizzier. Sit." She sounded just like Barb.

I sat at her vanity and looked at her in the mirror. "Thanks for doing this."

She switched on the curling iron and separated a piece of my hair. "It's better than staring at my bank account, counting my pennies."

"I'm sorry. I'd say I've been there, but I don't also have a Dylan, so I can't pretend to imagine what you're going through."

Summer teased and sprayed. "In case you're wondering, I do agree with Henry. But I'm just as stubborn as my mom. If I were her, I'm sure I'd do the same thing, so I really have no leg to stand on. No pun intended. My brother's got a thing for you, you know."

"He does not."

"He stares at you like Dylan stares at the presents under the tree," she said, combing a curl into frizz.

I glanced at her in the mirror, debating whether to ask my next question. "What's Liesel like?"

"Nice. Smart. Intense." Summer arched one thick brow. "Why?"

The heat radiating from me could have given the curling iron a run for its money. "Just curious."

"If you're his type?" She suffocated us both with hair spray. "Liesel and Henry fit together."

My expression fell—I caught it in my reflection.

"They fit like two books sitting next to each other on the shelf because they've got the same color cover," she clarified. "You and Henry fit like two books exchanged as gifts. You know what I mean?"

"Weirdly, yes. My ex gave me a book about crypto once and I probably should have ended it right then and there."

"I have a sense about these things," she said, pinning the front of my hair to look like bangs.

Like books exchanged as gifts. It was sort of magical to think about, like believing in Santa.

"So what's up with Lizzie? Is she single?"

Summer wasn't looking at me in the mirror, which made me smile. Even the coolest person in Chicago had to play it cool sometimes.

"She asked me the same thing about you," I said. "And yes. And by the way, she gives great books."

"I'd like to see her again."

"Do you want to come to this party? You'll need a costume."

"If my mom can watch Dylan, I'm in." Summer was teasing the finishing touches into my hair. "I'll be Randy. My brother's got a closet full of ugly sweaters. And tell her it was my idea. I'm not interested in playing games."

After yelling downstairs to her mom, Summer shooed me out so she could get ready. On the landing, I texted Lizzie:

Summer's coming because she likes you!!

Lizzie responded with the head-exploding emoji. *Exact words please*

"Tell her it was my idea. I'm not interested in playing games."

She emphasized the message. *But I was going to wear my pink bunny costume*

What are you going to wear now?

Probably my pink bunny costume but with the boobs cut out

Lizzie swung by to pick us up—in her pink bunny onesie with floppy ears—and as soon as Summer dropped into the back seat, the chemistry in the car was palpable. I kept catching them making eye contact in the rearview mirror and felt compelled to say something before they started undressing, so I cleared my throat and twisted around to face Summer in the back seat. "Tell us what it was like to live on the road," I prompted.

"Incredible," she answered. "And horrible. Picture a traveling circus, but everyone has way too much money."

While we drove thirty minutes to Ronald's house in the suburbs, she told us about the time a pop star adopted a bunch of kittens and every PA had to take care of one. And the time a ten-time Grammy-winning artist refused to play a sold-out show at Madison Square Garden because the scented candles he liked were missing from his greenroom. She described the grind of sleeping on buses for months, trying to help an eight-year-old with online school while cleaning up the messes of adults who acted like eight-year-olds. What it was like to spend days on the road with no place to shower, eating fast food, setting up and taking down stages in an endless string of twenty-hour days.

"Honestly," she said, "nothing sounds better than a bed that doesn't rock all night. I want Dylan to have a home like I did. Somewhere he really feels safe."

I was still facing the back seat, riveted by her stories. "Wow. That sounds really hard."

I wondered how Dan would fare. The man was very specific about his pillows.

Lizzie signaled to exit the highway—we were almost there. "So, does that mean you're sticking around?"

"Yeah," Summer said, the corner of her red lips turned up again. "I'm sticking around."

I looked out my window to give them a moment and watched Chicago slide by. Sometimes love was so complicated. It left for a better opportunity, it refused to pay child support, it moved to Florida. It took advantage of your youth, it ended in divorce, it died. But other times, two people met.

And it really was that simple.

Chapter 18

December 23

A holiday jam fest in Ronald's garage was exactly what I needed. We performed in our costumes—me as Mother, Lizzie as the bunny, and Ronald wearing a plaid bathrobe over striped pajamas just like Old Man Parker. It was so hilarious that I couldn't look at either of them without laughing. I had to focus on the audience gathered in a half-circle around us, and even that wasn't much better given that seventy-five percent of the guests were dressed as leg lamps. Summer was right about that.

The best part about playing Ronald's party was that we didn't get paid. We did it for fun, which meant we could relax without the threat of a bad Yelp review. We ran through the same set we'd played at the Signature Room but took more risks. Ronald and Lizzie both added in solos. I danced, or at least tried to. When we hit the last note, I emerged sweaty, dehydrated, and beaming, with no memory of what had happened.

Had it been like that for my mom onstage?

Ronald shouted, "Good night, Chicago!" into his microphone like we were closing down the Metro instead of a dimly lit garage with a wooden box stamped FRAGILE doubling as a cooler for Bud Lights. But everyone gave us a standing ovation, so we gave them a few more songs.

By the time we finished—really finished—it was getting late and Ronald's friends had started filtering out. He was hugging them goodbye as Lizzie and I put away the equipment.

The garage was nearly empty when Summer sidled up to us and cleared her throat. I'd forgotten she was here. If I'd remembered, I'd have been nervous. My career existed in the bubble of the Chicago wedding industry, but Summer was a professional from the industry with a capital I.

"I've got some pointers if you want them," she said.

We all stopped what we were doing and turned to her like disciples.

"You do?" Ronald asked, a drumstick hanging limp from each hand.

"I do." Summer began to circle Ronald's latest car project, peering in the windows. "And this ain't my first rodeo."

I exchanged a glance with Lizzie and Ronald. We'd never had a professional tour manager give us pointers before. Bettering ourselves had historically consisted of Dan being critical, Ronald being optimistic, and me singing in the shower until the neighbors complained. Now we were rookies, trying out for the big leagues.

"We want them," Lizzie answered for the rest of us, even though, as a classically trained guitarist with perfect pitch, she was the only one who didn't need them.

"You sure?" Summer asked, leaning casually against the hood.

"We're sure," Ronald said.

Was I sure? I didn't feel sure. But Summer was already grabbing Lizzie's hand and pulling her three steps forward. "Stop hiding behind the drums. Your finger work is stellar and your face emotes like you're starring in a silent film. You belong here, upstage. Ronald, you gotta cool it with the power solos, buddy. Don't get me wrong. I wouldn't want to meet you and your sticks in a dark alley, but, like, 'Silent Night' should have a softer touch. The pitter-patter of a gentle rain, if you will. And, Mel, you're belting out the high notes like you've got something to prove. When you stretch them, you force Lizzie to slow the tempo waiting for you to wrap it up. Don't ruin the song for the sake of singing it. And you've got to find a new bassist. Maybe if Mel played an instrument, you could get away with three of you, but like this, you sound thin. Do you play anything?" she asked me.

"A little piano," I said. "I'm not very good."

"Then you should be on keyboard. That's a no-brainer. But you should still get a bassist. I might know someone. Let me ask around."

"You on keyboards is genius," Lizzie said to me. "How did we not think of that?"

The truth was, I had thought of it but had never brought it up because I knew Dan would shoot it down. He wouldn't have wanted me to have two roles in the band, thinking that would give me twice the attention. "I don't know," I lied. "But let's try it."

Summer tapped her nails on the cymbal of Ronald's drum set. "If you're interested in playing gigs other than weddings, starting to put yourselves out there, I could make some calls for you."

"Why?" I blurted. I hadn't meant to sound so blunt, but honestly . . . why would she want to do that?

"Because you guys rock," she said. "Seriously."

The sound in the garage seemed to extinguish like a muffled bass drum.

"You'd have to start writing your own songs, though," she added.

Ronald twirled his drumsticks, ever game for a new hobby. "Sign me up."

"I'm in," Lizzie agreed.

I was the only one who said nothing. Why was everyone trying to get me to write songs when I was perfectly happy singing covers for brides and grooms?

I *was* perfectly happy singing covers for brides and grooms, right?

I shot Lizzie a look, imploring her. Whether she couldn't read my mind or didn't want to, she said, "Just don't be mean if we suck."

"I won't be mean," Summer said. "I just won't help you. A cover band isn't getting anywhere."

I shook my head. "But I'm not a songwriter." *I'm not my mother.*

Summer shrugged. "Suit yourself." She tugged on Lizzie's bunny tail. "Should we get out of here?"

On the way home, Summer took the front. They were going to drop me off and head to another party. "Why don't you come?" they'd asked, but I already had a date planned—with Graham from *The Holiday,* specifically in the scene where he puts on glasses—and couldn't stand him up. Besides, I was tired. I doubted I'd make it much past the glasses. The past two weeks had been a blur, but the days had been long, and some of the moments seemed to last forever. Sometimes it caught up to me, and I needed to be horizontal.

I leaned my head against the window and closed my eyes until something tapped me on the knee. It was Summer's maroon-polished fingernail.

"I'll be honest," she said. "When you told me you were a wedding singer, I pictured Adam Sandler getting wasted and singing 'Love Stinks.'"

I laughed. "That movie is the main reason I can't take myself too seriously."

"But you've got a voice," she continued. "You remind me of Rachael Price. Your band has serious Lake Street Dive vibes."

I sat up straighter. "Really? That means a lot coming from you."

"It gave me an idea. About Dash Whitney. You know the show *American Icon*?"

I hesitated. Where was she going with this? "Of course. I've been watching that show since you had to call in your votes."

"You ever consider auditioning?"

Lizzie slapped the steering wheel. "I've been saying this for years! But she doesn't want to camp in the snow for three days."

"I don't want to camp in the snow for three days *only to get rejected*," I clarified. "A very cold, wet waste of time."

"But you wouldn't have to camp out," Summer said. "My friend is their field manager. He works all the auditions."

The tempo of my heart sped up. Yes, I'd thought about auditioning before. I'd even googled the dates and locations a few times. But there was a big difference between the distant possibility that even if I waited in that cold, wet line, I'd get an audition, and the very real possibility that Summer seemed to be offering me now. I tugged at the seat belt that was suddenly too tight across my chest. "Meaning what?"

"Meaning I could guarantee you an audition."

Was this for real? They were smiling.

"But I'm just a wedding singer," I said.

"You're better than all the middle school show choir captains who try out for that show," Summer insisted. "But also, who cares? Do you want to know if Dash Whitney had an affair with your mother nine months before you were born? Ask him. And if that doesn't work, rip out a fistful of his chest hair."

I laughed. "I don't think a DNA test needs to be specifically chest hair. Anyway, no need. My dad's name is Philip Hart, and he likes deep-sea fishing."

"Okay, but you could still audition," Summer said. "And if you wanted, you could still rip out a fistful of his chest hair just because he deserves it."

I laughed again. "I'll think about it."

Summer untwisted to face the windshield. While she chatted with Lizzie, I let my head fall against the seat and closed my eyes. Audition for *American Icon*? When my mom used to beg me to audition, it bothered me. What was so wrong with a mother wanting to see her daughter on TV? But it felt, to me, like she didn't see my career as good enough. Like she didn't see me.

Only now a feeling tugged at my stomach, like the pull of a taut guitar string. Maybe the problem wasn't that my mom didn't see me. Maybe the problem was that she saw me differently than I saw myself. Maybe she believed in me.

Chapter 19

Christmas Eve

The first thing I registered on Christmas Eve was "I'll Be Home for Christmas" floating down the stairs.

The next thing I registered was a text from Dan.

I sat up, blinking at it.

Made it to New York. My mom would like you to have your stuff out by New Year's. Her friend is moving in while I'm gone.

Then, an hour later when I hadn't responded, *Please confirm.*

Sunlight slanted across the basement—I'd slept in, apparently past a deadline.

I hadn't spoken to Dan since that day in Ronald's garage. Hadn't even thought about him.

This text felt like a snowball pummeling me in the face.

If Dan wanted me to get my things—which was his right, obviously, I wasn't disputing that—then I'd need another place to put said things. Having another place to live meant moving out of here, potentially into my mom's.

It meant facing my ghosts.

I tossed my phone on the mattress and yanked the blankets over my head, curling into a ball like a potato bug when it senses danger.

Maybe it was a wake-up call. I couldn't hide out here forever.

I grabbed my phone and typed *no problem,* listing the many problems in my head. If living at my mom's was out of the question—and it was, considering I couldn't go inside—then I'd need to rent a place of my own. With what money?

I brushed my teeth and lugged my problems upstairs. If I had to make nice with the Chicago real estate market, at least I could do it with coffee.

When I entered the kitchen, Barb was standing over the sizzling stove wearing oven mitts and a silk robe with long, luxurious sleeves. That seemed like a fire hazard, but this was a woman who didn't like to be told what to do.

"Merry Christmas Eve," I grumbled, shuffling to the coffeepot.

"Merry Christmas Eve, sweet—" She saw my face. "What's wrong?"

I folded in half, banging my forehead on the counter. "I need an apartment."

"Not today you don't!"

When I peeked at her through one eye, she was flipping pancakes.

"Today is Christmas Eve," she said. "It's a day for eating chocolate and watching movies."

"If I don't reach out to some listings now, I'll run out of time. Where is everyone?"

Barb slid a plate of pancakes toward me. "They went ice skating. A Christmas Eve tradition with their father. I went once and broke my tailbone in three places, so now I stay home and make breakfast."

I dragged myself to the table and searched for one-bedrooms in my price range of zero dollars. At first glance, the options were bleak. "Yikes."

Barb joined me, holding out her palm. "Show me."

"Here's one with a triangle-shaped bedroom," I deadpanned, displaying my phone.

She pushed her red-framed glasses up her nose, tilting her head back to see through the bottom of her bifocals. "Pass."

I scrolled. "Here's one over a nightclub."

"So you can never sleep again? Pass."

I forked a bite of pancake into my mouth, scrolling and scrolling past doom and gloom. "Here's one that looks decent, but it's next to a fire station."

"Great for your love life but terrible for your blood pressure." She topped off my coffee and added another pancake to my stack. The yellow house, in all its warm shabbiness, was a five-star bed-and-breakfast compared to my grim future.

While I ate, Barb vetoed every listing I showed her. When I scrolled to the basement apartment with no windows, she plucked my phone from my hand and stashed it in her apron pocket. "Absolutely not," she said. "You can't live there. You can live here."

A high, surprised laugh escaped me. "What? You mean permanently?"

She opened her hands and looked around like, *What's the big deal?* "I've got the basement, no one uses it, and I'm an old lady who could use the company. You don't have to pay rent and I'll do all the cooking. What's not to like?"

I dropped my fork and hugged her, smelling cold cream and lavender bath salts. "Barb, thank you, but I can't."

"Why not?" she demanded. "Summer and Dylan are doing it."

I softened. Of course I couldn't move in, and of course Barb wouldn't see why.

"You're Summer's mom," I said. "They're family."

"So I'll be your mom, too," she insisted. "The job's been reposted, and I'm applying." She spread her arms and bowed. "I'll be Connie's understudy, rising to the occasion when she can no longer perform."

Her eyes held mine, tough and steady, like a mother with a lot of practice.

"You know I can't," I said.

"Give me one good reason why," she challenged.

I swallowed a bite of pancake, shaking my head. "Because it's too much to ask of you."

"But I'm telling you it's not too much. I'm offering. Try again."

Because it's kind of weird given that I have a huge crush on your son, I wanted to say. "Because I wouldn't feel right about not paying rent," I said instead.

"Why? I own this house free and clear. But if it makes you feel better, pay me a hundred dollars a month and split the groceries."

I pointed my fork at her. "That's not enough and you know it."

"Aha!" She snapped her fingers. "So you're considering it."

I opened my mouth, then closed it again. If I moved in, I could eat these pancakes every day, laugh with Barb every day, adopt her as my replacement mom. What was stopping me?

In the yellow house, I wasn't a one-woman show anymore. I didn't have a tuba strapped to my back and a harmonica taped under my mouth and a keyboard in my arms. I was part of a band, a family band, where siblings helped one another and mothers took care of their children and everyone lived together in the same house. Wasn't that the dream?

"You want to know what I think?" Barb asked.

I laughed. "I think you're going to tell me regardless."

Her strong, cold fingers cupped my hands, an iron grip. "You're trying to be strong, but you've got the definition wrong. Be weak. Being weak is stronger and scarier and harder than toughing it out in spite of yourself."

Her words sliced me open like a cut of raw meat. "I don't know how to do that."

She took off her glasses and tapped them against her lip, thinking. "You know what I do when I've got too many feelings to sort out? I write a song. It helps me process. I feel things I had no idea were waiting to be felt. It's revelatory. Believe me."

I had to laugh. Was the universe conspiring? Why did everyone in this house want me to write a song so badly? Did they not have Spotify accounts?

"I'll be really bad," I assured her. "I'm not a writer. I can barely write a birthday card."

Barb stood up anyway and extended her hand. "If you write a song about your feelings, there are no bad songs because there are no bad feelings. Come."

Before I could insist that I should really keep scrolling through listings, she pulled me out of the kitchen. All those years of ballet had stuck with her. She moved like she was crossing a stage, with grace, with attitude, with long legs. She could still put them behind her head, too. The other night, she'd demonstrated it for me while her pot pie was baking.

In the living room, I perched on the piano bench, pressing my hands between my knees.

"Scooch closer," she instructed, yanking my waist until her bony hip met mine. "What should we write about? Love? Sex? Politics? Those make for rich topics. Music nowadays is getting quite filthy, isn't it? I heard a song on the radio the other day about oral sex. I'm no prude, but come on. Whatever happened to 'New York, New York'?"

I smiled, shaking my head. "I'd prefer we not write a song about oral sex together, Barb."

She lifted her chin to read her sheet music through the glasses that had fallen down her nose. "Fine, sweetheart. But if you ever have any questions, my door's always open. Now, here's a love song I wrote about my late husband." She turned the page of her songbook. "And here's one I wrote about chicken."

"A love song about chicken?"

"Not all of them need to be masterpieces, dear. Sometimes it's just about having fun."

Backlit by the Christmas tree, she played a plucky, joyful tune. "Chicken—tastes like swine unless you brine. Chicken—does just fine with a splash of wine. Chicken—breast is best, but thigh is divine. Chicken!" She ended with a jazzy chord and smiled, her blue eyes warm and teasing. "What do you think?"

"I think I'm understanding why you need some company," I joked.

She turned to a clean page. "I've been thinking about writing basic recipes into songs for children so they can learn to cook. Like, 'Crack your eggs, but do well, to get no shell, and they'll be swell.' That kind of thing."

"I love that idea. Maybe I could even learn to cook."

She pushed her glasses up her nose and sniffed. "Just a silly pet project. More important, what should we write? An ode to your mother?"

The lightness of Barb's chicken song extinguished. I squeezed my hands between my knees. "How do we do that?"

"Just say whatever comes into your mind. Words, phrases, ideas. Let's start with the top of her head and move down. Hair. She ironed her hair. With an iron." On her blank page, Barb jotted down *iron.* "Now you go."

I nodded, but my heart had begun to pound. How could I write an ode to my mom when I'd rather live in a basement apartment with no windows than go in her house? When I felt all this anger? But I couldn't say that to Barb. She didn't know about the dark side of my grief.

So I closed my eyes. I pictured my mom's head. Her hair, which was once black but had turned gray. For years she'd dyed it, but eventually she gave up and let it grow out, and I thought she looked more beautiful than ever. "Her hair was gray," I said. "And gorgeous. Like yours."

"We did have the best hair in Tennessee." Barb wrote down *gorgeous gray.*

"Her white sunglasses, obviously." I worked my way down my memory of her, top to bottom. "She always wore lip liner, not just lipstick, and it was always red. She had every shade of red they sold at Walgreens."

I told Barb how she used to wear a velvet minidress to Clyde's Christmas parties, where all his teacher friends wore baggy khakis and clip-on ties. I told her about the letters my mom used to send me when I went to sleepaway camp, written in the voice of our dog. I told her how my mom loved reality TV because she cared about real people, not made-up ones, and how she liked dirty jokes but wholesome movies. I told her my mom never listened to music, and now I understood why.

It was easier than I thought. The details came faster than Barb could write them down. My hands weren't squeezed between my knees anymore. I was using them to demonstrate the size of earrings my mom liked to wear. "At least three inches long," I said. "With a matching necklace."

When I looked at the long list of traits in Barb's songbook, it hit me: I'd been thinking of my mom's life as sad because of the way it ended, because of her addiction, because of the ways she'd fallen short of what I thought a mom should be. But her life wasn't sad, it was full. Addiction was part of her, but she was also so much more than that.

She loved the small things in life, things most people took for granted or paid no attention to at all. She loved hot dogs on the

Fourth of July and pasta with cream sauce. She loved the salty sweet combination of popcorn and chocolate. She loved the fireplace in our house, which didn't even work anymore. She'd filled it with candles and called it her spa.

She loved sunsets. She used to sit in the driveway on a folding chair in the summer, watching the sun go down, texting me blurry photos of pink and orange.

She loved Christmas. And because of her Santa schemes, I still believed in him a little, if I was being honest.

She loved thunderstorms. When it rained, she'd open all the doors and windows.

She loved the rare occasions when I agreed to spend the night, begging me to stay up late and have one glass of wine with her. But I'd say no, that hyper-serious version of myself taking control. If she were here now, I'd stay up. I'd stay up all night.

I laughed, remembering how she loved rearranging furniture. Her own and everyone else's. Whenever she came to my apartment or the one I shared with Dan, I couldn't go to the bathroom without returning to find the couch in a different place. But she was right. It did look better over there.

She loved giving me creative gifts. Never did I receive a scarf. One year she gave me a bag of mustaches so I could host a fake mustache party, but I never did. At some point, I'd given them away. It hurt, how badly I wanted those back.

She'd wanted to make life special for me—with Santa, with sunsets, with mustaches. That was her legacy. To find joy in the mundane. To celebrate. To open all the doors and windows when it rained.

There weren't enough words to fully honor my mom or thank her for everything she did for me. Barb could fill up songbooks and we'd never get there. She was my mom. When I was little, she put my towel in the dryer so it was warm when I got out of the bath. She was my mom.

I loved her. I missed her. I was angry at her. All of those things were true.

I looked at Barb with tears in my eyes. My chin trembled; I couldn't hold it still. "I didn't appreciate her enough," I whispered. "And now it's too late."

Barb held me, stroking my hair like I was a little girl. "Why do you say that?"

"Because I was so mad at her," I admitted, my voice raw and broken.

"Everyone's angry with their mother sometimes," she whispered. "It's part of the deal. We're okay with it."

I pulled away, shaking my head, wiping my face. "No, that's not what I mean." I looked into her pale blue eyes to gauge her reaction as I admitted, "My mom drank. A lot. My whole life, but it had been getting worse. She lost her clients and had to retire. It killed her. She never told me the truth, but I saw it on her death certificate."

I hadn't realized I expected Barb to be surprised until she wasn't.

She released a long, slow sigh. "Oh, Connie."

I sucked in a small breath. "You knew?"

Barb picked a melancholy tune on the piano. "The unfortunate truth is that when we were young, no one talked about addiction. Drinking too much was considered wild, and everyone liked a wild girl until they didn't anymore. Everyone loved that Connie liked to party. She was a blast. She'd turn a bathroom line into a conga line, make friends with the bartender so our drinks were free, dance on tables in her white cowboy boots. We used to go dancing at a gay club hidden in the back of a convenience store. When the lights came on, I'd have to drag her home, and even then she'd suggest opening a bottle of wine. Connie had an on switch but no off switch. Sometimes I had to slam my door in her face to get some sleep. It seemed like she would do anything to avoid going to sleep sober, and I always wondered—what was she so afraid of dreaming about?"

I'd barely been breathing. "Did you ever do anything about it? Like, did you try to talk to her?"

Barb struck one low note on the piano that reverberated in the deep hole of my chest. "Sometimes I'd pour out her bottles of wine and she'd get angry at me. But by the time I was mature enough to have a real conversation, she wasn't speaking to me anymore."

So Barb had never tried to save my mom. I'd never tried to save her. Had anyone been there for her?

I looked down at my lap, my tears becoming dark splotches on my jeans. "We didn't talk about it. I tried for a while, but she'd get mad and change the subject, so I gave up. I thought I was doing us both a favor by pretending everything was fine, pretending we could get along like a normal mother and daughter. I never had an intervention. I just let it happen."

I felt Barb's fingers under my chin, lifting it, forcing me to look at her. "Listen to me. Are you listening? This is not your fault. There was nothing you could have done to change what happened here. But even if there was, it was not your responsibility. My children are not responsible for me, and that's coming from someone with a black belt in guilt. The best thing—the only thing—a child can offer her mother is forgiveness for her mistakes, empathy for her experience, and acceptance that she is human."

I wanted Barb to be right. But one question suffocated me in its grip, the one I could barely say out loud, so afraid to put the words out into the universe for fear of an answer I didn't want. My face crumpled as I asked, "But what if she died thinking I didn't care about her?"

Barb wore her heart on her face, and it broke. She cupped my cheeks. "It's a mother's job to love her child, not the other way around. It is your job to carry her love forward and project it out into the world. If you have a child someday, you will love her just as hard."

I sank my elbows on the piano, making a flat, harsh chord. My body was so heavy I couldn't hold it up. "If she loved me—" Each word hurt as it left my throat. "If she loved me, then how could she let it get so bad? Why didn't she want to be here for the rest of my life? When I get married or have a baby, she won't be here. How is that love?"

I was aware of Barb's hands on my back as I gasped for air, tears on the piano, finally writing a song nobody wanted to hear.

"Your mother wanted to be here," Barb said, soft but firm. "She loved you more than anything. She loved you so much it hurt. The person she struggled to love was herself."

The ache in my throat hardened, jagged. When I asked, "How do you know?" the words scraped against my soul.

Barb tightened her grip on me. "Because—" She was fierce in her conviction. "Because I am a mother."

I closed my eyes, sinking into her words, letting her promise wrap me like a weighted blanket, as heavy as my mother's love.

I focused on the strength of her hands, trying to breathe oxygen into them. Slowly the uncontrollable heaving of my chest subsided. I breathed.

When I could, I sat up and wiped my cheeks with my sweatshirt sleeve.

"Are you okay?" she asked.

"No," I answered. I was so drained, I had nothing left to lose.

"You will be," she promised. "It takes time."

I nodded, tasting a fresh wave of tears, but the slow, hot, weepy kind. "I miss her."

"I've been missing her for thirty-five years. She is a worthy person to miss."

I thought of my last conversation with her, when she'd hurried off the phone and I hadn't gone over to check on her. "What would you say to her if you had the chance?"

Barb sighed. "If I had the Gift, I'd say, Connie"—she looked up and opened her hands at the ceiling—"I'm sorry for everything. I was a selfish little bitch."

I managed to laugh through my tears. "Why are you looking up? She's in the basement."

"I didn't want to imply anything by looking down," she said, leaning in as if my mom might hear. "What would you say to her, if you could?"

"I don't know," I confessed. "I wish I did."

Barb took both of my hands and looked at me with such understanding, it was as if her hand had reached inside my chest and held my heart. "She's not here anymore. You don't need to worry about hurting her feelings. Go ahead and be honest."

I remembered one specific August storm when despite my protests my mom had opened all the windows and soaked the kitchen floor. *Better to let in the rain than no air at all,* she'd said. "I'd ask her for the truth."

Barb tilted her head. "What truth do you need?"

I had a memory. It was Christmas Eve. I was in my twenties and single. I'd suggested my mom and I go out for dinner, knowing she'd have nothing prepared and I hadn't felt like cooking. We went to a hip place in my neighborhood, a bar with *wine* in the name—the Wining Cow or something. I couldn't remember because I'd never gone back. She barely touched her food but drank seven glasses of wine. Seven. I was surprised they hadn't cut her off. And then I paid, and I was furious. I had no money, and they were fifteen dollars each.

As I drove us home, I called her out. "You had seven glasses of wine. We were only there for an hour and a half." She covered her mouth and giggled. "I got carried away," she said, defensive but joking, like a teenage girl. *Take this seriously,* I wanted to scream. *Take* me *seriously.* And then she added, "I did not have seven."

In the morning, I thought about showing her the receipt. But instead, she pretended like it had never happened, so I did, too. I wanted to enjoy Christmas morning like we used to when I was little, in pajamas by the tree, eating waffles from our Mickey Mouse waffle maker.

I was angry at her for ruining dinner, but I was angrier at the charade. And at myself, for playing along.

But there was a part of the story I liked to forget. After she'd gone to bed, I'd texted Gabby, who was home for winter break, to vent. She'd invited me over and we ended up getting drunk in her hot tub by mixing Baileys into Swiss Miss hot chocolate. An ice pick stabbed at my temples all of Christmas Day and I felt so queasy I couldn't eat my waffle.

Why did I think I was so much better than my mom? In lying to each other, we were lying to ourselves.

"I'd ask for the truth about what I saw and why," I told Barb. "I need to know I wasn't crazy. Maybe then I can forgive myself. And if I understand why, maybe I can forgive her."

Barb placed her elegant fingers on the keys. Her nails were bare, and her hands were marked—some from age, some scars from the kitchen. "You're here now," she said. "You're asking the right questions, even though it's hard."

When she began to play, I recognized the high chords that sounded like "Jingle Bells," but that wasn't it. Then the song crashed into me. It was Joni Mitchell's "River," the depressing Christmas song we both needed. Barb's voice was gritty and passionate, the sound of sand meeting ocean. She played with her entire body, eyes closed, swaying as her fingers brushed the keys, commanding the instrument, drawing heartbreak from this stand-up piano with its chipped wood and scratched keys. Energy shot out of her through a million tiny holes, like needles of light. I watched her, starstruck.

Barb had promised me the gift of knowing my mother, but she had given me so much more. She'd given me my mother's love, but also hers. They'd become intertwined. If I cried on Barb's shoulder, she'd wipe my tears. She'd given me permission to feel pain and ask for the truth.

She was Barbara Stern. A legend—if to nobody else, then to me.

Chapter 20

Christmas Eve

I helped Barb in the kitchen for the rest of the day, answering her questions, telling her everything I could remember about my life. She wanted to learn about her lost friend through me. What kind of mother she'd been. Who she'd become. We talked about her business, the absence of her love life, how she'd tried to convince me to live at home for college. And when we sat down for dinner, I told everyone about how many close encounters I'd had with Santa. Dylan still believed—ostensibly—so I didn't mention my mom was behind it all. Still, he eyed me with suspicion while he pushed mashed potatoes around his plate, pummeling me with pointed questions. I answered each one as reasonably as I could. Why shouldn't he keep believing in Santa as long as possible? He deserved uncomplicated magic in his complicated life.

"Why were only *your* presents left behind?" he pressed.

"Because Santa's bag refills at each house," I said. "Haven't you seen *The Santa Clause*?"

"If he crashed, why were there no marks in the snow?"

"I'm sure there were. But it was snowing that night, so they got covered up."

He narrowed his eyes at me, scooping a slow and scrupulous bite of potato into his little mouth. I lifted my eyebrows, waiting for whatever he'd throw at me next.

Summer had made a centerpiece using Barb's Yankee candles and branches cut from the tree. It glowed in the middle of our table, warming our faces in yellow light. Henry looked handsome by candlelight, I observed, like I was some kind of pioneer woman and this was Christmas in a log cabin. Still, he did.

When Barb made us go around the table and say aloud a Christmas wish, we rolled our eyes and teased her, but then we all cried.

One more song with my soulmate, Barb said.

A house as warm as this one for my son, Summer said.

To love again, Henry said.

For my mom to be alive, I said.

Dylan asked for LEGOs, giving us all an excuse to wipe our tears and laugh. My body was betraying me. I was supposed to be grieving, but instead I was smiling, laughing, light.

Barb had made penne all'arrabbiata for dinner. When she carried the pasta out of the kitchen in a huge steaming bowl, she handed Dylan a shaker of red pepper flakes. "Add a sprinkle for some extra kick," she instructed, doling out plates.

But when Dylan turned the shaker upside down, the plastic lid fell off, dumping out the entire bottle of red pepper flakes.

The table collectively gasped.

Then we burst out laughing.

The pasta was so spicy that for every bite, I drank a glass of water. Tears streamed down my face, both from the heat and from laughing so hard. I thought of Shelly, my mom's accountant, and her advice: *You need something spicy to bring you back to life.* I laughed myself back into existence.

After cheesecake for dessert, which finally calmed our burning mouths, I insisted on cleaning up, maybe to be alone with my thoughts, maybe to stare through the window over the sink at the magic of Christmas lights in the dark. But when Henry joined me with a dish towel, I moved over to make room.

We were quiet for a while—washing, drying, listening to Kenny G play instrumental holiday music on the saxophone. If the saxophone doesn't make you want to wrap your arms around another person and sway all night in the middle of your kitchen, then you don't have ears.

"I was wondering if I could take you somewhere," Henry said, his fingers brushing mine as he accepted a dish.

I looked up at him. Handsome, candlelight or not. "Do I need to change out of my sweatpants?"

He grinned. "Nope."

"Then yes," I said, my voice, I feared, betraying how badly I wanted to go anywhere with him.

We didn't say goodbye to the others. After dishes, we silently slipped into our coats and snuck out the back door. Henry grabbed my hand as we crossed the snowy front yard. In his Jeep, he cranked up the seat warmers, tuned to Christmas jazz, and we were off. To where? I couldn't have cared less.

Neither of us said anything as we drove through the quiet neighborhood. It was after ten. Most houses were dark, but I caught glimpses of some families still gathered around their tree or table or TV. Henry held my hand across the console and I hummed along with the radio. Everything felt so blissfully normal.

After a few minutes, he parked in front of a house that looked not just dark, but vacant. A FOR SALE sign rose out of the snow.

I sat up, peering through the window. "What's this?"

He leaned over me to see out. "I'm thinking about buying this house."

I frowned at it. It was a two-story Colonial with a screened-in porch, white wood siding, and a steeply slanted roof. While charming—and wasn't that Realtor code for "shabby"?—it looked like it had spent fifty years raising dozens of children and needed a long nap. The roof sagged. The garden beds were somehow both dead and overgrown. A stair to the porch was missing. You'd have to jump over it to get inside. I wasn't sure how to ask this question, but couldn't a doctor afford a house that needed less work?

I chewed my thumbnail. "I mean this out of genuine curiosity. Why?"

"I've always wanted to fix up an old house. It's got great character, and a guesthouse in the back where Summer and Dylan could live. If you can get past the spiders, the inside is incredible. All original, a hundred years old."

"Wow. I didn't think spiders lived that long."

He laughed. "I promise there are no electronic toilets. I'm pretty sure the fridge doesn't even work, let alone talk."

"There might be a necessary middle ground."

He unbuckled his seat belt. "Just wait until you see the banister. Do you want to go inside?"

"We can do that?"

"My agent gave me the code to the lockbox. There isn't anyone else interested."

I laughed. "Aren't they supposed to lie to you about that?"

Henry killed the ignition, grinning. "I'm a sucker for the underdog."

Since no one had shoveled, the yard was thick with snow. He held my hand again as we picked our way across, our boots sinking with each step. Our breath made white clouds. When we reached the porch, before I realized what was happening, Henry scooped me into his arms and carried me over the missing step.

After he deposited me on my feet, I raised a brow at him. "Are you a secret agent?"

"If I told you, I'd have to kill you," he said, leaning close to my ear, the words warm on my skin. "And that would be against my Hippocratic oath."

Goose bumps swept up my neck.

When he typed a code into the lockbox, the key that fell into his palm was so old-fashioned it looked fake. "Is that a key to the dungeon?" I teased. "Should I be scared?"

He held it up. "When I saw the key, I knew I'd have to have the house."

"You know it would probably be cheaper to buy a new house and install an old-timey lock."

"But that would be cheating."

He unlocked the door with a creak and a thunk, letting me into a dusty entryway. The air was cold and dry and musty. I could barely see anything until Henry flipped the light on. The banister revealed itself, curving elegantly to the second floor, thick and carved with an intricate pattern of leaves. I spotted only a couple of spiderwebs.

"Okay," I said. "I'm sold."

He clapped and rubbed his palms together. "Excellent. Let me give you the grand tour."

I trailed him through the dining room, wallpapered in peeling silk.

"I thought I could knock out this wall and replace it with windows," he said. "It'll get great light in the morning."

He led me to the kitchen next, tiled in pale green like my Lincoln Park apartment—very 1960s but in a cool way.

"I'll keep the tile," he said. "But replace the appliances so they actually work. And I was thinking French doors to the backyard would be perfect here."

He was right. This place had potential. If it were mine, I'd plant blue hydrangeas all along the backyard so I'd see them through the French doors every morning while I made coffee.

"Come see the living room," he said, extending his hand again. It was my warm refuge in this drafty house.

His excitement was contagious. By the time I saw the floor-to-ceiling bookshelves surrounding the fireplace in the living room, I'd mentally moved in. I'd tear down the floral wallpaper but keep the original molding and paint everything bright white. Hang a gigantic mirror over the fireplace so the room went on forever.

"I'd never leave," I said, awe in my voice as I longed for that fireplace to be mine. On the grate sat an old pile of half-charred wood. "Does that still work?"

Henry stuck his head inside and opened the flu. "Should we try it?"

I scrunched up my face. "That feels illegal."

"Yeah," he agreed, then grinned. "But I'm feeling a little bad tonight."

"Watch out, everybody," I teased. "Bad Henry is here to create ambience."

"Bad Henry is a romantic," he said, pulling a book of matches from his back pocket.

I laughed. "Ah, Bad Henry came prepared to be bad. So he's a Bad Boy Scout."

When he looked at me over his shoulder, there was nothing Boy Scout about it. It was a bona fide smolder, so hot I started sweating.

The flame caught. He turned around, facing me. He was too far away. I wanted to move closer, but I wasn't sure what this was.

We stared at each other until the heat building in my neck was too much. I broke the moment by taking off my scarf.

"Do you want to join me on my invisible couch?" he asked.

I sat beside him on the floor. "What, no fur blanket?"

"It's in the car. Didn't want to be too presumptuous. But I do have something for you." He reached into his coat and produced a thin gift-wrapped square.

I turned it over in my hands, noticing how neatly he'd folded and taped the edges. "A Christmas gift?"

"More like a grief gift. It's silly, but it helped me when my dad died."

I peeled back the corners, nervous I was going to start crying and ruin our impromptu date. But when I saw what it was, a laugh danced out of me. "*Broadway's Greatest Hits*?"

"I grew up with my mom playing this constantly. My dad would always complain, but really he knew every word. We all did. We'd catch him humming 'Don't Rain on My Parade' while he cleaned wet leaves out of the gutters. After he died, none of us could play it for a long time. And then one day Summer put it on and turned up the volume high like my mom used to do when we were kids and we all felt so much better. It was like he was there with us, singing along, and this fog had lifted and we realized he was still with us. I know you used to be in musicals, so I thought it might work for you."

My heart grew three sizes, like the Grinch. I held the CD tightly with both hands. I didn't own a CD player, but I didn't care. I'd drive around in Barb's van all day so I could listen to this.

"Henry . . ." I'd rehearsed a little speech earlier about how I liked him—a lot—but we were both recovering from breakups and my relationship with Barb made this complicated if something went wrong, so we should take it slow.

But I never got to give my speech because he kissed me.

I was so surprised that at first I didn't react. But then the romantic girl in the secret garden tucked away behind my heart swooned, and

I remembered to kiss him back. My hands found his neck, his found the skin just beneath my sweater. My entire body whispered *yes.*

It was my idea to take our clothes off, but when he got the hint, he didn't object. We ditched our coats and boots like we were racing against time, like this was our last chance to repopulate the earth. I lifted his sweater and threw it aside. We were a clumsy mess of removing clothes. His button got stuck in my bracelet. My teeth hit his shoulder, an accidental bite. We laughed when I said, "I'll do that again later but on purpose." We laughed out of sheer relief. I had been, if not waiting, then hoping.

Maybe, in those last moments before all the clothes were gone and there was nothing left between us, I should have asked myself whether this was too good to be true. Could we all live happily ever after? Me, Henry, Barb, the yellow house?

But I didn't. Instead, I let Henry kiss me on the floor in front of the fire. I welcomed his fingertips flexing into my back. I listened to him whisper my name, asking me to look at him.

Afterward, we lay on the dirty floor, facing each other, Henry's fingertip trailing up my rib cage.

"I really should have brought that blanket," he said.

"I do think I have spiderwebs in my hair." I sat up to investigate and gasped—smoke was pouring out of the fireplace. "Oh my god. Your sweater!"

The one I had so desperately thrown aside was engulfed in flames, carrying the fire into the room. I watched, frozen in panic, as it spread to my jeans, my coat, my scarf, and the oily, grimy mat on the hearth.

But Henry jumped into action, calm and in command. "Open the windows," he said, kicking the burning clothes into the fireplace. The smoke was thicker than I would have expected—black and opaque, like liquid.

I hurried to the first window and wrenched it up. The warped wood squealed. All the windows were stuck, painted over at the seams. Henry and I opened them one by one, releasing smoke into the dark, cold night.

When the air had mostly cleared, I slumped against the wall. "Thank god."

Then a piercing beep from the kitchen made us both jump.

"Shit," he said. "The fire alarm."

"At least you know it works?"

He ran to the kitchen as the high-pitched, earsplitting beep cried relentlessly. I opened the front door, thinking I could fan in some fresh air, but the heavy oak creaked as it yawned open, then creaked as I heaved it closed. There was no point. I gave up and ran to help Henry in the kitchen and found him standing on the counter, pressing his thumb into the reset button and waving smoke away.

The alarm stopped.

A loud silence took its place.

We looked at each other—and burst out laughing.

Henry was completely naked on the kitchen counter. I was naked in the doorway, my arms and chest covered with grime from the decaying windows that probably hadn't been cleaned in a decade. It was saying something that Henry looked sexy up there, even from this unflattering, ball-forward angle.

After he climbed down, he asked, "Did that ruin the moment?"

"No," I said, pulling his body against mine. "It was hot."

He laughed and kissed me against the counter, then swooped me up to sit on it and wrapped my legs around his waist.

"Now I have to buy this house," he said.

"Why, so you don't get sued?"

Henry tipped my head back and brushed his mouth just beneath my ear. "So we can do that again."

I curled my fingers into his hair. "I would do that with you again anywhere, anytime. I'd do it with you in the back seat of your Jeep. I'd do it with you in your twin bed."

"But what if I like the house?" he murmured against my skin.

"Then buy the house." The way he fanned my hair away to brush kisses down my throat, I'd have agreed to just about anything.

"But do you like the house?" he asked, lips grazing my jaw as he worked his way to my mouth.

"I like the house," I breathed, surrendering to his kiss.

When he released me, he held my face, keeping his mouth an inch from mine. "Mel."

"Yeah?"

He looked into my eyes. "I'm going to fall in love with you. Is that okay?"

In this old house, on the precipice of a new beginning, between the cold tile and the warmth of his body, I understood how life could be both beautiful and devastating at the same time. Maybe healing was just learning how to live with both.

I tucked my face into his neck and nodded against his skin, feeling the steady comfort of his pulse. "Yes," I promised. "That's okay."

Chapter 21

Christmas Day

I opened my eyes on Christmas morning like I was seven years old, ready to leap out of bed and sprint to the tree to see what gifts I'd gotten. Only the gift was right next to me, naked and asleep.

When we got home last night—Henry in his T-shirt and jeans, me naked beneath his coat like I'd nearly burned his house down as an excuse to seduce him—Henry snuck downstairs. We watched half of *It's a Wonderful Life*—I did not remember how long that movie was—then pretended we were going to sleep, started kissing, had sex again, then actually fell asleep. Now his skin warmed mine.

I tried to gently extricate myself for the bathroom, but as soon as I moved, he murmured, "Good morning," into my neck.

I smiled at him over my shoulder. "Were you waiting for me to wake up?"

"Just lying here staring at the back of your head. Didn't want to disturb you. Nice hair, by the way."

I rolled over to face him. "I am disturbed. That's creepy."

He grinned, sitting up. "Not as creepy as my breath. Please allow me to brush my teeth before I devour you."

Abandoned by his body heat, I burrowed into the warm spot he'd left behind and closed my eyes.

I'd wondered whether I'd ever feel normal again, let alone happy, let alone joy. But when Henry returned from the bathroom and the mattress shifted as he lay down beside me, I glimpsed life after grief. He circled my waist with his capable arms and drew me in. I breathed in Henry and breathed out the pain.

Our plan was that I'd go upstairs first, make sure the coast was clear, then text him. Quietly I eased the basement door closed and listened. Barb was in the kitchen, humming. The scrape of plates, the clank of pots, the sizzle of breakfast.

I peeked in the living room. The tree was plugged in, colorful and happy its day had arrived. Barb had lit a fire and cranked up the heat. The windows were so fogged, I couldn't tell whether it was sunny or snowing. Nothing existed in this little nest but us.

I walked in to Barb whisking eggs. "Merry Christmas!" I greeted her.

"Is my son down there or did he fly the coop?"

My face fell into my hands. "How did you know?"

"He could have at least closed his door. It's like he wanted to get caught."

"Are you mad?" I asked, peeking through my fingers.

"Furious!" Her whisk twirled so fast it was practically blurry.

I'd been teasing. Now I dropped my hands. "You are? Oh, shoot, I—"

She lifted her chin. "I'm furious I can't take credit for this. Who made the first move? I bet it was my son. Was he respectful? Who am I kidding, he probably sent you a handwritten invitation."

Relief softened my shoulders as I laughed. "Given that you basically kidnapped me, I think you made the first move. You get all the credit." I poured myself coffee and carried it to the basement door. "You might as well come up," I called. "She knows."

"Of course she knows," he called back. "She's probably taking credit for it as we speak."

On my way back to the kitchen, I paused when I noticed a figure through the frosted glass in the front door. The shadow of a person raised a fist and knocked.

"Are you expecting anyone?" I called to Barb at the same time she called, "Can you get that?"

I opened the door to a UPS guy. It was snowing, it turned out. Thick flakes swirling, like feathers in a pillow fight. "Hi there."

"I've got a package for Mel Hart that requires a signature," he said, holding out an envelope and a tablet.

"That's me." A bright cold pricked my hand as I signed with the stylus. "I didn't think you delivered on Christmas."

"If you pay enough, we do. Merry Christmas."

"Merry Christmas," I echoed, taking the envelope.

The UPS guy flipped up his hood and crunched through the snow to his truck. I closed out the wind and looked down at the return address—it was from my dad. The postage said he'd paid a hundred dollars to overnight it.

An unexpected swelling expanded in my rib cage, compressing my heart.

Delicately, I opened the envelope and shook out a brown leather notebook with a card. *Your mom gave me this in 1984. I hope it makes you feel closer to her. Merry Christmas. Love, Dad.*

"Who was it?" Barb called.

"UPS," I answered, but mildly, not loud enough for her to hear. My heart pounded in my ears.

Henry emerged from the basement. "Everything okay?" he asked, bending to kiss my cheek.

I nodded, though I wasn't sure the answer was yes. I ran my thumb over the hundred-dollar postage stamp, struck by a new loss. How much time had my dad and I wasted not being there for each other?

"My dad sent me this," I explained. "It's a book of songs my mom wrote. Do you mind if I go read for a while? Tell Barb I haven't flown the coop."

He swept the hair off my shoulder. "Of course."

I retreated to the living room. The book was so lightweight I almost suspected it was empty, a fake book, one of those trick things where people hide their remotes. But when I opened the first page, words greeted me, written in pencil.

I lowered myself onto the couch and began to read.

The early pages had a wide-eyed gaze, reminding me of myself at twenty-two, fresh from my breakup with Kamil, wanting the whole world. The middle pages were angrier. More questions, more fear. I saw Ernest in them, toying with her self-esteem, pitting her against Barb. The later pages spoke of a woman in love with a man who gave her little of himself in return.

I didn't realize I was crying until a heavy tear blotted the paper, smearing the words.

I turned a page, expecting more tearjerkers, but instead, my senses pricked. *Cowboy, king of thieves.* It reminded me—

I'd sung those words before.

Mister bad medicine, miss big sugar

Trade my body for ashes

But carry my heart

Rudy's ears lifted when I said, "What the hell?" He cocked his head. *Did someone say "ball"?*

The fire was suddenly too hot. I moved to the window to read the lyrics with better light. They matched the words of "Carry My Heart" almost exactly. Humming along, I confirmed only two lines were different.

From the kitchen, I heard dishes clattering and Barb singing to "A Marshmallow World." Then, "Breakfast is ready, sweetheart!"

she called. But I ignored her and instead pulled my phone from my sweatshirt pocket.

"Hello, there!" my dad answered. "Merry, merry!"

Despite the unease in my gut, I smiled. When I still spent summers with him, we'd have a fake Christmas in July since we didn't spend the real one together. That was how he'd wake me up on fake Christmas—with cloves stuck into an orange and a cup of hot chocolate, saying, *Merry, merry!*

"I can't believe you paid so much to send me this book," I said.

"I'd have paid a lot more," he said. "But don't tell UPS."

Wherever he was, it was loud. Maybe he was hosting a party, at a house I'd never been to, full of people I'd never met. "Thank you. This really means a lot."

He murmured something, probably to Susan, *a few minutes.* Then a door closed and the line was quieter. "I remembered what was bothering me about the name Barbara Stern," he said. "Before you were born, I suggested your mother and I go back to New York to celebrate our anniversary and stay at the Waldorf-Astoria. She'd always wanted to do that. I hired a travel agent named Barbara Stern, and when your mother found out her name, she refused to go on the trip. I told her the travel agent was an old lady, but she couldn't be convinced. She said Barbara Stern was the cruelest person she'd ever met, and she never wanted to hear that name as long as she lived."

That made sense, considering. "Barb was her best friend, then had an affair with her boyfriend."

"Who, Ernest?"

My head jerked back. "You knew about him?"

"Ernest wasn't the reason your mother was finished with Barbara Stern. She was smarter than that. She knew Ernest was a bad man."

Worry lit up my spine, one vertebra at a time, like a string of Christmas lights.

I tried to keep my voice even as I asked, "Did it have something to do with 'Carry My Heart'?"

"Bingo," he said. "I listened to that song after we got off the phone and realized it was familiar. I opened the book and there it was. Your mom gave me that book in 1984. I googled it, and 'Carry My Heart' was released in 1985."

I glanced over my shoulder. Why did it feel like I was being watched? "What are you saying?"

"I'm saying your mother wrote that song. Not Ernest. And sure as hell not Barb Stern."

The book was no longer light. Suddenly the lyrics weighed a thousand pounds. I saw an image of my mom onstage, beaming under a spotlight, only for the spotlight to go dark.

"Maybe it's Barb's notebook," I reasoned, hoping to convince myself. "Or maybe they wrote it together."

"You'll have to ask her," he said. He sounded excited, like he'd discovered a key piece of evidence in a cold case. Maybe he had. But he didn't understand how badly I wanted him to be wrong.

From the kitchen, I heard a huge crash—something had shattered. "We're okay!" Barb called, and a vacuum turned on.

"I should go," I said. "I'll call you later."

I hung up. My legs were numb but full of static, the fuzzy feeling of electrical current. Rudy trotted behind me, still hoping *ball* was on the agenda.

I found Barb vacuuming while Henry swept the floor. They looked up when I walked in, smiling identically. It struck me for the first time how similar they looked.

But when Barb saw my face, she switched off the vacuum. "What happened?"

"I don't know," I answered, my voice too wooden to be mine. "I'm wondering the same thing."

I held out the book with both hands, like an offering, and maybe it was. My gift to her being my willingness to believe—my hope—that this was all a mix-up.

But when her eyes fell to the book, the light left them. I knew then that what my dad suspected was true.

How? How was this possible?

I worked hard to lighten my voice, but it trembled anyway. "The lyrics to 'Carry My Heart' are in here. Did my mom write that song?"

Even Barb's wild spirals of hair seemed to lose their fight, falling limp. "You have to understand that I was going to tell you."

Panic rose up my throat. "Tell me what exactly?"

When she didn't answer me right away, I said her name, *Barbara,* a formal address. Like we didn't know each other, because it turned out we didn't.

"The truth," she said. "But I suppose I wanted you to need me first."

That Dean Martin was cheerfully singing "Let It Snow!" was all wrong. I wanted to shut it off, shut this noise out.

I sensed Henry watching me, but I couldn't look at him now. I couldn't bear to think of what I was about to lose.

When Barb took a small step forward, I took an automatic step back. If this was a dance, the Broadway show she'd always wanted, the performance was almost over.

Barb slumped against her vacuum, gripping the handle like she might fall over. "Connie wrote 'Carry My Heart' for the two of us to sing. It was going to be our song, the one that got us famous. We all knew it was that good. When she left, Ernest wanted to record it without her. He said the industry was a game with no rules, and all I had to do was play along."

I tightened my grip on the notebook. "So you stole it from her. And then you got famous and she got nothing."

Barb nodded. "When the song was released, Connie hired a lawyer, but I took Ernest's side. It wasn't so much that we were two against one, but that he was a man versus a woman."

The panic rising up my throat turned to acid. "You lied to everyone. Including me."

She reached for my hands, but I pulled them away. She flinched, withdrawing hers like she'd touched something hot.

She had. I was flaming.

"You're right. I was incredibly selfish. I still am, or I'd have told you the truth sooner. But I didn't want to lose you. When I had you, I had Connie back."

That sliced right through my heart. Barb had convinced me I had a second chance at the mother I'd wanted. I thought she wanted me too, but I was just a stand-in.

"Sweetheart—"

"Please stop calling me that. You're not my mom."

I turned to leave, to run away, but she caught my elbow. "Wait. Connie wanted us to be together, so let's fix this. For her."

I grabbed my boots from where I'd left them by the bench, scattered on the floor like this was my house, and struggled to put them on. "How do you know? She didn't speak to you. For good reason, by the way."

"Because she told Henry I should call you."

I looked up to see her gesturing at Henry, who stood in the corner, color draining from his face. "What?"

Briefly he closed his eyes, his chest falling as the air left him. Then he swept his gaze all over my face, like he was trying to memorize it.

"I'm the doctor who called you," he said. "I was with your mother the night she died."

My brain crawled to a stop. For several moments I stood there, staring. It was so hot in the kitchen. Why was it so hot? I peeled off my sweatshirt and grabbed a holiday card to fan myself, the family in the photo smiling at me as if to rub their ridiculous joy in my face.

"When she came into the hospital that night," he said, "she asked for me. She knew who my mother was. She knew I worked there. She must have looked me up."

I teetered, dizzy, as I dropped the card and steadied myself on the counter. Henry rushed forward to help, but I held out my palm to stop him.

This wasn't a home—it was a scheme. And Henry wasn't my person—he was a liar.

Just like his mother.

Slowly I straightened, brushed off my cheeks like I planned to brush off these people, this house, this holiday from hell.

Before I left, I looked at them, wishing my hot tears weren't giving me away, wishing my voice didn't break as I said, "You realize you both tricked me into loving you, right?"

At their silence, which spoke of their inability to explain this all away, the last whole fiber in my chest snapped. Because I'd still been holding on to the hope of an explanation, but the only explanation was that these people I'd trusted had broken my heart.

In the basement, I shoved my things in my purse—my jeans, my photo album, my mom. I yanked the sheets from the fold-out couch and balled them up for the laundry along with Summer's borrowed clothes. I wanted to leave no trace behind. In the bathroom, I splashed cold water on my face, itchy from the salt of my tears, and cried into a towel. I should never have come here. I should have told Barb to get off my mom's porch. I should have gone with Dan, who was at least honest about who he was.

I couldn't bear another look at Barb's floury hands or Henry's arms reaching for me, so I waited in the basement until my Uber was outside, then snuck out with a quiet click of the latch, closing the door on what could have been.

Chapter 22

CHRISTMAS DAY

I was right back where I started.

Shivering in the cold at the front door of my childhood home, willing myself to unlock it.

The curtains were still drawn, the clay pot still full of snow. But one thing was different. I had no escape anymore. The only way out of this house was through it.

My heart held its breath as I slid my key into the lock and turned. I opened the door an inch and waited, but no one came, of course. What had I expected? The house was empty.

Inside, the air smelled stale. I flipped the light switch—nothing happened. Was the bulb out? I flipped the next switch, in the hall—nothing. "Weird," I said aloud, before walking around flipping on and off switches. Nothing worked. The microwave clock was off, the fridge wasn't cold.

I returned to the front window and swept the curtains aside. Our neighbors' colorful Christmas trees lit up their living rooms, and the strings of lights around their windows twinkled and blinked. Ours was the only dark house on the block.

This happened sometimes when I was a kid. Homework done, TV dinner, Nick at Nite, and suddenly, lights out. Where did Lucy go?

"Dammit," I'd hear my mom say from the kitchen, because the cordless phone had stopped working, too. She'd call the power company from her phone in the bedroom, pay what she could, and Lucy would be back.

But the power company wouldn't turn off the electricity because the bill was a couple of weeks late. Had she not paid it for months?

Zipped to my chin, I ventured back into the wind and around the side of the house to check the breakers, just in case. A few inches of snow had piled on top of the silver box. When I opened it, tangles of black wires and orange switches mocked me. Who was I kidding?

Flipping them all off and on again was the only approach I could think of. But when I went back inside, the house remained dark and lifeless.

I walked back to the front door, considering leaving. But where would I go? It was Christmas Day and I was alone.

I sensed a shift in the dark, a brush of air, like someone had walked by or the house itself was breathing. "Hello?" I called.

"The candles."

I jumped. My mom's voice, as clear as I'd ever heard her. I spun around, searching for the source.

Emptiness.

I'd imagined it.

I leaned my back against the door and sank to the floor, heavy and tired.

Then, "Our emergency stash."

My eyes sprung open and I scrambled to my feet. Was I losing my grip on reality? I searched the house—kitchen, bathroom, bedroom.

Empty.

Her voice had come from everywhere and nowhere at the same time.

Traipsing back to the front door, I stopped short.

There she was, standing next to her urn.

Only it wasn't the mother I knew. It was Connie at twenty-two, straight hair, short skirt, tall boots, white sunglasses.

"They're in the pantry, remember?" she asked.

This isn't real, I told myself. *This is in my head.* I already knew the candles were in the pantry.

Silently, as if I were the ghost, I collected as many as I could carry, plus a book of matches. Before reentering the hall, I shook myself out of it.

But there she was again. Suede tassels hung from the hem of her miniskirt. "You didn't have a funeral for me," she teased, youthful and light, just a girl.

Because there was no one to invite, I thought, but Connie answered, like she'd heard me.

"What about Barb?" she asked. "I sent her to you."

She ruined your life. My heart tightened just thinking of Barb, how she'd lied.

Connie walked to the couch and sat down. Somehow she had a glass of wine in her hand. Again, she answered like I'd spoken out loud. "What makes you think my life was ruined? I had an incredible life. I lived in New York in the seventies. I wrote the most infamous country song in America. I fell in love, I had a soulmate, I had you. Don't simplify my life down to the way it ended. Go look in my closet if you need a reminder that I was someone other than the disease written on my death certificate."

As she talked with her hands, wine slipped over the edge of her glass, but it didn't leave a stain. I couldn't take my eyes off the couch, searching for a purple splotch, some evidence that this was real, that she existed, that I didn't have to say goodbye.

"Why did you send me Barb if you knew what she'd done?" I asked.

Connie was already refilling her glass. "Because she wouldn't let you push her away no matter how hard you tried. And you needed someone."

"But she lied to me." I was clutching my candles like a life raft. "I trusted her."

"Don't repeat my mistakes," Connie warned. "You're stronger than me."

"Because I had to be," I said, decades of simmering anger making me harden.

"I know that," she agreed, and somehow she became both twenty-two and also my mom, both the person who inspired me and the person who hurt me.

"Do you?" My words felt like pushing against a brick wall. "Because you never acknowledged that when you were alive. You tried to convince me you were fine and then you died."

My tears came hot and gushing and relentless. I wiped my nose with the back of my hand, furious and breaking and aching and alone. Wanting someone but having no one. Wanting her to come back to life just so I could yell at her and then hug her and ask her to hold me. I was thirty-three, but I was a child. And this was it. This was everything I'd needed to say, bubbling up, because this was my last chance.

When she sipped her wine, my fingers tensed with the desire to grab it and throw it against the wall.

And then I realized: I could.

What was stopping me?

This wasn't real.

So I stormed to the couch, grabbed her glass and the bottle, too, and threw them, hard.

They exploded, deep purple spray and shattered glass, leaving behind no stain or fragment.

I breathed into the relief. The problem was gone. I'd fixed it.

But by the time I faced her again, she had another bottle and another glass, sipping like nothing had happened.

I laughed, bordering on hysterical. "Tell me, please," I begged. "What should I have done?"

"Nothing. It was always going to end like this."

"I could have been honest."

"It wouldn't have worked. I couldn't be honest with you if I wasn't being honest with myself."

The brick wall I'd been pounding my fists against crumbled, and I could see through it to the other side, where I was whole, where I'd forgiven myself. Because Barb was right. There was nothing I could have done to change what happened. Maybe I could have talked to my mom about sobriety or even dumped out her bottles of wine. Maybe I should have. But I'd chosen to pretend because that was what she'd wanted, and I wanted her to be happy.

I sat beside my mom on the couch. "I was angry because I loved you so much. If I didn't care, it wouldn't have hurt."

Her body radiated warmth, warmer than human. "The fact that you knew what I was trying to hide is the only regret I have. I wanted to be the perfect mother for you."

I lifted my feet onto the coffee table, matching hers. "Is that why you didn't call me from the hospital?"

My mother, beautiful and sad and finally honest, set her glass in the air, where it disappeared. "I didn't call you from the hospital because I wanted to die holding on to the last shred of hope that you still had no idea I drank. But I'm sorry. I should have given you the chance to say goodbye even if it meant telling you the truth. So here I am."

I held her hand. It was papery and dry, even though it looked young. "I love you. I didn't tell you that enough."

She cradled my face and kissed it everywhere—my cheeks, my nose, my hair, my forehead. "I love you more than you could ever possibly know."

"Is this the last time I'm ever going to see you?"

She nodded, suddenly sixty-five, waxy and frail.

It was the strangest feeling—wanting to memorize her, knowing it was my last chance, but hating to look at the evidence of her illness. Wanting the goodbye to last forever and also to hurry up. But this was the goodbye I hadn't gotten, so I studied her details. Her thin nails, her pale knees, the line through her earlobe where earrings had dragged it down.

The clouds must have thickened because the light through the window was shaded and gray. I could barely see her anymore, so I lit the candles and arranged them in a half-moon around her urn. Their flames twirled in little halos of golden yellow. My breath caught at the beauty of it—this was the vigil I'd never planned.

When I looked up—*no*—she was gone.

Then an explosion of light in the dark, and she was everywhere: Hanging my school pictures on the wall, decorating our tree, shouting, "You're here!" and kissing my hair, pouring a glass of wine, catching Santa on camera, and loving me. Loving me, always.

I watched every version of her, recording each memory as candle wax melted on the floor. With each wick that snuffed out, she faded, until I realized I was losing her—

"Wait!" I begged. "I have more questions."

"I've got time for one more," she said, wrapping lights around the tree.

One more? But I needed to know everything!

"Hurry," she said.

So I blurted the only one that mattered now, the one that decided the future instead of the past. "What do you want me to do with your ashes?"

She was translucent, almost gone. "Nothing overly sentimental. I don't want to float away on a river or lay in a garden or be scattered in an ocean. Try not to worry about it so much. I'm in no rush. Just make sure that wherever I go, I go out with a bang."

I scrambled for another question. "And did you send me Henry, too?"

She shook her head. "No, I think the universe did that."

I dove after her, desperate for one more whiff of her lipstick, one more kiss on my hair. *"Please don't leave me,"* I cried, falling to my knees.

But the house was dark.

I slumped against the wall and wiped my eyes. What more could I ask for? I'd gotten my truth. I'd felt her kiss. What I wanted was more time, but nobody could give me that.

The last candle was dwindling, clinging on to life, still burning, still here.

I took a deep breath, filling my lungs with oxygen.

I'm alive. I am breathing. I am still here.

And I wasn't alone. I had a house full of people who'd taken me in.

I hunted in my purse for my phone and saw dozens of missed calls from Henry and Barb.

I don't deserve a second chance, Henry had texted, *but I'm here if you want to talk about your mom.*

I didn't know if he deserved a second chance, but I did have more questions, and he had answers.

What do you know about circuit breakers? I wrote back.

He must have been waiting by his phone. *Little to nothing but there's always YouTube. Why?*

I'm at my mom's and the power's out.

What's the address?

I gave it to him.

Look in my closet if you need a reminder that I was someone other than the disease written on my death certificate.

While I waited, I went into my mom's room and pulled the door of her closet wide open, letting the stale air out. It was a mess—we had that in common. *A messy closet is a messy mind.* Someone had said that once. Someone on HGTV probably, who had a lot of matching, neutral-colored baskets on shelves. So what if we did have messy minds? We liked collecting lipsticks, saving clothes just to look at them and laugh later. Upstairs, I had boot-cut jeans, a bunch of going-out tops, and a long pleather coat from Charlotte Russe with holes in both pockets. I used to lose all my favorite lip glosses in those holes. If I stuck my hand in one now, guaranteed I'd find a sticky old tube.

I'd never snooped through my mom's things before. What was it about death that gave you permission to comb through the drawers in someone's metaphorical nightstand? And, for that matter, the literal drawers of their nightstand? When I was ten, *Harriet the Spy* inspired me to keep a secret notebook with tabs on my mom. With a mirror angled around corners, I spied on her in the kitchen, in her office, putting on makeup in the bathroom. *Drinking wine,* I wrote. *6/12/97, 3:16 p.m., office.* It wasn't a judgment, just an observation. When she found the notebook, in which I'd written *drinking wine* over and over again on every page, she said I was making fun of her and cried and threw it out. But I'd only wanted to know her.

What was that saying? You can't know a person until you walk a mile—

I dropped to my knees and reached into the back of the closet where the shoeboxes were piled, throwing the lids aside, searching. But they were just boring sneakers, summer sandals, pumps from before her business closed. I wanted the sequined miniskirts from her photos, the knee-high boots, the white sunglasses. Where were those?

I grabbed hanger after hanger, box after box, chucking it all out of the closet and onto the floor. It was exhilarating to make a mess after two weeks of trying to fit my grief into a neat little box. I touched my face and realized I was smiling.

Then I found the gold mine. Far in the back, draped over the handle of a suitcase, a pair of bell-bottoms wide enough to swallow a watermelon. The denim was soft and worn as I ran my fingers down the leg, imagining who she was in them. I wanted to feel close to that person.

With a quick glance over my shoulder like Henry might be standing there, I hurried out of my leggings, the cold biting my bare skin, and shimmied the bell-bottoms over my hips. The button slid smoothly closed, a perfect fit. I looked down and laughed. The two legs were so wide they looked like one big skirt.

I dragged the suitcase into her bedroom and knelt beside it, unzipping. It was full of clothes I recognized. The tall boots, the fringe jacket, the yellow halter top. Up close, the clothes were even cooler and more beautiful. I lifted the yellow halter top—mustard knit, embroidered with white flowers. I smelled it—cigarettes, cedar, campfire, like she'd worn it to Woodstock. Maybe she had.

Goose bumps raised my skin as soon as I lifted my sweater off. My fingers were so cold in the heaterless house that I fumbled tying the strings of the halter behind my neck. When it was on, I looked in the mirror and laughed—the halter left no secrets. At twenty-two, my mom had pulled it off way better than I could. *I'm too old for this,* I thought, and covered up the whole ensemble with my puffy coat.

A knock on the front door made me jump. Henry.

He must have broken every speed limit to get here this fast.

I surveyed my mess, considering shoving it all back in the closet and closing the door. But why hide? That was what got us here in the first place.

So I left it all and went to let him in.

He waited several feet back, snowflakes landing in his hair. My chest hurt just looking at him. I missed him, even though he was right there.

"Hi," I said.

"Hi," he said.

I stepped aside. "Come in."

When he brushed past, I smelled smoke from last night on his coat and briefly closed my eyes, the reminder sacred but searing. "The circuit breaker's outside. I'll show you."

I led him through the kitchen, sensing him taking in my lonely, quiet house, with its fridge full of olives and half-empty bottles of wine, nothing like the abundance at Barb's.

As soon as I opened the back door, the wind swept snowflakes inside as it whipped through the yard.

Henry turned up his collar and dug his hands in his pockets before stepping out. "The storm must have knocked it out."

"Probably," I said. *Probably not,* I thought, but followed him outside anyway.

The snow was blowing sideways. At the box, I stamped my feet and shivered as he flipped all the switches on and off, just like I had, frowning at the wires, just like I had. "I don't know what I'm doing," he admitted. "I didn't really come here to fix the power." He looked at me, snow in his eyelashes, that thoughtful line between his brows. It was comforting that this hurt him, too. I wasn't just another patient's daughter.

At some point, I'd huddled near him for warmth. I was close enough to see the individual green and gold flecks in his eyes. "I didn't really invite you here to fix the power."

"Are you okay?" he asked, dropping his voice so only I could hear, even though no one else was around. The question was meant for me, an intimate vibration.

My hands ached so badly to touch him I had to cross my arms. "No," I said. "But I will be." The hems of my bell-bottoms were soaking up snow. "Let's go inside. I want to show you something."

Back in the kitchen, we stamped off our boots and swiped snow from our shoulders. Then I walked him through the house, giving him a tour. "My room's up there," I said, gesturing at a narrow, carpeted stairwell.

He peered up into the darkness, wearing a small smile. "What's it look like?"

"I'd say the theme is fairly described as 'Seth Cohen.' "

He laughed. To the extent Seth Cohen was a nerd, he was a hot nerd who looked like a really good kisser, and Henry fit that profile exactly.

I showed him into my mom's room, which looked like the scene of a robbery cut short. Enough gray light filtered through the windows to reveal half-emptied closets, open boxes, clothes strewn everywhere. It was strange having a man where no man had stepped foot before.

"I wanted to find the clothes she was wearing in her photos," I explained. "I thought I could wear them and feel closer to her. Is that stupid?"

"Not at all. Did you find anything?"

Slowly I unzipped my puffy coat to reveal the yellow halter top that barely covered me. Henry's eyes practically bugged out of his head. I had to laugh. A shy smile spread across his face as he rubbed his jaw and cleared his throat.

"Sorry," he said. "That was not an appropriate reaction for the moment. I'll try to contain myself."

"Don't worry." I held up a leather tassel bikini. "My mom was hot."

His expression sobered and his eyes locked on mine. "She was beautiful, but you light up every room you're in."

My hands fell limp at my sides, surrendering. Because that was our truth. We'd found each other and surrendered. We'd become each other's new beginning.

The way I saw it, I had a choice. I could dump him. I'd dumped a lot of men for a lot less. But none of them were Henry. None of them were worth it.

Life with Henry in it was better.

I leaned my back against the wall and slid to the floor. He sat beside me, but at a careful distance.

"After everything you'd already been through," he said, "I made you hurt more. I'm so sorry. I understand if you can't forgive me."

I sighed, tipping my head back to contemplate the ceiling. "What I want to understand is why you didn't tell me."

The line between his brows smoothed out, like telling the truth was a relief. "I don't know if I made the right choice, but the reason is that your mom asked me not to. She was adamant about it. That's why it took us so long to call you—she'd refused to give us your number. If you were anyone else, I wouldn't have questioned maintaining her confidentiality. But you're not anyone else."

I scooted closer, until my leg was against his leg, my hip against his hip. The secret he'd kept, he'd kept for my mom. I could get behind that.

"Were you planning to come clean before Barb spilled the beans?" I asked.

"When I first realized who you were, no. Speaking to you, a stranger, was no different than speaking to a patient's family member in the hospital, in which case I wouldn't have revealed anything about the patient's condition that they didn't want me to. When we became friends, I considered telling you because I thought you might find the information helpful for your healing process. Then when we became more than friends—"

I squirmed when I noticed him hiding a smile. My stomach may as well have been a helium balloon. *I'm still angry with him!* I reminded my body. Still, no one could blame it for having flashbacks of last night, when we'd been more than friends, more than once.

"—I realized I'd have to tell you," he continued, tamping down his boyish grin, "not because I wanted to—I knew it would probably end our relationship—but because it was a betrayal not to. I'd earned your trust on false pretenses. So I just kept putting it off." He held my gaze. "I guess I am my mother's son."

I slipped my fingers into his and wound ours together. "If you could start over, come clean now—what would you say?"

"I'm still not sure what I can say to be both an ethical doctor and the man I want to be for you." He looked at me sideways, lifting one corner of his mouth. "I called my mentor about it."

I raised a brow. "What was the verdict?"

"She said to treat you like I would the family of any other patient, which I said was impossible."

I nodded. Henry and I couldn't have been anything other than this from the moment we met in the café. "How about you give me the version as Dr. Samuels and the version as Henry?"

He folded his hands in his lap, looking academic in a way that spoke to the student-professor fantasies I'd consider divulging to him later. "Okay, I'll try. Your mother came into the emergency room that evening presenting with severe abdominal pain. She was displaying weakness and confusion. She was admitted to the ICU, and tests confirmed signs of a heart attack, jaundice, and liver failure. It was advanced. Her treating physician took steps to keep her stable, but the only true treatment would have been a liver transplant, which she wouldn't qualify for."

Hearing him describe the end of my mom's life in such clinical terms made her sound so human. For most of my life, I'd seen my mother only as my mother. Not as a person. But that was dangerous. At the very least, it wasn't fair. She was human, trying her best to survive.

"As liver failure becomes advanced, the toxins that are no longer filtered out cause multiple organ failure, and the blood struggles to pass through the liver, which can lead to high blood pressure and heart disease. Cardiac arrest is a leading cause of death in patients with liver failure." Henry paused to look at me. "I was sitting with her when her blood pressure spiked and she became nonresponsive. But she'd signed an advanced directive not to resuscitate."

"So you were with her? When—" I couldn't finish the words because I couldn't picture what those final moments looked like. I'd never seen anyone die before. Was it sudden, like a key change? Or did life fade slowly out, like gently lifting your foot from a piano's pedal?

He nodded. "I was."

I closed my eyes, letting the information wash over me. I finally knew the whole truth, and it was what I'd suspected all along. Now I could let go of the doubt that haunted me, the voice that said this was my fault, that I'd missed something, that I'd placed blame where it didn't belong. The truth hurt, but it had hurt worse to be angry at myself for what I could not control. That clenched fist around my heart seemed to let go, and I breathed out.

"Do you think she knew?" I asked, my eyes still closed, bracing for more truth.

"This is the part I struggle with," he said. "If you'd come to the hospital that night, I'd have told you what I just told you. While I can't reveal a patient's confidential medical information, of course when someone comes into the hospital and dies, I can explain what happened to their families. I don't have to say, *Sorry, your mother died, don't ask any questions.* But I wouldn't have speculated about her medical history or what might have caused what happened."

I turned my face to look in his eyes. As we sat this close together against the wall, our noses were inches apart. "Then how about you give me the version as Henry?"

He held my gaze. "Which is what I should have done from the moment I fell in love with you, which was pretty much the second I met you, since we're finally being honest."

My eyebrows lifted. My toes even lifted. Everything inside of me lifted.

For a moment, I let that different kind of truth resonate. A happy truth. How lucky I was, to have found love out of deep sadness. But that was the yellow house—a blessing, a refuge, a home, if just for the holidays.

"If you had," I said, "I would have left right away. I would have felt like the walls were closing in. I'd never have spoken to you or Barb again, probably. And then I'd never have gotten the chance to fall in love with you eith—"

Henry kissed me before I'd finished the word. It was his apology, his relief, his need, all mixed together, and I drank it in.

I was horizontal beneath him by the time I caught my breath. "We're not finished talking," I said. "The truth, the whole truth, and nothing but the truth."

He laughed, low and breathy. "You're right, I'm sorry." He pushed himself back to seated. "The version as Henry. Okay. I wasn't her doctor, and I'm not an internist or a hepatologist or a cardiologist. That night, I was just a guy whose mother she used to know. I wasn't even supposed to be at the hospital, but I wanted to check in on a patient. I was in the cafeteria when I got paged to the ICU."

"What time was that?"

"A little after five-thirty."

I flinched. Right when I thought the worst was over, these tinier truths shook me like aftershocks.

My mom had been in the hospital for hours before I found out, and by then it was too late. I'd been singing Christmas carols the whole time she was dying.

"She knew," Henry said gently. "She'd known for a while. When I got to her room and the nurse told me she'd asked for me by name, I read her chart."

Another truth, another shock.

A needle to my open wound, my open heart.

I wanted to die holding on to the last shred of hope that you still had no idea I drank, she'd said. In keeping our secrets, we were both trying to protect each other. That was out of love, maybe the best evidence I had that she loved me.

When Henry noticed me swiping away tears, he said, "I ended up talking to her for two hours. She told me all about New York in the seventies and all about you." Henry lifted our intertwined hands and kissed my knuckle. "I wanted to meet you after everything she'd said."

I laughed. "Stop. You did not."

"I did," he insisted. "That's why I waited so long for you to come to the hospital."

My laughter slipped away. "You must have thought I was a horrible person when I didn't show up."

He shook his head, tracing his thumb up my arm. "A lot of people prefer to remember their loved ones the way they looked when they were alive. I'm a doctor and I don't like seeing dead bodies."

My memory of that night was so hazy it still didn't feel real. "I was in shock. I'm not even sure I really heard you. But even if I had, some part of me knew my mom didn't want me there. This was what she wanted. Goodbye on her terms."

Henry took me in his arms, kissed my forehead, and rested his chin on top of my head. I closed my eyes and breathed his skin. "What she wanted was for you to be happy. She told me you were beautiful and talented and smart and the pride and joy of her life."

Tears burned my eyes—hot and fast and aching—for the devastation of what we'd lost as much as the beauty of what we'd had. I was learning to live with both, and that was healing, but that didn't mean I wasn't going to sob from the deepest part of my soul about it. I'd cry forever. I'd cry in the small moments that reminded me of her, and in the big ones when I wished she were there. I'd cry when it hurt that she lied, when it hurt that she hadn't been there for me in the times when I'd needed her. I'd cry because she'd never quit drinking, I'd cry for no reason but missing her. I'd cry for the rest of my life.

I wiped my cheeks with the heels of my hands. "I don't know how to move on from this grief."

He spread his fingers across my back, guiding my breath into his hand. "You don't move on," he said. "You move forward."

Grieving didn't just happen—grieving was hard work.

So I would try. I would try to live the life she'd want me to live.

I rested my head on his shoulder; he leaned his head on mine. We sat like that for who knew how long, until suddenly the lights turned on. A Christmas miracle.

He rose from the floor and reached out his hand.

"Henry," I said, sliding my palm into his in a way that felt like sliding into bedsheets, "if we have a future together, I'm glad you got to meet my mom."

He smiled, helping me up from the floor. "We wouldn't be here without her."

He was right. Whatever happened next was all thanks to her. How could a person be gone if their love survived?

Chapter 23

DECEMBER 27

When I invited Lizzie over for pizza, she responded that "we" were free. She and Summer were a package deal already, two for the pricelessness of one. They showed up as the sun was setting, orange and pink splashed across the clouds. I opened the front door to welcome them, throwing my hands wide and yelling, "You're here!" We hugged like we hadn't seen each other in a year.

"It looks incredible in here," Lizzie said, stepping inside and shedding her coat. "Are you getting ready to sell?"

For the past two days, I'd been a one-woman cleaning crew. Vacuuming, scrubbing the bathrooms, washing every linen in the house, dusting the curtains, cleaning out the pantry, and finishing the garage. And I'd done it all wearing my mom's yellow halter top like I was raising money washing cars in a bikini. "I've been busy. You'll be shocked, but I'm thinking about moving in."

Summer admired the living room, stepping out of her boots. "I love that. Your mom's got some great stuff in here. Is that an antique sewing machine? Did your mom sew?"

I laughed. "Not a chance. But she had cool taste. I have no taste, so you'll need to help me redecorate."

I gave Summer the highlight tour before we sat on the carpet around the coffee table, where my mom and I used to eat Campbell's tomato soup and watch *Miracle on 34th Street.* Lizzie lifted the pizza box lid.

"This looks like a knife-and-fork situation," I observed. "I'll be right back."

I went to the kitchen for plates and utensils and returned nudging a cardboard box I'd found in the garage. "You have to look at this box of records. It's full of all the classics."

While Lizzie doled out the pizza, Summer thumbed through the box. "Okay, I love your mom." She pulled one out of its sleeve and examined it under the light. "This is a nearly perfect Dylan from 1963. This is worth money."

"Do you want it?" I asked. "Dylan doesn't do it for me."

"I named my son after him," Summer said. "Does that answer your question?"

"It's all yours."

"Consider it my thank-you gift," she said, one corner of her red lips turned up again.

It took me a second to pick up on her implication. "What am I thanking you for?"

She and Lizzie exchanged a knowing smile.

"I got you an audition for *American Icon,*" Summer said, leaning back on her hands. "If you want it, which you do."

Immediately, my nervous system sounded the alarm. "An actual audition?" I asked, an octave above my normal voice. "On camera, in front of the judges?"

"In front of Dash Whitney," she said. "If that's what you're asking."

I pushed away my plate, shaking my head. "I can't."

As I pictured the lights, the a cappella performance, the commentary, my heart thumped in my ears, my ankles, my scalp. I'd watched two decades of contestants face-plant in front of America while I cringed for them. What if the entire country *cringed* for me?

"You *can*," Lizzie corrected, my best cheerleader, the voice I wished were in my head. The voice I actually had was running around in circles, forgetting the number for 911.

"I'm not good enough," I insisted. "I'll bomb. On national TV. In front of the guy I'd deluded myself into thinking could be my dad. It's all too embarrassing."

Lizzie gripped my shoulders and looked me straight in the eyes. "You are good enough. But even if you weren't, don't you want your chance to confront him?"

"I thought I'd hire a lawyer," I said. "Maybe write him a nasty letter, threaten to sue. Isn't that how these things work? Intimidate some cash out of him?"

"You can write your little letter if you want," Summer said. "But I guarantee you Dash Whitney will have a better lawyer and a better letter. I know from the shit show with Mitchell that what's right and what's wrong doesn't matter. Who pays their lawyer the most money is what matters, and as far as I know, you don't have any money. Am I wrong?"

I pointed at the box of records. "How much will those get me?"

"That's what I thought," she said. "This is your opportunity to confront him so he can be tried in the court of public opinion. And guess what? It's free."

"I like free," I assured her. "I do. But will this even work? All I've got is a handwritten copy of the song. It's not even dated. The whole thing could be fake."

"You're right," Summer agreed. "That's why you've got to take my mom."

I waited to see if she was kidding. When she didn't budge, I raised a brow. "Does she know that? She's willing to come clean?"

"It was her idea," Summer promised. "She's a wreck. Have mercy on us all and call her."

My shell hardened at the thought of Barb. "I don't know if I can forgive her." The part of me that had wanted a clean explanation for my mom's death still wanted to blame Barb for all of it.

"I get it," Summer said, with none of the edge that always made her sound so tough. "I really do. This is the woman I grew up with, and believe me, she's impossible. But for once, she's actually willing to admit she was wrong. That means something from the most stubborn woman on earth."

I laughed a little. "I do miss her."

"We all miss you," Summer said.

What was forgiveness? Had I forgiven my mom, my dad, myself? The pain was still there. It hadn't been erased. Convincing myself I didn't care about the past would be a lie. But I'd found peace. If not peace, then acceptance. If not acceptance, then empathy.

I looked at Summer, but she resembled her mom so much it hurt my eyes. It was like looking at an eclipse.

"My mom never spoke to Barb again after what she did," I said.

"And she regretted it," Summer said.

My hardened shell cracked. Anger didn't erase love. It was always there, beneath.

Summer pushed her plate aside and fixed her elbows on the coffee table, pinning me with her gaze. "I'm going to sound like my mother here, but I worked hard to get you this audition. Pulled a lot of strings, called in a lot of favors. Pretty sure Lizzie and I owe a guy free dog-sitting while he goes on a world tour with Pink. And Pink is *always* on a world tour. So the least you can do is show up."

"I'm scared," I admitted. "I thought Dash Whitney was going to be the hero of my story. But it turns out he's the villain."

"And this is your chance to make him pay," Summer said. "Figuratively, but also literally."

If you're not going to do it for you, my mom had said, *then do it for me.*

I grabbed my glass of water, chugged it, then grabbed Lizzie's and chugged that. Summer was right, but that didn't make this any easier.

"But hold on," Lizzie said, reaching across the table for my hand. "This isn't just about Dash Whitney. Fuck that guy. Even if he weren't going to be there, this audition belongs to you. You're good, Mel. You're so, so good. You deserve to be on camera, shooting your shot."

An audition for *American Icon* that belonged to me. Mine.

My mom and I used to play the what-if game. What if a fly got in my milk? What if we found a million dollars? What if I ate through my nose and smelled through my eyes? She always answered every single question.

One time I asked her, what if I died?

I'd never get out of bed again, she said. She lived for me. The least I could do was live for me, too.

You've got to live your life. That's the whole point.

I was auditioning for her legacy. But what if I also auditioned for me?

What if, what if, what if.

The thumping bass of fear in my veins became more like an excited drumroll. "When is the audition?" I asked.

"New Year's Eve," Lizzie said. "In LA. Obviously I'm coming."

"I am also coming," Summer pointed out. "As your manager."

I felt a smile creep across my face. "Before I agree to anything, I have one really important question: What if I get rich and famous?"

Lizzie gasped and clasped her hands. "Does that mean you're in?"

My heart was full of helium, lifting me off the ground. This was the house where I'd discovered my voice, where I'd belted into my karaoke machine, where I'd announced to my mom I was going to be a singer. My house. My dreams.

I nodded. "I'm in."

Lizzie jumped, threw her hands in the air, crawled across the floor to tackle me with a hug. "You're going to kill it!"

Without missing a beat, Summer said, "Let's talk wardrobe."

I laughed. "I guess you mean I can't wear these leggings."

We draped my mom's clothes over the back of the couch. In honor of the Secretaries, I wanted to look like I'd stepped out of a VW van in a cloud of smoke, but with a twist of Nashville and a dash of New York City. An unlikely blend of ingredients, but my mom's vintage treasures delivered. Blazers, cowboy hats, miniskirts, leather vests. We played dress-up until snow started falling and Summer had to get home to Dylan before she got snowed in.

At the door, Summer stepped back into her boots. "If he wakes up in the night and I'm not there, he thinks I've left for a tour without telling him."

Underneath Summer's unwavering confidence and laid-back vibe, sometimes I saw her gritting her teeth or closing her eyes for a long, private breath. She loved her son desperately, and they'd already endured so much.

I stopped her with my hand across the door. "Wait. Whatever we get out of Dash Whitney, I'll split with you fifty-fifty. So Dylan can go to school."

Her expression broke open, and between the pieces, I glimpsed her vulnerability. "Are you serious?"

"Of course. I wouldn't be going if it weren't for you. And I wouldn't have the guts."

Summer hugged me. Her curls swept across my cheek, her hands strong and solid on my back, like Barb's. "You've got yourself one hell of a deal," she whispered.

"Before you go," I said, "let me give you something."

I hurried into the kitchen to grab a cherry pie I'd baked using a recipe my mom had printed out before one of Clyde's parties. Even though she hated baking, she'd always wanted to be a good neighbor and show up with something homemade. She'd buy the ingredients and arrange them on the counter, but then she'd open a bottle, and the pie wouldn't get made. I'd found the recipe in the garage, and it spoke to something about her I didn't want to forget: that she'd always had big plans.

On a Post-it note, I scribbled a message before wrapping the pie in a kitchen towel.

Back at the door, I gave it to Summer. "For your mom."

My mom's life was over, but ours stretched ahead like the open highway from New York to Nashville, windows down, bleached sky, music so loud we felt it beating against our ribs.

Watch out, Hollywood, the note said. *Trouble's on her way to town.*

Chapter 24

New Year's Eve

When I emerged from the terminal through the automatic glass doors into the concrete turmoil that was the arrivals level of LAX, the sun was so bright I had to squint, even though I wasn't looking anywhere near it. The acid-washed sky and mass of shiny cars seemed to amplify the UV, turning up the wattage and shining it directly into my eyes. And it was freezing—a chilly, harsh wind swept my hair off my neck. How could it be this bright and this cold? I gripped the lapels of my blazer and closed it around my chest as a shiver ran through me. My legs were bare, and they erupted in a wave of prickly goose bumps.

"This weather feels like false advertising," I said.

Barb wrapped her arm around me, a human coat. She was the only one dressed appropriately, wearing her velvet jacket and riding boots. "Taxi!" she yelled, flinging her free hand in the air. I smiled. I was pretty sure it hadn't worked like that for a while, but better to let Barb do her thing.

Summer stood on my other side with Lizzie, ordering an Uber. "Mom, that was an airplane, not a time machine," she said without looking up.

Summer led the way to the designated parking lot where rideshares picked up, speed-walking between bumper-to-bumper cars, over bridges, and through parking garages, all of us dragging our suitcases, jogging to keep up. "Traffic keeps getting worse!" Summer called over her shoulder more than once. When we finally made it to the parking lot fifteen minutes later, I shucked my blazer and wiped sweat off my forehead. So much for being cold. So much for looking decent on national TV.

"This one's ours," Summer said, somehow managing to open the front door, the rear door, and the trunk in under three seconds, then load all our bags one-handed while holding her phone in the other, texting. I exchanged a smile with Lizzie and Barb. Summer had stepped right back into the role of Tour Manager, and I was honored to be her comeback.

"Sit in the middle," Summer directed me. "I need to do your makeup while Lizzie does your hair."

She held the door open, waiting. I took one last look at the curving white spider legs of LAX—my last chance to abandon this crazy plan and go home to where there were no judges, no cameras, and the sunlight wasn't so exposing. I could bury my mom's ashes in the backyard where Santa's sleigh crashed, wear the clothes in her closet, and accept that while I couldn't change the past, at least I understood it. I understood her. Barb had given me that gift. And that would be fine. I would be fine.

Or I could wear the clothes in my mom's closet into a TV studio and sing my heart out. The gift of justice for my mom. The gift of a dream coming true for myself.

You've got to live your life. That's the whole point.

She loved me. My mother loved me, and she didn't want to be buried in the backyard. She wanted to be flung around, scattering her love in the sky, letting it settle on my skin and hair.

She wanted my dreams to come true and so did I.

So I got in the car.

The fact that LA was one giant traffic jam did not help me channel my Zen place. I'd never been to LA before. The sky wasn't richly blue like Chicago's in the summer, but bleached and hazy. There seemed to be no neighborhoods, just endless stretches of red lights and strip malls and auto shops. My view through the windshield was half sunshine, half billboard. Chicago was by no means rural, but the vast congestion was unmooring. I searched for the Hollywood Sign to tether me to this city of recklessness where people chased impossible dreams, and sometimes they came true.

"You're sweating off all your makeup," Summer said. "You need to calm down. Sir, can you please crank the AC?"

She was right. My knees bounced; I was wringing my hands. I wasn't backing out, but that didn't mean I wasn't terrified.

"I barely practiced," I said. "I'm freaking out."

"You've sung this song five hundred times," Lizzie said. "You've been practicing your whole life."

"Go ahead and sing it," Summer said. "People rehearse in Ubers all the time here. The Uber drivers are rehearsing. Sir, are you a writer or an actor?"

"Neither. I do stand-up."

"Do you have any jokes for us? This one needs to laugh."

The stand-up launched into his routine as I closed my eyes and tried to draw slow breaths through my nose. Summer sponged makeup on my face and Lizzie braided my hair into a complicated crown. *This is just another show, this is just another show, just another show.*

If the driver was telling jokes, I didn't hear any of them.

American Icon taped on a huge lot in Fairfax, surrounded by palm trees that scraped the clouds. Our car stopped at the security gate and Summer stuck her head out the window. She gave her name, a building number, her contact, and my audition time, and he waved us through.

I'd never been to Disneyland, but I imagined it looked like this. We drove through a block in New York, an arrondissement in Paris, the sandy dunes of another planet. But none of that was as shocking as the crowd of people waiting in line outside an airplane-sized hangar armed with folding chairs, tents, costumes, instruments, coolers, and umbrellas—the hopefuls who'd been waiting in line for days to sing for Dash Whitney.

And I was leapfrogging all of them.

I crushed Summer in a hug. "Thank you," I whispered, my voice breaking.

"You're welcome," she said back. "Don't blow it." I could have been wrong, but I thought I heard her voice get raspy, too.

As soon as we got our bags out of the car, a security guard approached the driver and pointed him toward the exit. Summer asked the guard for a Matt and he walkie-talkied someone. Seconds later, Matt appeared in flip-flops and a T-shirt like it was beach weather. Was everyone in Los Angeles just too hot to be cold?

"You're kind of late, but it's fine," Matt said, like it wasn't fine. "You're going to be first after the break. Who's the one auditioning?"

Lizzie and Summer shoved me forward.

"It's me," I said. "I'm the one auditioning."

"You'll wait until the door PA tells you to go in. You'll be immediately on camera, so smile. Or don't. Whatever. It's up to you, but you should smile. There's a blue X on the floor where you need to stand. Don't look directly at the camera. That's weird. It'll make everyone uncomfortable. Look at the judges or look at the back of the room where the sound guy is. Turn around."

The directions came so fast I had no time to overanalyze. I turned around. Matt clipped the mic to the back of my dress beneath my blazer, then looped the wire under my armpit to clip it to the lapel. "Sing at normal volume," he said. "If you scream, they won't air your audition because of the feedback. They're counting you down. Stand here. Wait for the green light. Good luck." Matt gripped my shoulders and spun me around so I was facing another guy with a clipboard and a headset, counting from five on his fingers. My body felt clunky and mechanical, like I was trying to operate a forklift instead of my own hands. When I opened my mouth to sing, I'd probably sound like a meat grinder. Where were Barb, Summer, and Lizzie? I had tunnel vision, seeing only the PA's fingers counting three, two, one—

He opened the door and someone shoved me inside, where the lights were even brighter than the LA sun. The hot beam of a spotlight trained to my head, the camera's blinking red dot, the washed-out faces of dozens of people staring at me. I shielded my eyes and swallowed the sand in my throat. What was I supposed to do again? When my eyes adjusted, the judges' table materialized. There was the pop star, even more dewy in person. There was the manager in a black leather jacket, scowling. And there was Dash Whitney. He leaned back, one hand slung around his Pepsi cup and the other loosely draping over the pop star's chair. His casual confidence was paper-thin, an act I would tear in two. The sight of him cleared my mind. I breathed. I smiled.

"Hi," I said, walking to my blue X. "I'm Mel from Chicago."

"Hi, Mel from Chicago," the pop star said. She had straight blue hair and pink lipstick, with gems curving above her eyebrows. "What are you going to sing for us today?"

"My favorite song," I said, remembering to smile. "It meant a lot to me growing up, and recently it took on an even deeper meaning."

The pop star pressed a hand of sparkly rainbow nails to her chest. "I love that. What's it called?"

I looked directly into Dash's glittering emerald eyes as I said, "'Carry My Heart.'"

The pop star cackled. "Oooo! I love it when we have a showdown."

I waited for panic to set in, but I was eerily calm when Dash leaned forward on his elbows, a challenge. "You sure, young lady? I admire your guts, but it's not easy to sing a song in front of the man who wrote it."

I cocked my head, simmering, pitying, like he was a child. "It's a good thing I don't have to do that, then."

He chuckled, still so confident it made my organs burn and boil. "I guess you skipped Music History 101, little miss, but that's my song."

Behind my plastered-on smile, I clenched my teeth. Now wasn't the moment to strike. I had to earn America's trust first. *Breathe. This is just another show.*

"What else are you going to sing?" the pop star asked.

That caught my attention. "What else?" I asked. "Don't I get one song?"

"New rules this year," she said. "You can sing two songs as long as one of them is original."

I blinked, swallowed. "Right. I was not prepared for that, but we'll see if inspiration strikes." Barb's song about chicken popped into my head.

Lizzie and Summer waved from the back. They'd snuck in. They were mouthing something, hands cupped around their cheeks, but I had no idea what they were saying. I widened my eyes and shook my head, the tiniest movement. *I don't understand. What?*

The mean manager was refilling his water. "Are you going to sing or are we going to grow old and die here?"

"Don't worry," I answered, tearing my eyes from the back and smiling at him. "I'm going to sing."

It occurred to me then that everyone was staring at me. The cameras, the judges, the clipboards. I'd sung "Carry My Heart" hundreds of times in my life, but everything hinged on this one. This wasn't a performance, it was an offering. To my mother, to myself.

I had to nail it.

I closed my eyes and pretended I was at a small wedding, the intimate kind I loved. Lizzie and Summer were slow dancing, and Barb was twirling with her hands raised to the starry sky, and Henry was waiting for me in the back. My mom was there, too. She'd come to see me sing. She sat at a table, alone. When I opened my mouth, I didn't sing for revenge or money or a golden ticket to Hollywood. I sang for her, to make her proud. I sang my beating, bloody heart right out of my chest. And she beamed.

When I finished, the air had gone out of the room. I felt disembodied, as if I'd sung out all my life force and there was nothing of me left. I worried I might fall over. Gravity seemed backward, pushing me up instead of pulling me down. I looked at my feet. They were still on the ground.

The judges were stoic, but that was part of the shtick. They had to keep their impressions secret, so poker faces were expected. If all three voted yes, each judge got an extra vote for the contestant of their choice in the next round. If only one voted yes, that judge lost a vote, so the game was not to influence each other.

Breathe. This is just another show.

Except that was a total lie.

The pop star unpopped her lollipop. "Thank you. Have you decided to sing anything else?"

"Yes," I heard myself say. "I'm going to. But can I have a minute to get a drink of water?"

"Sure," she said. "I need to pee. Cut!"

I craned my neck to see Lizzie and Summer in the back. *Where's Barb?* I mouthed. They pointed toward the hall.

I bolted through the door and found her pacing. If we were in the yellow house, she'd be cooking out her nervous energy. Without the channel of her furious whisk, she was lost.

"Barb," I said.

Seeing me, she burst into tears and threw her arms around my shoulders. It was so surprising that I laughed, a much-needed relief. Warmth bloomed in me, and then tears, the good kind.

"Let me love you," Barb begged in my ear. "Please."

I tasted the salt of my tears as I smiled, the bittersweetness of losing a mother and gaining something like one. Because what were mother and daughter if not two women trying to love each other in the best way they knew how? Barb and I could spend the rest of our time on earth flinging love on each other like my mother's ashes.

"I will if you will," I promised. "But right now, I need you."

"If that isn't music to my ears," Barb said.

"Sing me something of my mom's. Something great."

She lifted her chin and corrected me. "They were all great."

"The best one, then. Please. I'm desperate. The second song has to be original."

"Now? I need time to warm up. Have a cup of lemon tea." Barb looked around, as if searching for a kettle.

"I literally have thirty seconds."

She sighed, relenting. "Fine. I'll sound like a grandma at Sunday mass, but here goes. This is a song Connie wrote about us."

I listened, recording the sweet, sorrowful melody in my mind. It was my job to learn songs on the fly to make brides happy. I could do this. I made her sing it twice more through and hurried back inside with my mom in my purse, ready.

Back on my blue X, I zeroed in on Dash, set my shoulders back, and did what he'd never had the guts to do. "I'm going to sing an original song, but to be honest, I didn't write it. My mom did."

The mean manager snorted, refilling his water again. "Is your mom here? Maybe she can sing it for us."

This is it. My heart played a fast tempo as I reached into my purse. "She is, actually."

When I debuted the blue urn, the pop star gasped, the mean manager recoiled, and Dash Whitney chuckled. "This just got interesting," he said, reclining back and crossing his ankles.

"It was already pretty interesting," I said, sensing the cameras following me as I marched up to Dash and deposited the urn in his lap. "Why don't I let her haunt you for a minute?"

When he saw the name written on the white label stuck to the lid, his cocky amusement drained right off his handsome face.

"My mom was a songwriter," I said directly into the camera. "She wrote one of the greatest songs of the last thirty years. 'Carry My Heart.' Maybe you've heard of it. If not, I can sing it for you again."

The pop star pointed her sparkly thumbnail to her right. "Dash's song?"

"That isn't Dash's song," I said. "It's Connie Blanchfield's song. If her name sounds unfamiliar to you, that's because Dash Whitney broke her heart, stole her music, and lied to the world about it."

Everyone turned to Dash. You'd have missed the blanching of his lips, the twitch of his shoulders, if you weren't searching for it. He was so practiced, so smooth, so obvious. He'd been conning women his whole life. "Young lady," he simpered, his hand over his heart, "I'm so very sorry about your mother. But a lot of people have claimed I owe them money over the years. That's part of the deal when you're famous. So forgive me if I don't go running to clear out my bank account. If I did that for everyone, I'd be the Giving Tree with no more leaves."

That made me tip my head back and laugh out loud. I probably looked maniacal on camera, but I didn't care. My mom used to read me that book, and I knew the ending. "You're not the tree, you're the boy. My mom was the tree. You are nothing but a predatory cowboy hat."

Dash smiled, unaffected and amused. But when I revealed my mom's notebook, I caught it: a fraction of a second of dread, like I'd opened a door to the truth only for him to slam it shut. "I've got proof."

"And what's that?" he drawled. "A handwritten journal you found hidden beneath the floorboards of your dead mother's dusty attic, Miss Indiana Jones?"

"Yes," said a voice. "But she's also got me."

I turned. It was Barb, standing on my blue X, back beneath the spotlight where she'd always belonged.

With grace and a commanding calm, she set her fierce blue eyes on the camera. "My name is Barbara Stern. Imagine me without all the wrinkles and you'll recognize me. When I was twenty-five years old, I recorded 'Carry My Heart' with that man right over there. He didn't write that song. Neither of us did. He did, however, convince me to lie about it and sign my name on a contract giving him all the credit." She reached into her velvet pocket and withdrew a set of papers. With her signature dramatic flair, she tore them in half, then in half again, and flung the paper slips in the air where they drifted to the studio floor like snow.

My heart exploded. I leapt, clapping, beaming. Whatever happened now, it didn't matter. Whether the audition aired was irrelevant. Barb had changed her story on camera. Dash Whitney was in trouble, and everyone in this room knew my mom's name.

Dash stood up, his chair legs scraping. "This is obviously a witch hunt," he said to someone I recognized as the woman in white. "Can we get them out of here?"

"But I have one more song," I said, feigning innocence.

"She does have one more song," the pop star agreed, conspiring with a smart smile.

Dash waited, and when no one came to his rescuc, he stormed out of the studio, texting—probably in all capital letters, probably to his team of lawyers.

I joined Barb at the blue X. "What do you say we sing this one together?"

My pulse was so loud in my ears I couldn't hear the giant ticking clock counting down. I couldn't hear my own thoughts.

It was customary that after a contestant auditioned, the judges had thirty seconds to cast their votes. They always made a big show of thinking about it, then scrambling at the last second before the buzzer rang. I loved the thrill of watching it on TV, watching someone's dreams come true in real time.

Being on this side of it was not thrilling. It was torture. Time had never moved more slowly. My heart pounded. My skin was slick. The lights were hot and my hands were shaking. *You're not going through,* I told myself. *But that's not why you came.*

I felt Barb's hand slip into mine, gripping it tightly, steadying me. I breathed. We'd done what we'd come to do. Whatever happened now was just the gold star on top of the tree.

Five seconds left.

Overhead, three huge gold stars waited, one for each judge, ready to light up if the judge voted yes.

Four.

Three.

A bead of sweat formed at the base of my neck and dripped down my spine.

As the timer ticked from two to one, the pop star and the manager hit their buttons—Dash had never returned.

A second passed, and—

Two stars lit up.

I gasped. I flew into Barb's hug, shaking and laughing. Tears sprung to my eyes, the happiest ones I'd ever had.

Had my mom's life flashed before her eyes in the moment before she died? Could life flash only in the seconds before death? Because mine was flashing now. I saw myself as a kid in my bedroom, belting out Céline Dion. I saw Lizzie and Ronald rocking out in the garage, and Barb swaying at her piano, and Henry on the sled, and my mom onstage, my mother, my mother, my mother, shading the radiance of her spotlight with white sunglasses.

Acknowledgments

This book would not exist without the unconditional support and encouragement of Jamie Carr and Caitlin Landuyt. They believed in this story when it was nothing but a glimpse of hope. The best part about being an author is working with incredible women I'd never have otherwise met and being inspired by them every day. Jamie and Caitlin, I can't thank you enough. Writing this book helped me heal, and without you, I couldn't have done it.

This book would also not exist without my mom, who passed away on February 2, 2022. What Mel remembers about her mother while writing a song with Barb is a version of what I read at the celebration of my mom's life. There are not enough words to fully honor my mom or thank her for everything she did for me. She was my mom. When I was little, she put my towel in the dryer so it was warm when I got out of the bath. She was my mom. I miss her every second of every day.

Last but not least, this book would not exist without my husband, Michael Simeone. My decision to write novels while working a full-time job and being a parent affects every aspect of our life together.

Without his contribution to our household to allow me the gift of protected time, in addition to his unwavering love and support, this dream would never have come true. If he hadn't believed in me with such conviction, I wouldn't have believed in myself.

Thank you to Jennifer Close, Kimberly King Parsons, Stefan Merrill Block, and Crystal Hana Kim for reading this novel and helping me uncover the story that needed to be told. Thank you to Jenny Bowen Storey, my therapist who taught me that it's possible to hold many feelings in your heart at the same time and that they are all valid. Thank you to Lydia Golitz for taking such loving care of my baby, giving me the mental space to write. Thank you to Maris Dyer and Elisabeth Weed for embracing this novel and guiding it to publication. And thank you to everyone at Knopf for treating this story with such care: Samantha Bryant, Elora Weil, Kelsey Micah, Eddie Allen, Jenny Carrow, and Mike Collica. This book is my heart and soul, and you made it beautiful.

A Note About the Author

Taylor Hahn is the author of the novel *The Lifestyle* and the novella *The Wedding, the Winery, and Will.* She is a graduate of Loyola Marymount University and Fordham University School of Law, and lives in Los Angeles with her husband and daughter.

A Note on the Type

This book was set in a typeface named Bulmer. This distinguished letter is a replica of a type long famous in the history of English printing that was designed and cut by William Martin in about 1790 for William Bulmer of the Shakespeare Press.

Typeset by Scribe,
Philadelphia, Pennsylvania

Printed and bound by Berryville Graphics,
Berryville, Virginia